"I'VE BROUGHT SOMETHING FOR YOU, BROTHER. A GIFT."

Calum suspected this was another one of Eachann's sick jokes. "A gift?"

"Right in here is the answer to all our troubles of late. Something I decided we do need after all." Eachann leaned down and lifted the latch cover.

There was a muffled noise that sounded like a loud sea cawing gull trapped in the middle of a haystack.

"Look for yourself."

Calum held the lamp low over the holding tank and cast a glance inside. He stared down at what looked like some kind of monster—a huge lump. A wet bundle of rich silk and white skin, of four flailing arms and a kicking foot here and there.

It took a moment to see the lump wasn't a loch monster, but two gagged, sopping wet women dressed in expensive silk gowns and wrapped up tightly in an ancient mackerel net. They were wiggling and elbowing one another, each fighting to try to sit upright.

Calum swore graphically and looked at Eachann. "Women? You brought *more* women?"

"Aye." Eachann leaned against the railing with his arms crossed. "Not just more women, but something better." He nodded at the women. "Those are our brides."

Praise for the Breathtaking Novels of

JILL BARNETT

IMAGINE

"Jill Barnett has written a wildly romantic story! Just 'imagine' if it could really come true!"

—Gloria Miller, *The Literary Times*

DREAMING

"Barnett has a rare knack for humor. Her characters are joyously fresh and her style is a delight to read—a ray of summer sun."

—*Publishers Weekly*

"There is so much happiness, magic, and pleasure in the pages of *Dreaming* that you'll believe in the magic of love!"

—Kathe Robin, *Romantic Times*

"Positively stellar! This book is not only funny, it's caring, and compassionate . . . and magical!"

—Julie Meisinger, *Heartland Critiques*

BEWITCHING

"Jill Barnett has a sophisticated sense of humor and is an author not to be missed!"

—Megan McKinney, author of *Till Dawn Tames the Night*

Books by Jill Barnett

Carried Away
Imagine
Bewitching
Dreaming
The Heart's Haven
Just a Kiss Away
Surrender a Dream

Published by POCKET BOOKS

JILL BARNETT

CARRIED AWAY

POCKET BOOKS

New York   London   Toronto   Sydney   Tokyo   Singapore

This book is a work of fiction. Names, characters, places and incidents are products of the author's imagination or are used fictitiously. Any resemblance to actual events or locales or persons, living or dead, is entirely coincidental.

An *Original* Publication of POCKET BOOKS

POCKET BOOKS, a division of Simon & Schuster Inc.
1230 Avenue of the Americas, New York, NY 10020

Copyright © 1996 by Jill Barnett Stadler

ISBN: 0-671-52144-6

First Pocket Books printing September 1996

10 9 8 7 6 5 4 3 2 1

POCKET and colophon are registered trademarks of Simon & Schuster Inc.

Cover art by Gerber Studio

Printed in the U.S.A.

To Dewey Weber surfboards and '57 Chevys,
Palm Springs at Easter
and cruisin' Hawthorne Boulevard,
those food fights in the cafeteria
and crooked smiles in geometry class;
to Beatles' songs and prom nights,
skiing the face of Heavenly
and still dancing the surfer's stomp.
To fast cars and old gas pumps;
the thrill of that very first marlin
and the joy of fatherhood;
to tears and touches,
snoring and really bad jokes.
To a man who knew how everything worked
because at sometime in his life
he must have taken it apart;
the same man who over all those years
showed me what love is.

JOHN CHRISTOPHER STADLER
May 14, 1948–February 8, 1996

I hope there are hot rods in Heaven, my love.

The common cormorant or shag,
Lay its eggs in a paper bag.
The reason you will see no doubt
Is to keep the lightning out.
But what those unobservant birds
Have never noticed is that herds
Of wandering bears may come with buns
And steal the bags to hold the crumbs!

Anonymous

On the last clear day in August, seven great black cormorants flew in a wedge out over the Atlantic and lit on a rock in a lazy cove on Arrant Island. Now that wasn't particularly unusual; cormorants were sea birds and sea birds landed on rocks all the time. Except those birds had done the same thing, at the same time of day, for the entire summer. Every morning they lit on that rock and just stood there with their wings spread-eagle, as if they were drying out their laundry. They didn't move, even when a tasty school of alewives swam by; all they did was stare, for hours, like they were waiting for something to happen.

If the birds had been crows, their antics could have been easily explained away. New Englanders knew that the number of crows seen at one time could foretell the future:

one for sorrow,
two for mirth,

three for a wedding,
and four for birth.

But these birds weren't crows. They were cormorants, ravens of the sea. The locals claimed them to be the most annoying birds to ever fly the Maine skies, because more often than not, they ruined both the fishermen's catch and the island trees. Had anyone ashore known about the birds perching on that rock, they'd have probably said it was only "like attracting like." The island, it seemed, had as bad a reputation as did those birds.

From the shoreline, on a clear day, when the seas were calm and blue-green, if you were to cast a quick glance at Arrant Island, it looked as if it were a proud medieval castle built upon a high crag. But when the weather changed, the island did too, for it appeared to be only a mysterious blue cloud floating on the horizon.

At times when the winds were southernly, the ledges around the isle broke hard and dangerously; seafoam sprayed over its rocky headlands. But always the island stood stiff and unyielding, oblivious to the moods of the wind and seas, like a stony face that must hide secrets.

It was only a scant seven leagues off the jagged Maine shoreline, where huge summer estates and elegant compounds were only down-the-coast-a-ways from fishermen's shanties and the sea-worn wharves that dotted the mouth of the Kennebec. The isle was just a short sail in fair weather for the sleek schooners built in the Bath shipyards and not far from where fishing boats chased cod, mackerel, and the huge schools of silver herring, which, when the moon was high, made the water shimmer as if the Milky Way had fallen right smack dab into the ocean.

Still, with the bustling coast only a whistle and a lick away, there was an aloneness to the island, a sense of isolation. Not just because of the water that surrounded it, but because it was almost as if Arrant Island were another world, hidden away, until the mist rose and you saw with a second look that it truly did exist.

The island had long been the stuff of idle talk. Children of the fishermen huddled around winter fires and told tales of the wild Scots who lived there, men who were not real, they claimed, but instead the ghosts of those who had died long ago on Culloden Moor, ghosts that fled clear across the Atlantic to a craggy, cold, and rugged plot of land that was like their beloved Highlands.

Others called the MacLachlans who owned the disappearing island those "mad Scots." And children grew up afraid of nights with a full moon, convinced that unless they placed a pale feather from the down of a puffin chick beneath their pillows, a mad MacLachlan might charge up on a white horse with its mane flowing and *snatch* them from their warm beds!

When the wind grew fierce and blew the shingles off the fishermen's shacks, it was said a MacLachlan was out riding that night, stirring up the wind. Some nights the willows would moan from that same wind, a sound exactly like someone crying. Mothers would tuck their children back under warm woolen blankets and assure them that no one was there. The noise was only a wind tunnel formed by the branches of the trees.

But the imaginations of children spun as wildly as the wind in those willows. They pressed their small heads together and wrapped their arms tightly around one another as they whispered that the sound *was* crying, crying from some poor soul who had seen a white MacLachlan horse come thundering out of the mist.

So that summer the odd behavior of those annoying black sea birds went unnoticed. There were already too many yarns to tell, the stuff of nightmares and dreams, dark and fierce tales about wild Scotsmen who would ride up on their white horses and carry you away.

I wonder if perhaps I might
Suddenly see a shining knight
Winding his way from blue to green
Exactly as it might have been
Those many many years ago . . .
Perhaps I might. You never know.

A. A. Milne

For Amelia Emerson, it was one of those bright days when the sky looked like the inside of a big blue bowl, the earthenware kind the cook used to mix bread dough every Saturday morning. Even the clouds played to her fancy, because they streaked across the blue bowl sky like thin white strips of bleached flour.

Amy turned her face toward the warmth of the August sun and closed her eyes. In her mind's eye she imagined God standing in the heavens above her dressed in a white smock and apron, His long gray hair tucked under a crisp linen kitchen cap as He dumped the sky upside down to give those on earth the gift of a perfect day.

In June there had been a blue bowl sky, just like today, when William De Pysters had taken her canoeing on the Kennebunk River. As their canoe moved silently on the glassy water, the red maple blossoms drifted down and floated alongside of them like a red velvet carpet set before a queen. That day had been as close to a perfect day as she could ever remember; for a few smiles, some small talk, and a sweet kiss later, and Amy left the canoe with her hand on William's strong one, the same one that had placed a soft red blossom behind her ear and the emerald engagement ring on her finger.

It was strange how one's life could change. Her parents had died three years before and that was why she had spent her summers in Maine. One of her executors had suggested the sea air might help her, and the others had quickly agreed.

The summer coterie came from many places—Boston, Philadelphia, New York, wealthy caravans of "good society," all summering in Maine, where the blueberries were plump and sweet, where the light sea breezes made the living easy and free, where they sailed and socialized in an idyllic world of their own, one of blue blood and money.

Amelia Emerson had money, lots and lots of money. Enough money to have her name placed highly in *Beach's*—a social register that listed the amount and origin of each Yankee fortune. Enough money to open the hallowed doors that cloistered the closest thing America had to aristocracy. Enough money for Amy to receive all the right invitations watermarked with names like Cabot and Livingston, Dearborn and Winthrop, the old money families. She went to their parties, even after she realized she wasn't truly welcome, but instead was a pariah because her family had actually had the audacity to earn their millions rather than inherit that money from some great-grandparent who left the old country a couple of hundred years before to come to America and eat speckled corn with the Indians.

She still didn't understand how wealth that had been earned through hard work and ingenuity could be considered of less social value than money that had been moldering in a bank or bonds, or in vast amounts of land for the last hundred years or more.

The concept of old money versus new money escaped her understanding.

But Amy understood very little of people. She had been very close to her parents, who had kept her safe and sheltered within their tight little family where she knew she was loved.

As if it were yesterday she could still recall the image of her father with his long legs bent at odd angles while he sat in a tiny white chair with pansies painted on the arms. He had been a very tall man, but he could balance a miniature china teacup and saucer on his knobby knees while he ate cucumber sandwiches with his pinkie finger stuck out in the air.

He had taught her to appreciate the beauty in the trees and flowers, the call of a bird and the brilliance of a summer sky. He had a strong sense of what was right and wrong and what was important to him.

Sometimes, when he was walking with Amy, he would shake his dark head and say he would never understand how anyone could look at a rose blooming, at a red maple changing color, or listen to the song of a starling in the morning and not believe there was a God. He would get that same look of wonder whenever he looked at her and Amy's mother, as if he couldn't believe they were real.

Amy's mother made her feel whole and comfortable. She had knack for knowing the exact moment when Amy needed a hug, advice, or just a soft touch of a comforting hand. She knew with one quick glance when Amy was feverish. She never even had to put a hand or her lips to her forehead.

Amy couldn't count the number of times when she had suddenly realized she was hungry, had turned around only to find her mother standing at her bedroom door with a bowl of fruit or a plate of teacakes. Her mother would come into Amy's room on some pretext moments before exhaustion could hit her. In a blink

Amy was in her nightdress and tucked into a warm cozy bed while her mother turned down the lamps and said good night in a voice so soft and soothing it sounded as if it came from straight from Heaven.

When she was barely seven, she and her mother had seen a doll with an exquisite trousseau in the window of F A O Schwarz. Amy could remember standing on her toes so she could look in that shop.

Her breath had fogged the window because she had her nose pressed against the icy cold glass, but her mother had bent down with a gentle and amused look on her face, and she had wiped off the mist with her good lace handkerchief just so Amy could keep looking at that display. They must have stood there for at least a half hour with the snow falling on their fur mufflers and velvet coat collars. But her mother had never hurried her away, she had just let Amy look.

For Christmas that year Amy opened box after box of doll clothes, not the ones from the toy-shop window, but velvet gowns with brocade trim, miniature bonnets with bows and feathers, even little velvet purses with silk braided drawstrings, all exact duplicates of the dolls' clothing and all handsewn by her mother.

Her parents could have simply purchased the clothes in the shop—her father was successful even then—but they hadn't. Her mother had spent hours making those clothes for Amy's own doll, which made them more valuable to Amy than all the money in all the banks in Manhattan. Each pearl in the trim, each ribbon and tuck had been sewn with a mother's love.

As wonderful and joyful as those years of tender memories were, her parents had made one mistake: they had never exposed her to any world other than the one they'd created for her—a place where she was loved and protected, where she was taught goodness and love and thoughtfulness, values that had nothing to do with money.

Her childhood had been a special world that centered around their family, a world that suddenly, in one tragic instant, no longer existed. Because the moment her parents died, the only world she had ever known died too.

Amy was left in the practical hands of her estate executors who were really strangers. Her father might have trusted them, but to her they were just men of law who couldn't understand what it was like to be a young woman and suddenly left completely alone in the world. So they had packed her off to Maine each June.

Quiet, shy, and out of place was how she felt whenever she was in a large group, especially the social group that each summer escaped the heat of the crowded Eastern cities to the freedom of the cool Maine coastline. To them, values were business assets and the cost of something; its hallmark and monetary worth. Cachet was in *the name,* whether it be that of an old respected family or a Worth gown.

Everyone always seemed very different from her, so right and in place, complementary, like a drawing room decorated to soft and subtle perfection. Among them she felt obvious, a glaring swatch of shocking red in a room full of soft pinks.

And yet, something magical happened after her canoe ride through the bright flowers on a fine June day. It was almost as if Amy were a part of someone. She began, a little at a time, to feel whole again. In her heart and her head she believed she would have the power of the De Pysters name behind her instead of the bourgeois taint of new money. She wouldn't be glaring red any longer. Because of William, wonderful strong William, Amy would soon be a soft pink, the same subtle color as everyone else.

To her, it was days like this last Saturday in August that sparked those special one-of-a-kind events,

events that would change one's life forever. On a day like today one of Amy's dreams had come true.

So it was with some reluctance that she turned her face away from the warm sunshine and looked out at the sea, blue-green and calm. In the distance, the northernmost island stood silhouetted against that cornflower blue sky. For just an instant that hard craggy island looked like a castle in a fairy tale, tall and gray and majestic. She could imagine knights on white horses riding over the island in search of dragons to slay for the heart of a lady.

However, the only dragons in Amy's life were the bright lacy-winged dragonflies that buzzed around her. They darted in and out of the August air, then shot down the hillside toward a copse of wild blueberry bushes. She followed them past the vine roses that laced themselves into the thickets, waving away the honeybees that hovered before her in bright specks.

Nearby in the tall willow trees whose papery trunks were thick with clinging ivy, she heard the lyrical song of a starling and indigo buntings flew from branch to branch, their bright blue feathers melting into that wonderful sky.

Humming her own light tune, she knelt down beside those highbushes where the wild blueberries were so ripe and heavy with juice that one could touch them with the tip of a finger and they would tumble right into a cupped palm. She poked a couple of berry clusters.

Like pearls falling from a strand, the blueberries with their dark and frosted skins cascaded into her hand. They lay there for only a second before she weakened and popped them into her mouth, chewing so her cheeks bulged like a mouse that had found the Christmas pudding.

She was starved, because in her rush to go berry picking, a rush she'd had to make so the others would have no opportunity to leave her behind, she had not eaten even a bite of breakfast.

Her knees sinking in the soft brown dirt, she picked more berries and let them roll off her palm into a wicker basket that sat next to her forgotten shoes and stockings. Within a few minutes, the basket was half full and Amy had burrowed into the thicket, her bare and muddy toes the only thing showing from beneath the bushes.

Male voices and the crunching sound of boots on gravel drowned out the starling's song and the faint buzz of the dragonflies and honeybees. Amy froze at the sound of that laughter, unsure if she should say something or just stay still. Through the leaves of the bushes, she could see nothing but a few pairs of trousers.

"I doubt anything could be that bad, Drew. Even I haven't the stomach for such a sacrifice."

Jonathan Winthrop had a sharp and distinctive voice she immediately recognized and "Drew" was Andrew Beale. Both were friends of her William. She listened quietly as she counted legs through the leaves. There were six men.

"'Tis a far, far better thing you do . . . for all that money," quoted one of them, and the men laughed again.

"I'd rather exile myself out on Arrant Island with that band of mad Scots than shackle myself to that one."

"Plaids have never been your best suiting, Drew." There was more laughter. "And your family doesn't need those millions."

"Even if my family did, I doubt I'd become the sacrificial lamb."

"You'd do it. If you needed the money as badly as William does."

Amy froze the moment she understood they were talking about her. She held her breath and listened.

"When does the sacrificial lamb, or should I say ram, go to slaughter?"

There was more laughter. "Sometime in December."

"December." Someone laughed. "December is the doom and devastation of the De Pysters."

"Say that six times quickly."

Amy sat there and could almost feel her insides shrivel up, as if her hopes and happiness were just sucked from her until she was nothing more than an empty being. The men laughed again and made a word game of that last insult. She flushed with embarrassment.

"You know what they say, you can marry a woman for money and sex and still have love. . . . Spend her money, spend her body, and love every minute of it!"

With each burst of laughter, each joke that continued, her cheeks grew hotter, her eyes burned with humiliation. She sat there hidden away and crying silently as she listened to William's friends making fun of her. These were people who didn't stop to watch a bird fly, to see a sunset, or to smell a rose. Handsewn doll clothes wouldn't do for them. Things needed an expensive price tag or "a name."

Amy didn't have the right name, just enough money to cover any price tag they'd ever encounter. It was almost as if right there in the blueberry bushes she had changed from a person into not even half of a person, or a bad person, but something much worse: a bank account.

She closed her eyes and for what seemed like the thousandth time in the past three years, she wished her parents were alive. She wished her mother were there with that lace handkerchief, not to wipe away the fog from a window, but to wipe away the tears she couldn't stop.

She wished she could feel her mother's arms around her, just once more, just this time, to make her feel whole, like a person again. She wished her father were alive so she could look in his eyes and see to someone, she *was* special. She wished she were anywhere but there, and she wished she had William's strong arm to hang on to.

When the men stopped laughing, she opened her eyes and stared at the blurry expanse of blueberry leaves around her. She realized then that she really wouldn't want William, the only man who cared for her, to hear his friends' jests and the laughter. She couldn't bear for him to see the shame she was feeling. Shame she didn't know how to overcome, shame she carried because she wasn't born with the right name.

A few more moments of cruel and cutting jokes and the men moved on down the path toward the Cabot house, where an *al fresco* meal would be served in Chassy Cabot's formal rose gardens before everyone would leave to attend the last event of the summer, the annual gala at the Bayard Estate.

Amy moved out of the bushes and stood slowly, not caring that leaves, dirt, and crushed blueberries clung to her blond hair and to the welts of her silk skirt, or that mud oozed up between her bare toes. A deep male voice carried back to her—something about deserving a medal of valor for the sacrifice.

She turned quickly, stunned and unbelieving, and stared at the curly brown hair and broad back of William De Pysters, the one man Amy had thought cared for her. She felt as if she were having one of those lucid and horrid moments just before you fall, the moment when the revelation of what's happening smacks you in the face.

Her throat tightened, as if it had been coated with cold grease. She took deep breaths so she wouldn't do something foolish like burst into loud sobs she couldn't control. Her hand covered her mouth as she watched the men continue walking down a tree-lined path toward the broad green lawns beyond.

Deep inside her chest, her heart just seemed to die.

Her world, her foolish little wish-filled world, the one that didn't really exist, had again suddenly come to an end.

Because it was William's voice she had heard, claiming he deserved a medal. So she watched him from behind as he stood in the middle of his group of cruel friends. He was still as tall as he'd always been. He still looked as strong standing there in the sunlight.

She had thought he was the man who would slay her dragons. But as she raised her chin and swallowed the thick lump in her throat that felt as if it were her heart, she saw the truth: it was her William who was laughing the loudest.

Life is like pudding.
It takes both the salt
And the sugar
To make a good one.
Old New England proverb

There were holes in the upholstery. Georgina Bayard grabbed an embroidered pillow that had once belonged to Marie Antoinette and shoved it onto the sofa so it covered the worn spots.

Across the room, a tall clock chimed the hour. She spun around and stared at the clock. Nine more hours. She snatched a honeybun from the breakfast table and ate it while she paced in front of the large French doors that led out to the gardens.

She swallowed the last bite and looked out at the horizon where today the sky met a calm Atlantic sea. But Georgina knew the sea was as mercurial as her brother's luck. One day the waters were flat and calm, unmoving, as if the ocean could never roar and spit and crash so hard against the rocky Maine coastline that the local fishermen called howlers.

They crept up on one, those howling storms, right after days like this, perfect days. Idle days. Days that lulled one into a sense of well-being and peace, as if all were right with the world and could never be any different. But those who knew the coast, who had spent as much time in Maine as she had, knew the end of summer like any other season could be fickle.

If there was one thing Georgina Bayard understood, it was that life was fickle. Only fools believed in fate and luck. Her brother had been the biggest fool of all, chasing his dreams only to end up dead and broke, leaving her nothing but a trail of bad investments, a business with stacks of debts, a mansion in Boston, and a summer home she loved, both with huge mortgages that she couldn't pay.

She finished off three more sweet buns, nervously biting and chewing, biting and chewing, and not tasting anything. Disgusted, she plopped down in a nearby chair and stared out the window where the vista was marred by that ugly gray clump of an island, the place the locals said was run-over with ghosts of mad Scots who had been driven from their homes.

Mad Scots . . . oh, certainly. She laughed. As if anyone could believe that tripe. But as she sat there, she realized that she did have something in common with those "mad Scots." She was about to lose her home.

She lay her head back to ease the tightness in her neck. Her grandmother had always done that, slung her head back for a few minutes when she was sitting in this chair, the same chair from which she would say, "Georgina, you should have been a boy. That brother of yours is nothing but a spineless wastrel. There are only clouds in his head and a new scheme to dream. He'll come to no good. You'll see. He's weak, but you're the strong one—stubborn, hard, and cold. You're like your grandfather and his father, a true Bayard. A survivor."

Her grandmother had been right. Her brother Albert never thought about the consequences of anything he wanted to do. He just did it. He was only a year older than her, but in the eyes of their parents he was years ahead of her; he was important because he was the son.

One Sunday afternoon when she was six, they had all climbed into the family vis-à-vis and driven to a park, where there was to be a concert, confectionery booths, and a special puppet show to entertain children. But before long Albert had dragged her off to chase a pond frog, then to feed the pigeons that he swore would eat nuts right from the palm of her hand. The next thing she knew they were lost in a mad crush of very tall people who were all in such a hurry to hear the concert that they never noticed the small girl who looked lost.

It had seemed like hours before her parents found them, sitting on a bench near the duck pond. Their mother ran to coddle Albert, who was crying. Georgina just sat there with her hands knotted in her lap to stop them from shaking. She was so terribly frightened she couldn't even find any tears to cry. Her father and grandmother mistook that paralyzing fear as strength, and for the very first time her family spoke her name with approval and with pride; they had claimed she was the strong Bayard.

One hot summer day when they were a few years older, Albert had lured her out to swim in the too-deep waters of the bay. It had been Georgina who had fought the undertow and brought them both back to shore. While she'd sat in the eel grass on a sand dune trying to cough out all the burning seawater from her throat, her hysterical mother had grabbed Albert, sobbing that they had almost lost their son.

Her parents swept her brother back up to the house. Since Georgina was the strong one, she didn't need them like Albert did, so she was left behind. Later, when her brother was tucked into warmed sheets and fed hot whipped chocolate and creamy chowder, Georgina got a pat on the head because she was so strong and levelheaded, then she was left alone again to put herself to bed.

When her brother cried out at night because he was frightened of the dark, her mother ran to him. But Georgina, the strong one, didn't cry out in spite of what horrible things she thought might be hiding in that dark room with her.

In time, she had trained herself to ignore the things that came from her imagination: dreams and hopes and other such fanciful emotions. Those emotions were only monsters that hid in the dark, things that didn't really exist in life.

Life was not thinking about things that were, or could have been, or those things that even might be. Life was becoming what everyone thought you were. Life was living each day trying to be what you are not. Because you were so terribly afraid. What would happen if they found out that deep inside you were not that strong person they thought you were?

Georgina learned at a young age to be what they wanted her to be. She learned to hide her fears behind a facade of sheer will. Over the years, whenever her world began to crumble around her, like when her mother was dying and only said goodbye to Albert, or when her father died and left the entire Bayard estate to her brother alone, Georgina became stronger and fought harder to hang on the same way she had fought those many years ago to hang on to Albert when the sea had tried to push and pull them under.

And now, for weeks she'd been quietly fighting again. Tonight she would know if she had won her latest battle. She stood up abruptly, as if by sitting down for those few minutes she had done the unforgivable and had given up. She turned, then paused at the glass doors and watched a crew of fifteen men working in the gardens, pruning back the overgrowth so the stone benches were clear of wild branches and sucker shoots, shaping the bushes and spruce hedges until they were perfectly symmetrical, cleaning up crushed lilacs and roses, and the fallen leaves from the flagstone walks and marble fountains. Lanterns were being strung from the top-floor balcony, high enough to softly light the grounds below yet not shine on the mansion's cracked wood and scattered patches of peeling white paint.

For the last day and a half, the brick-paved drive had clattered with the constant sounds of delivery wagons filled with crates of live lobster, prime cuts of beef, sweet hothouse fruits, exotic flowers, beluga caviar, and case after case of Veuve Clicquot champagne. Georgina had spent the last of the Bayard fortune on tonight's gala, a Bayard tradition.

Every summer, for as long as anyone could remember, the Bayard gala closed the summer season in Maine. Men pomaded their hair and wore jeweled studs in their silk shirts. Women laced up China silk dancing slippers and saved a Worth gown for this annual farewell night, when French champagne flowed endlessly from a heavy silver fountain, when delicate pieces of sweet lobster were wrapped in buttery pastry and served with wonderfully exotic bananas glazed in honey and hazelnuts, and when Russian caviar speckled the creamy platters of new potatoes. There would be lively music and dancing in the Bayard gardens; and though there always were lanterns hanging to light the way, the gardens never ceased to glow under a traditional August moon.

Anticipation ran high among the attendees, for it was well known that there had been more sealed engagements, more merging of wealthy families at the Bayard gala than at any event ever. Ladies dreamt of a long look, a long kiss, a short question, and an impressive four-karat diamond set in precious platinum. Young men practiced love lines on bended knees, and in their sweaty palms they held celluloid ring boxes lined with blue velvet to protect the jewels that were hidden inside. Tonight could change the life of at least ten couples.

Within two weeks all of Maine's summer society would be back in Boston, New York, and Philadelphia. Back home until the next June when Maine became home again, another Camelot to those legendary American names and bank accounts already living in a private world almost as fantastical as an Arthurian tale.

But Georgina wouldn't be going home. The bank had taken the Bayard townhouse. Within three months she could lose this home too. In fact, unless John Cabot proposed tonight, Georgina would have no home here or in Boston. Once everyone went home they would know about the foreclosed townhouse, the broken business, the bonds gone bad, and the shipping losses. They would know about her foolish and frivolous brother. They would know that the Bayard fortune was no more.

A few minutes later a rosewood regulator clock chimed; its gong rang one . . . two . . . three . . . four times, before the shelf clock went off. Soon all twenty clocks were chiming at different moments and different hours as if they needed to mock the chaos in Georgina's life. She stared at the clock wall where the Bayard collection was artfully displayed.

The first Bayard had been a clockmaker from the old country, a man who came to a new world and here he made his fortune and his name. Ironically, they were the things that were more timeless than his famous clocks, prized because they never lost even a minute's time in an entire year. Elegant, rare, and some even whimsical, the clocks had always been a part of this house, part of Georgina's heritage. Yet now, when her life was ready to fall apart, not one clock in the entire room kept the same time. No matter how often she wound them. No matter how often she reset them, the clocks would chime at different hours.

She gave the bell pull an angry yank. For one brief second a small rip sounded, then the other end of the bell pull fell to the floor, the old silken cord so rotten that it had just unraveled. She stared at the tattered end lying on the carpet and looking as if it had been chewed. In her right hand she still held the other end. She took two deep breaths, then hollered, "Mrs. Cartwright!"

Nothing.

"Miss-sus Cartwright!"

An older woman came scurrying into the room, wiping her hands on her apron. "Yes, Miss?"

"Please have someone fix the bell pull and check all the other pulls. Every single one of them. Tonight is too important. I want everything perfect."

The old woman nodded and took the bell pull from her.

Georgina crossed the room just as a clock with a mother-of-pearl face like the moon chimed six. What time is it? she thought, then scowled at that clock. "And Mrs. Cartwright. Reset all the clocks. Every one of them is wrong."

"But Miss Bayard, we did. We reset them this very morning and still they run at different times."

"They are Bayard clocks. A Bayard clock never loses time. Everyone knows that. I said . . . reset them." Georgina left the room and marched down the hallway, barking out orders to three maids before she stopped to fiddle with a bouquet of fresh flowers that sat atop a two-hundred-year-old French console table with gilt edges and three ink marks from Louis XIV. She plucked out a rose, then a lily, a chrysanthemum, and two fern leaves, then put them back exactly as they were. She eyed them critically and muttered, "Much better."

A moment later she was inspecting the rooms, all twenty eight of them. Before too long, maids with feather dusters and mops in tow were running this way and that like confused birds that had been locked in a small cage. They polished the heavy silver candlesticks that had belonged to emperors, cleaned imaginary spots off one of the fifteen crystal chandeliers, scrubbed off the small dark specks on the French carpet in the smoking room, and used thick beeswax and almond oil on the mahogany banister, stairs, and all the wood crown moldings—*again.*

Having snapped out her last order, Georgina stood in the middle of the foyer, her hands planted on her hips while she stared up three stories to the gallery above. She knew one thing for certain: she had to save this house. At her darkest moment, when Albert was dead, when she found out that everything was gone, that moment when she was completely alone and the undertow was threatening to drown her, the answer had come to her like knowledge from above—if she were to believe in such things, which she didn't.

The house, this house and everything in it, stood for all she was. Within its walls of plaster and wood were the rhythms of life, all the Bayards were and ever had been. It stood for the survivors. With calculated desperation she had done whatever she had to do in order to save this house, because if she lost the house, she lost Georgina Bayard, she lost herself.

No one knew of her circumstances yet, and if John Cabot proposed, no one need ever know. Everything was ready. And tonight, if all went smoothly, she would have her marriage offer. Her future and her home and her name would be secure.

Georgina rearranged the flowers on the table for the

fifth time that morning, while a constant litany of *Tonight! Tonight! Tonight!* rang through her head like the chiming of an overwound clock. Everything had to be perfect, absolutely perfect, especially when she felt as though she were swimming harder than ever before. Because for Georgina, tonight was swim . . . or sink.

Now my brothers call from the bay,
Now the great winds shoreward blow,
Now the salt tide seawards flow;
Now the wild horses play,
Champ and chafe and toss in the spray.

> *Matthew Arnold,*
> The Forsaken Mermen

ARRANT ISLAND, MAINE

The rider burst over the crest of a lawny hill as if he were atop Pegasus. The August air, warm and quiet only seconds before, now trembled with the thundering sound of Eachann MacLachlan on his white stallion. Down the dirt road they flew, past a rocky island point where on a clear day like today black shags stood spread-eagle atop the white crusted rocks and gulls screamed at the constantly shifting waves.

Eachann sailed over a fieldstone fence, down a lush glen where his horse splattered through a cool brook, then jumped another rock fence twice as high as the first one. They sped past a pond with harlequin ducks and white whooper swans gliding over the glassy surface toward a small wooden bridge that arched over the water like a rainbow.

When he rode like that, his horse's hooves eating up the damp green earth, together, he and his white stallion looked like one unique beast of incredible grace and power, seeming to almost drink up the salty air. At the edge of a thick mossy forest of cat spruce and pumpkin pine, they dipped suddenly and turned down a trail lined with birch, maple, and aspen trees whose leaves had already begun to change color. Each year when those leaves fell to almost a foot deep, the trail turned red and orange as if it were on fire.

He slowed his horse as the trail wound downward toward the sea where a small inlet was hidden by an arm of rock that curled protectively around the northern edge of the cove. But once on the white sand, they took off again, pounding through the shallow rush of surf, the water spraying up behind them and sparkling in the brilliant sunlight like a trail of fireflies.

At the squat wooden dock near the far end of Piper's Cove, a coaster sat with its sail just being furled. But they didn't ride toward the quay. Instead, they turned and rode swiftly up another circular trail, past a tall hemlock that stuck out from the rocks and hid the spot where the trail flattened and led toward a sprawling stone house.

From the cove the house below looked as if it were built right into the hillside. Along the rear entrances were a series of granite arches that scalloped the entire back of the house in a smooth sleek way that made the windows and doors look as if they had been cut out from one solid, mammoth piece of salmon-pink granite.

At the rear of the house, Eachann stopped. He was a tall brawny man with blond hair that gleamed gold in the sunlight and shoulders nearly as wide as the wingspread of an osprey. But he swung a long leg over the saddle with casual ease for one so large and slid to the ground.

For a moment his stallion tossed its head and pawed the ground as if it were still hungry for a run. But he clicked his tongue twice and the horse tossed its head once more, then stilled with an eerie acquiescence that for a brief second silenced everything around them but the distant rush of the sea.

For only the time it took a gull to scream, he stood as still as his horse, staring at the cove and at the coaster docked at the quay, then he disappeared into the deep dark shadow of a stone archway.

Follow love and it will flee thee,
Flee love and it will follow thee.
Old Scottish proverb

There were some things even Calum MacLachlan
wouldn't do for his name. Which was why he was
hiding behind an island spruce in the forest that
edged the north end of Piper's Cove. The trees on the
forest rim were covered with fat burls that bulged
from the trunks like Rip Van Winkle's bowling balls.
They hid him well, yet he had a clear view of the dock.

He watched five women step from the boat deck
and walk up the quay. The women stopped abruptly
when Fergus MacLachlan shouted to them from the
deck.

There was no doubt; these women were the latest
batch of brides. That stubborn old devil wanted
Calum married.

When it came to Fergus MacLachlan, a distant
cousin and constant thorn in the side, Calum had no
say in what the old man did. Fergus did what he
wanted, claiming that age, experience, and a close
kinship to the old laird, Calum's father, had always
awarded him the freedom to do what he thought best

for "the spawn of his guid friend, the auld laird, MacLachlan of MacLachlan, God-bless-him-in-spite-of-his-fasheous-sons." The fact that Fergus had been a surrogate father and helped raise both Calum and his younger brother Eachann only added to Fergus's zeal.

And for the past few years, his zeal was to see Calum, laird of the clan MacLachlan, married. The old man started his matchmaking slowly at first, but when Calum refused to take him seriously, canny old Fergus began to lure women to the island with promises of winning a husband who was a "braw mon of property."

To Calum, marriage was like death. He knew he had to do it someday, but he was certainly in no hurry to experience it.

Calum adjusted his spectacles, stuck his head out from behind the tree, and really looked at the women.

He had the sudden urge to run like hell.

Immediately he hid again, whipped off his spectacles, and polished the glass lenses on his shirt. He held them up to the sunlight, then polished them again. A few minutes later he put the glasses back on and peered out from behind the tree.

The first woman was so old her shoulders had begun to stoop. The second he couldn't see because the third woman's red hair was in the way. In fact, her red hair was in the way of everything within three feet of her head. It took him a minute or so to notice that every few seconds she would twitch. He strained his neck out a little farther. Still he could only see three of the five women.

"There he is!" a woman shouted from behind him.

"Ya! Das ist him!" screeched another one.

Calum whipped around. The two missing women, the two with the most man-hungry expressions, stood back in the pine trees. He heard the others on the dock scream, "Wait for us!"

An instant later in a flurry of pine needles and sand, of wild red hair and even wilder and determined expressions, they were all charging straight at him from three different directions.

He turned and ran like holy hell.

When turtles tread, and rooks, and daws,
And maidens bleach their summer smocks,
The cuckoo then, on every tree,
Mocks married men; for thus sings he,
Cuckoo . . .

William Shakespeare

Calum slammed the library door closed and leaned against it for a moment, trying to catch his breath. Pine needles clung to his damp shirt and Spanish moss hung from his pants and belt. His spectacles dangled off one ear. He slipped the frame over his other ear, positioned the glasses on the crown of his nose, and the lenses immediately fogged from the heat of his sweaty face.

"I'm going to kill Fergus," he muttered, cleaning his spectacles again, then picking needles, stringy gray moss, and damp leaves from his clothes. "With my bare hands . . . around his thick old neck . . ."

"I take it Fergus brought you more brides."

"Aye," Calum said, plucking a dead maple leaf off his white shirt while he turned toward the sound of his brother's voice.

Eachann sat sprawled in a leather wing chair near the windows; he had to sit sprawled, his size gave him no other choice. While Calum was considered tall at six feet and plenty brawny, Eachann was over half a foot taller, with wide shoulders, and hands so big that he could almost palm the base of a caber. He could throw the hammer farther than anyone Calum had ever seen, but he was nimble enough to skate like the wind when he held a shinty stick in his huge hands. Also, there were Eachann's horses. Atop one of his prized white horses Eachann MacLachlan was a sight to see.

Calum didn't have his brother's skill with animals. But he could run. He ran so fast he could race any one of Eachann's horses down the beach. As children, it was Calum who won every foot race. It was Calum who could change direction and never lose an inch of ground.

Eachann used to brag that his older brother could wheel about in a blink. And he was right. Calum never skirtit anything. He would run right into the woods and never break stride, even where the birch trunks were so thick that anyone else would have to sidle through. Calum ran like Eachann rode—with every ounce of skill that God had given him.

However Fergus's brides were giving him more practice running than he wanted, or than he had time for.

"How many women this time?"

"Five." Calum picked the last of the forest from his shirt and dropped the moss and needles into an empty brass ash can that sat near the fireplace. He thought he heard Eachann give a quiet snicker and Calum looked up.

His brother was grinning at him the way he always did when Calum was cleaning up.

"I like things neat," Calum said defensively, then walked over to his desk and started to sit down, but he stopped and picked some lint balls from the chair.

"Aye, that you do." Eachann paused and stared at Calum's head with that same smirk. "You might want to take that pine cone out of your hair. Makes you look like a boarhound with one ear cropped."

While Eachann was laughing at him, Calum patted his hair and a small pine cone fell onto the neat stack of papers on his desk. He was just cleaning up the mess when a hollow clop . . . clop . . . clop came down the hallway.

Both brothers looked up. Eachann's horse trotted into the library, stopped, looked at Eachann, and then tossed its head.

Calum groaned and sank into his chair. "Can't you keep that damn horse of yours out of the house?"

Eachann shrugged. "He doesn't hurt anything."

Calum watched the stallion's long tail sweep back and forth, just missing a crystal and silver whisky decanter. "Not yet he hasn't," Calum muttered to himself and watched his brother stroke the horse's muzzle. "That beast thinks it's a lapdog."

A sudden loud and furious pounding came from both the back and front doors.

The women called out, "Let us in!"

"Let us in!"

The brothers exchanged a knowing look.

"I'll take care of the women." Eachann unfolded himself from the chair and stood.

"Be sure to bring Fergus back with you."

"Aye. I'd already planned on it." Eachann crossed the room in a few long strides, a trail of grass and dirt crumbling onto the carpet from his crusty riding boots. His horse whickered, then pranced after him.

Calum opened the bottom desk drawer and took out a whisk broom and dustpan. A minute later he was on his knees sweeping up the grass and dirt and mud clumps in the shape of horseshoes from the carpet. He emptied the dust pan, shook out the whisk broom, and while he polished the pan with a dust cloth he critically eyed the dark carpet. Satisfied, he turned and checked the tall polished red oak bookshelves that his great-grandfather had built into two walls of the room.

Each leather-bound volume was aligned perfectly with the next. No dust. No lint, and every piece of crystal and brass in the entire room, from the decanters to the walnut bowl, sparkled brightly. The windowpanes were so clean that if it weren't for the frames and the slight waves in the glass you would think there was nothing there at all.

Calum put the broom and dusters away in their drawer and he sat down at his desk. He restacked his papers three times, and when he decided they were perfect he took a deep breath and leaned back in the chair. Everything was in its place.

A few minutes later the door blasted open and slammed against the wall with enough force to dent the crown molding. Calum's papers flew all over the desk.

Eachann strolled through the doorway in his usual careless fashion. "All taken care of," he said, as if handling women were as easy as breathing.

Calum was lying atop the desk with his arms spread out like a cormorant and his hands clamped to the desk edges so his chest held down his paperwork. He looked up, his spectacles perched on the edge of his nose. His younger brother looked as if he had just done something as easy as take an exhilarating ride through the meadows.

Calum straightened, pushed his glasses back up his nose, and scooped up the papers into his arms. He began to restack them into neat and precise piles while his brother sprawled into his favorite chair again as if nothing was wrong with the world. He supposed that for Eachann, handling those women was that easy.

It wasn't that easy for Calum. Women scared the hell out of him. He and Eachann were opposites, but their differences never made Calum feel uncomfortable. With women, Calum felt as if he were in another world, one he didn't understand, one that didn't make any sense at all.

Women were just too complicated for him, the way they would say one thing and do another. He never knew what to believe: what they said, or what they did . . . or worse yet, what they never said and what they wanted you to know you should do. They were completely illogical, and whenever he was around them he became irritable and crusty, the same way he reacted to Fergus's matchmaking.

He finished tidying up, then stared pointedly at his brother's muddy boots. "There are boot jacks by all the doors."

"I know. I keep having to step over the blasted things. Damn nuisance if you ask me." Eachann picked up a walnut from the bowl by the chair and cracked it with his huge hand. He picked out the nut meat and let the shells fall on the table and chair. A second later, clop . . . clop . . . clop, and his horse moseyed back into the room.

Calum gave up. He shoved his glasses back up his nose with a stiff finger and shuffled the stacks around his desk until they were aligned and in alphabetical order, then he looked back at Eachann who was dusted with walnut shells. "Where are the women?"

"In the kitchen."

"The kitchen? Why the kitchen?"

"Women belong in the kitchen." Eachann cracked another nut. "Besides, I told them your favorite foods were doughnuts and blueberry pie."

"*Your* favorite foods are doughnuts and blueberry pie."

Eachann grinned. "I know."

"I want to get rid of those women and you've got them cooking pies?"

Eachann shrugged and tossed a piece of nut in the air and caught it with his open mouth. "I was hungry." He looked at Calum. "Stop your worrying. They're too busy trying to impress you with their recipes to be following you around. Besides, I locked the kitchen door."

"Where's Fergus?"

Eachann used a piece of walnut shell to point at the open doorway.

Calum looked, but the doorway was empty. He waited to the sound of cracking nuts and the annoying patter of walnut shells on his clean carpet. Finally he called out, "Fergus!"

Nothing.

"Fergus MacLachlan, I know you're bloody well out there!"

Nothing.

"Get in here, old man."

"I'm coming . . . I'm coming . . ." A tall old man with shoulder-length hair as white as seafoam came walking through the open door. He scowled at the room in general from a craggy time- and sea-weathered face. "Do ye ken I canna hear ye? Ye're bellowing like a foghorn. Ye need tae respect yer elders, laddie." He squinted at the stallion, then his gaze shifted to Eachann, who pointed toward Calum. Fergus planted his hammy fists on his hips, turned, and scowled at a bust of Robert the Bruce that stood on a mahogany column pedestal near Calum's desk. "I dinna be deaf, dumb and blind, ye ken."

"I'm over here," Calum said dryly.

Fergus turned again and squinted at him. He didn't say anything, but his whiskered chin jutted out like a mule.

"I told you no more women."

"Aye, that ye did, laddie, that ye did."

"Take them back, old man."

Fergus only stood there as if he had grown roots.

"I'm going to tell you this once more. Do not bring women to this island. In fact, you won't be going ashore again."

"I wouldn't have sent him this time," Eachann said.

"I didn't send Fergus. I sent David. Do you think I don't know what I'm doing?"

Eachann just shrugged and tossed his horse a piece of nut.

"If ye ken what yer were doing, Calum MacLachlan, ye'd have wed a long time past. 'Tis a puir thing ye've done, laddie. A puir thing . . ."

Eachann groaned under his breath. "Oh God. . . . Here it comes again. . . ." He sank deeper into his chair. His horse rested its muzzle on his shoulder and watched Fergus from heavy-lidded equine eyes. Calum just stood there waiting for the same old lecture.

". . . All the auld lairds must be a writhing in their graves. 'Tis a sad day for the clan MacLachlan." Fergus took a deep breath and shook his big white head. "Yer great-great-grandfather, the MacLachlan Himself, dying at Culloden Moor, spilling his blood for the sake of the clans, and here ye are with no woman, no bairns." Fergus shook his white head. "Och! This world is no' for the auld ways."

Calum glanced at his brother who was mouthing the words as Fergus spoke.

". . . And yer great-grandfather, but a laddie he was when he fled to France with the Bonnie Prince, and lived in exile, he did. But did he think of Himself? No, he dinna. He spent years finding a new home for his people. He sailed across the sea, coming here to this wild place and searching till he found this island."

Fergus paused, then waved his arm around like an evangelist in a room full of sinners. "Aye, will ye look around ye? At yer isle? 'Tis like a bonnie Scots' isle. Then the puir mon sailed back to Scotland and brought his starving clan. Lost his wife he did, yer ain wee grandmother died on that voyage.

"Here ye are, over a hundred years after yer great-

great-grandfather, yer own namesake, the great Calum MacLachlan who died for his prince at Culloden, and ye canna even honor the dead MacLachlans by marrying one puir, awee, little woman." Fergus sighed dramatically.

By then Eachann was quietly snoring, his stallion's muzzle resting on his head.

Calum planted his hands on his desk and leaned forward, enunciating each word. "Take . . . the women . . . *back.*"

"If ye dinna ken when ye need a thing, well, I ken when ye do." Fergus raised his chin, crossed his arms and just stood there. "And ye need a wife, Calum MacLachlan."

"One of those women?" Calum shouted so loudly that Eachann woke up with a start.

"And what 'tis wrong with them?"

"Fergus can't see worth a damn, brother," Eachann said. "He has no idea what's wrong with them."

"I'll have ye ken, Eachann MacLachlan, I can see as weel as ye!" Fergus bellowed at the bust of Robert the Bruce.

"Fergus."

"Aye." Fergus turned toward Calum's voice.

"One of those women is old enough to be my grandmother."

After a few silent seconds, he admitted, "Aye, I suppose Sallie's a tad long in the tooth."

Eachann gave a sharp bark of laughter. "She doesn't have any teeth."

"Ye need a wife, Calum MacLachlan. Ye need a family. Ye need wee bairns. MacLachlan bairns. Like Eachann. Yer brother's four years younger than ye and he has bairns."

"Two bairns," Eachann added with a grin that was cut short when Fergus muttered something about another letter, scowled, and began to fumble through his coat pocket.

"Ooh, here it be." He handed Eachann a vellum letter that they all recognized. There had been at least ten such letters from his children's school in the last year.

Fergus slapped the letter in his hand and gave Eachann an equally quelling "you need to be married" look. "Ye've no wife, either."

Eachann only shrugged. "I've already had one."

"Yer bairns need tae be here, with MacLachlans, not at some auld school where strangers are raising them into wee heathens. They need a mother."

"Why? I never knew mine." Eachann cracked another nut, tossed it into his mouth, then scowled and spit it back into his hand.

Calum shook his head. Perhaps Eachann did need a woman. He needed something.

Eachann looked up at them. "Like I was saying, I never knew our mother and look how I turned out."

"I am, laddie. That I am."

Eachann said something to his horse, then stroked the beast's muzzle.

"Ye have more caring fer yer horses, Eachann MacLachlan, than fer yer ain wee bairns."

Eachann froze and was silent and tense. All his cockiness had fled. He just stared down at the unopened letter with an odd and shuttered look.

Fergus had gone too far this time, Calum thought, looking from that bullheaded old man to his equally bullheaded brother.

But Fergus must have realized his mistake because he too was silent. The air grew thick and for just a moment there was no sound in the room except for the perennial ticking of the Bayard mantel clock.

Finally Eachann looked up, his jaw tighter than it

had been a moment before, his eyes narrower. "I'll take care of my bairns, old man."

"They need a woman's touch and they need tae live here, with the MacLachlans. The bairns need tae live with their ain father, lad."

Eachann didn't say a word.

Fergus turned to Calum again. "And ye're the laird of the clan MacLachlan, the last Calum MacLachlan and ye dinna have any bairns. Eachann's bairns dinna have cousins. Bairns need family, lads. If ye dinna be wanting to do a thing about it, I will."

"Tell me old man. You expect me to get bairns from that old woman?"

Fergus shrugged. "She was the first one I could find."

Calum stood there completely silent.

But Eachann wasn't. "Where did you look, under a rock during a full moon?" He glanced at Calum. "Perhaps he found her out scavenging for eye of newt."

Fergus scowled at him.

"Skin of toads? Bat wings?"

"Jest all ye want, Eachann MacLachlan. But ye and yer brother still need wives."

"And you want someone like that hausfrau to be the mother of the next MacLachlan laird?" Eachann began to laugh.

Fergus scratched his chin thoughtfully. "Weel. . . . She came for free."

"Free?" Calum's head shot up and he stared at Fergus.

"Aye."

Stunned, Calum remembered all the different women Fergus had been bringing to the island, and in his head, he began to mentally count them—money and women. "You mean all this time you've been *paying* them?"

Fergus said nothing, which meant that was exactly what he'd been doing.

"You paid them money to come here when I told you no bride, no wife, no women?"

"I dinna have tae pay all of them."

"How many?"

Fergus was quiet, but his lips were moving as he counted. Finally he looked at Calum. "Sixteen."

Eachann burst out laughing and Calum knew why. Fergus had brought eighteen women to the island on the past year.

"Two came for free, brother," Eachann said, his expression showing that he was trying not to laugh again.

"Those puir foolish mainlanders think the Mac-Lachlans are ghosts," Fergus said indignantly. He paused for a minute, as if he were waiting for Calum or Eachann to speak. When they didn't, he picked Calum to glare at. Then he jammed his fists on his hips again and said. "Why are ye shouting at me, Calum MacLachlan. Ye were the one who paid the last one tae leave."

"That's because she kept climbing into his bed, old man." Eachann looked at Calum. "You should have married that one. Then even Fergus here couldn't say you weren't carrying on an old clan tradition."

Calum didn't know what the hell Eachann was talking about and one look at Fergus said he didn't either.

Eachann gave them both a wicked grin. "Like our forefathers you'd be sleeping with a battle-axe by your side."

When neither one of them laughed, Eachann just shrugged and muttered about the sad lack of humor in the MacLachlan clan.

Calum turned back to Fergus. "How much did you pay them?"

"I dinna keep count."

Calum began to pace, running a hand through his

black hair as he thought about how he'd spent those two months running from three different women when the unpredictable weather had prevented them from returning to the mainland. It had been absolute hell.

"The red-haired lassie, now she be a MacGunnagh from Nova Scotia," Fergus said proudly. "She'd be a perfect wife fer ye."

Calum stopped pacing. "The twitchy one with the wild hair?"

"Wild hair? You should have seen her eyes," Eachann mumbled, then shuddered.

"Pure-blooded Scots, she is." Fergus stood a bit taller and puffed out his chest. "Her mother was—"

"Her father's sister," Eachann finished, then cracked three nuts in one hand and gave Fergus a grin.

Fergus fumed for a silent second, then turned and marched angrily toward the door. He muttered something about the great laird MacLachlan's no-guid spawn, then he smacked right into the door molding.

Dazed, he stood there for a moment, his forehead against the molding like he was nailed to it. He muttered something inaudible and looked all around him to get his bearings, then turned back and glared at Eachann first, then locked his squinting eyes on the bust of Robert the Bruce. "Ye need wives. And I'll no' stop till ye have them. Someone has tae care about seeing tae the MacLachlan blood." And with that he stomped out of the room.

Calum called out after him, "If you bring another woman to this island, the only MacLachlan blood anyone will be seeing, Fergus, is yours."

There was a crash and a loud Gaelic oath. A few seconds later the front doors slammed shut.

Neither brother said anything for a moment, then Calum unlocked a drawer and took out a bag of money. He tossed it to his Eachann. "Pay them off again and have someone take them back to the mainland."

"I need to go to the school." Eachann stood and held up the letter. "I'll take them back." He moved toward the doorway, but stopped at the bust of Robert the Bruce and patted it on the head. Imitating Fergus, he said, "Don't worry, Robbie me lad. Ye need a wife, and old Fergus will be bringing ye the Venus de Milo any day now."

"You wouldn't think this was so damn funny if it was you they were chasing."

Eachann just laughed the way he always did when Calum was in this fix.

"Look. Just get rid of the women. Pay them off. And hurry. I don't relish having them stuck on the island like the last ones were."

Eachann clicked his tongue twice and his horse trotted over to his side. In one swift motion Eachann was up in the saddle. He rested one arm on the saddle pommel and grinned down at Calum. "Stop your worrying, brother. I'll take care of it."

He ducked down low over his horse and they started to ride out of the library, but Eachann stopped halfway through the doorway and turned back around. "I'll see those women are off the island." He gave Calum a cocky salute and added, "Just as soon as those pies are done."

If a person offends you, and you are in doubt as to whether it was intentional or not, do not resort to extreme measures; simply watch your chance, and hit him with a brick.

Advice to Youth, Mark Twain

The arithmetic master was unconscious for almost five minutes, Mr. MacLachlan." Miss Hebsibah Harrington's distinct and nasally voice pierced through the walnut door between the schoolmistress's office and the small salon next door.

Seven-year-old Kirsty MacLachlan jabbed an elbow into her brother Graham's bony ribs, wiggled in front of him, and peered through the keyhole in the salon door.

"I was there first," Graham whined in a whisper.

She turned around and stuck her scowling face just an inch from his, which always worked in her favor. "Shhh! I can't hear them."

Graham called her a troll under his breath, but she'd let that pass this time. If she kicked him, he might holler and give them away. She shifted so she could block her brother with her backside and petticoats, then she turned her head just a bit to better see her father.

He stood with his arm resting easily on the marble

fireplace mantel in Harrington Hall's genteel office, which was filled with skinny-legged tables and oval chairs painted gold on the edges and with ugly feet that curled up like fists warning you to stay away. The cold wood floor had Turkey rugs with some odd dark blue patterns that were supposed to be trees—which made Kirsty wonder if the trees in Turkey were blue—and frail-looking imported porcelains sat everywhere and gave her an uneasy feeling whenever she was in the room. Those china figures looked as if they would crack into little pieces if you spoke too loudly.

Her father looked as out of place in the office of Harrington Hall as Kirsty felt in this school. It was odd to see him standing there. She knew the room; she'd spent many unpleasant moments standing before Miss Harrington's stiff-looking desk while the schoolmistress lectured her on conduct becoming a proper young lady, especially a *Harrington* pupil.

So to see her father standing there with pastel French porcelain figurines next to his thick arm was very odd. In her mind he belonged on the island, riding one of his horses or standing next to that tall hemlock tree where his head almost touched the highest branches. She hadn't many memories of him, but she remembered how wonderfully her father could ride. She thought perhaps he had taken her for a ride on his horse once, but she wasn't certain if it had happened when she was barely old enough to remember, or if she just wished it to be.

Her memory seemed real; she could imagine his tanned hands on the thick leather reins of one of his powerful horses, before he had pointed up at the bright pearly ball of a moon and told her the misty ring around it was a sign that rain would come soon. Sometimes, in the middle of the night while the other children were sound asleep, Kirsty would wrap herself in woolen blankets and sit cross-legged beneath the window, looking up at the vast dark sky above her. If there was a ring around the moon, she always thought of her father.

But now she could look at him, see him in person. She wedged her eyeball a little closer to the keyhole. In one of those hands of his, he held a letter which he'd been staring at with a serious and thoughtful look. Kirsty wondered what he was thinking about when he looked at the letter. Did he think about them? Graham and her?

They thought about him and whispered about what they imagined he was doing when they were supposed to be studying geography. Kirsty didn't give a holy cow where the Himalaya Mountains were or what direction the Ganges River flowed.

She cared where her father was. He was all she and Graham had left. If they could just wake up one day and suddenly have no mother, that meant the same thing could happen to their father. To anyone.

After that realization, Kirsty never slept well and woke up shaking and crying a lot. She hated that weakness about herself and stole pillows and blankets from the other children so she could muffle the sound when she would wake up already crying.

She wondered if her father ever had nightmares. Did he think about their mother sometimes like she did? Did he cry when she left them? She couldn't imagine her father crying.

The sad truth was that she didn't really know her father. But she desperately wanted to, so she just stood there with her eye pressed to that brass keyhole and watched him.

It was odd how he looked different to her, and yet the same. His hair had grown longer than the last time she'd seen him and it was darker than her own pale gold hair. Her father's hair was deep golden, the color that the tops of the puffy clouds turned when the sun set over the western hills. He wore his hair combed back from his broad forehead, which made his face look like the rocky cliffs on Arrant Island with their sharp granite edges.

She could remember trying to mold his likeness from the clay they'd made from wheat flour in art class one day, but she could never form her father's strong features with her small pudgy fingers. She had needed something sharp like a knife to cut the clay. But knives were against the school rules, even in art class, something which made her so peevish that instead she'd made a likeness of Miss Harrington riding a broomstick, then had to spend the next few hours printing "I will not be disrespectful to my elders" on the blackboard a hundred times.

That was last spring. Now it was the end of summer and she could see the last of the warm season on her father's face. His skin was tanned from the intense summer sun that crawled over the islands. She was glad her father's skin was the color of the hickory nuts that fell on the grounds outside and wasn't the milky pale skin color that made the arithmetic master look so sickly and weak, even when he wasn't unconscious.

Her father wasn't sickly or weak. One look at him and anyone could see that. He was an enormous man. The top of her head barely came to his wrist. When she would tilt back her head so she could look up at him, he seemed as tall and straight as those island pine trees, almost as tall and straight as she imagined God Himself must be.

Her father hadn't been to the school in months, not since the last really bad letter, when she and Graham had dunked Chester Farriday's head in the mop bucket. Chester's father was the governor of the state, so there had been a lot of brouhaha over that prank. But Chester was wrong. He was dumb and said stupid mean things. Her family was not a bunch of spooky ghosts and monsters that scalped men with claymores and wrapped women in their plaids, then rode off in the mist to have their way with them. She wasn't certain what having-their-way-with-them was, but she knew MacLachlans didn't do it because Chester Farriday was a big old dummy.

He had to be. MacLachlans didn't eat small spit-roasted children and boil bat wings and toads for supper. Although she had wished she were really a witch so she could turn Chester Farriday into a toad, then maybe someone else would boil him.

Chester had caused the whole thing anyway. He had tried to get the other boys to pin Kirsty and Graham on the ground and yank off their shoes and stockings to see if they had cloven feet. But Kirsty had pinched him really hard and scrambled away. She had to do something. Graham didn't fight back with those boys and, besides, it was dumb old Chester who was standing right next to the mop bucket. If he didn't want to get his head stuck in the bucket, he shouldn't've been dumb enough to stand next to it.

"Lemme see." Graham was pestering her and poking his finger in her shoulder blade.

"Just a minute." She turned her head sideways and could see Miss Harrington's skinny freckled hand twisting a silver letter opener while she spoke. Also on the desktop was *the* wooden ruler, the same one that her knuckles knew so well that they cried out "howdy-do" when they met each other. At least in her mind they cried out "howdy-do." If she pretended something silly like that then it didn't sting so terribly much and she could keep herself from crying and showing anyone that the cruel smack from that ruler truly did hurt her.

Miss Harrington was jabbing a silver letter opener into the desktop's green ink blotter over and over again as she spoke. After a minute Kirsty realized she was using the opener to accentuate each of her nouns and pronouns—grammar was Kirsty's very best subject.

"Your children have a severe discipline problem."

After the words "your children," the letter opener stuck in the desk and wiggled like an arrow did when it hit the archery target bull's-eye.

"Harrington Hall has an exemplary reputation, Mr. MacLachlan. We are known as one of the finest boarding academies in New England. Harrington alumni have become pillars of society. We have never failed to mold even the most headstrong of children into proper young ladies and gentlemen. Our history of success, as I told you when you enrolled your son and daughter, has been one hundred percent." Miss Harrington cleared her throat and there was absolute silence for so long that Kirsty could barely keep her breath in her chest.

"Until now." Miss Harrington planted her thin white hands on the desk and stood up stiffly. "The situation has gotten completely out of hand. I'm sorry, Mr. MacLachlan, but I must ask you to withdraw your children from Harrington Hall immediately."

Kirsty turned back to Graham and whispered excitedly, "We did it!"

"I wanna see!" Graham whispered and tried to shove her aside.

Kirsty ground her heel into his foot and glared at him until he winced. "Not yet," she said through gritted teeth and looked back through the keyhole. Her father opened his coat pocket and took out a money pouch.

She heard him say, "How much?" Her breath froze in her chest and grew thin like the cold winter air did.

"This isn't a monetary issue."

His expression changed suddenly. He shoved away from the fireplace and crossed the room with three long and quick strides. "My children need to be in school. I'll have another talk with them."

No! No! No! Kirsty's hand tightened on the glass doorknob so tightly she could feel the diamond-shaped facets press into her palm.

Miss Harrington, bless her ruler-thwacking, blackboard-writing, and corner-sitting old soul, shook her head and handed him an envelope.

Her father stared at it.

"It's a bank draft refunding the balance of the tuition," Miss Harrington explained, then added, "less damages, physicians' fees, and the like."

Now he was the one who braced his hands on the desk and leaned toward Miss Harrington. "There are no other schools available. There must be some solution." His jaw was so tight, like when he and Uncle Calum had a fight, and his words sounded fiercely quiet and strained. Was he angry? Suddenly their pranks took on new meaning when it looked like their father might actually care enough to be angry.

"I'm sorry, but you'll have to take your children home with you."

"I can't take care of two children." There was a thread of something that sounded like panic in her father's voice as he pinned Miss Harrington with one of those "listen-to-me" looks that all adults got when something wasn't going as they wanted it to.

Kirsty chewed her lower lip for a second. She had never heard him sound like that—almost scared—and it confused her a little, got her thinking until she remembered their plan had worked.

She and Graham were going back to the island. Back home. She'd accept the consequences of what they had done because the only way she could even try to win over her father was if she and Graham were with him day after day, instead of locked away at a dumb old school with people who hated them.

"You *are* their father, Mr. MacLachlan. You'll have to take care of them." Miss Harrington stepped around the desk and moved ahead of their father toward the door. "Your children are waiting in the next room."

Kirsty moved back quickly and turned to her brother. "Okay, Graham. Now it's your turn." She stepped back and Graham scrambled to look in the keyhole.

Boys were such silly and impatient creatures, she thought with a sigh.

A second later the door opened . . . and Graham fell flat on his face, right at their father's feet.

> You should never do anything wicked and then
> lay it on your brother, when it is just as convenient
> to lay it on another boy.
>
> *Advice for Youth, Mark Twain*

Kirsty stood there looking all the way up at her father. However, he wasn't looking at her. Both he and Miss Harrington were staring down at Graham, who was still lying flat on the floor while his face turned redder and redder, almost as bright a red color as his hair. He slowly turned, his expression a little dazed, until he focused on her.

Her brother's gaze narrowed. His lower lip and chin jutted out. She knew that look. She made her eyes as wide as she could and shrugged her shoulders.

He wasn't hoodwinked at all, so she looked up quickly and gave her father that same wide-eyed look, which worked. She captured his attention long enough to get in two whole blinks *and* a saintly look.

Then Graham tackled her. They hit the carpet hard, but Kirsty got in one good sock. She wiggled out of his grasp, and at exactly the same time . . . she pinched him. While he was hollering, she sat on his chest. Graham might be bigger and older than she, but she would *not* let him best her. He was a boy.

She heard Miss Harrington shriek. She sounded like a barn owl. Out of the corner of Kirsty's eye, she saw her grab two china bluebirds that wobbled on a nearby table, then hug them to her bony old chest.

Before Kirsty could get in one more good sock, her father lifted her off Graham and set her on her feet right next to him, so close she could feel the heat from him and was aware of his scent, like the sea and leather. If she really tried, she could almost smell that sharp pine scent of the island. Her father smelled like home.

She looked up at him.

His brow was creased and his eyebrows were almost touching—a really stern look.

"Do. Not. Move," he said with force, but not anger, then turned his attention to Graham.

Kirsty took two wee little steps, then froze when her father whipped back around with a suspicious look.

Standing perfectly still, she gave him her most brilliant smile.

He blinked once and stood there for the briefest second, his expression odd, as if she were a stranger to him. He looked away and shook his head slightly, then scowled down at her brother who was still on the floor. "Stand up, Graham."

"My belly hurts. She socked me."

"I saw the whole thing. You started this."

"But she—"

Her father held up his hand and Graham shut right up.

Kirsty was amazed. She had to pinch her brother or grind her heel into his foot so he'd shut up.

"Boys do not hit girls."

"But she's not a girl, Father." Now Graham was whining. "She's my sister!"

Boys *always* whined, Kirsty thought with disgust. Grown up men did too. The arithmetic master whined whenever the class didn't understand what he was trying to teach them and the school janitor whined when Chester Farriday had pulled his soaked head out of the mop bucket and messed up his clean floor. The pastor even whined when they didn't know their Bible verses.

She wondered if God whined, then remembered the Bible story about the creation they'd read in Sunday school. Adam had whined to God that it was Eve who had given him the fruit. Considering that, Kirsty figured God probably whined too, since He made Adam in His own image and since men whined in the Bible and the Bible was God's own word.

Kirsty just stood there very calmly watching her father's face while he stared down at her brother, who blinked a couple of times before he slowly looked directly at their father and swallowed so hard Kirsty could almost hear the gulping sound of his Adam's apple. She actually felt a wee bit sorry for Graham. She did play a trick on him after all. It was just so very hard for her to pass up on such a perfect chance to best someone, especially her brother, who so often called her a troll under his breath.

She sighed.

Her father turned to her, his face unreadable, but he ran a hand through his golden hair. He looked away and stared at the floor for a long tense second while he rubbed his forehead like Miss Harrington did when she had one of her many headaches that seem to happen whenever Kirsty was in trouble.

"I will leave you to reacquaint yourself with *your children*, Mr. MacLachlan. Their belongings are packed and by now should be waiting at the front doors. Good day, sir." Old Miss Harrington stuck her pointy chin in the air. She turned and "perambulated"—one of last week's spelling words—out the door with those fragile-looking porcelain bluebirds still clutched to her chest like she was one of those mid-evil knights who had vowed to save holy relics from the heathens. Kirsty always remembered the story of those knights 'cause she never understood why evil men, even if they were only halfway evil, would make a vow to save things for God.

Her father watched the door close, then finally and slowly turned back and looked from her to her brother, who was still sitting on the floor.

"Get up, Graham" was all he said.

As her brother got up, Kirsty stepped forward before he could do or say something dumb. Besides, she supposed she owed him. And he was her brother.

"Father?"

"What?"

She smiled as brightly as she could, held it for a second or two, then said, "I didn't drop that brick out of the window onto Mr. Appleby's head."

Her father didn't say anything, but watched her as if he were trying to see the lie or the truth on her face. She was telling a little of both, as usual, so she figured she was safe.

"And Graham didn't do it either." She stepped a little in front of her brother and covertly pressed her elbow into his ribs. "Did you, Graham?"

Her brother's eyes grew wide from the jab of her elbow and shook his head perfectly. He wasn't as dumb as some boys.

"I suppose that brick fell right out of the sky."

"Well, not exactly."

Looking into her father's eyes was not easy. He seemed to know more than most adults and more than she wanted him to.

After a minute, he gave a bark of laughter that was not at all humorous. "I think for once in his meddling old life, Fergus was right."

"Right about what, Father?"

"About what I need," he said distractedly.

There it was: the perfect opportunity for her to change the subject. "What do you need?"

He just stood there for a long silence that to her seemed to stretch endlessly. The whole time he stared at his hands and absently twisted the gold ring he wore. His thoughts weren't with them. She could see that. He had a faraway look, the same look people got when they were lost and trying to figure out which way to go. She wondered what Fergus had told her father he needed, and if it had to do with them, Graham and her.

Now she was curious. "You need something, Father?" She had her hands clasped demurely behind her back, and she rocked slightly from the heels to the toes of her red leather button-top shoes.

He looked down at her as if he were surprised to see her standing there.

Could he really forget her that quickly? Her heart felt a little tighter deep inside of her chest and she realized she had stopped rocking and was standing still and stiff. She lifted her chin a notch to hide her feelings.

He shook his head. "It's nothing either of you have to worry about."

She just stood there. Scared.

He gave her an odd look. "Are you all right?"

She nodded.

"You look pale. You're not sick, are you?"

"No." She paused, then realized he must care if he looked so uneasy. "It's just the stuffy old air in here."

Her father looked around, puzzled.

"Why sometimes it's so stuffy that we can hardly breathe." She poked her brother again. "Isn't it Graham?"

He nodded, then gave her a questioning look she was afraid her father would see, so she pinched him.

"See. Even Graham looks poorly."

Now she had her father's complete attention; she could tell because he was staring at her so sharply. "The classrooms have no fresh air a'tall and there are no windows and . . ." She crooked her finger at him so he would bend down to her. When he did, she whispered, "The children faint sometimes. They do." She nodded. "They truly do. Why Alice Whiting passed out right in the middle of history class. Bam!" She clapped her hands. "Right on her pig fa—" She clamped her lips together, then swallowed. "Right on her face."

She searched her father's expression for some reaction, and when she got none she added, "And it wasn't just Alice, either. There were lots more. I can tell you all the stories, Father."

"Yes." He nodded his head and his face had a pensive but odd expression, as if he knew a secret. "I expect you have plenty of stories in that head of yours." He continued to look down at her.

She realized at that moment that perhaps there were times when having her father's complete attention was not such a wonderful thing.

"What I want to hear is the story of what happened to the arithmetic master."

Neither she nor Graham said anything.

Her father crossed his big arms and looked down at her. "I'm waiting."

"Well . . ." She gave a nice big weary kind of sigh and stared at the toes of her shoes. She thought it might make her look less guilty, just in case the fib showed more than she thought. "It's kind of a *long* story."

Her father opened the door and gestured for them to leave. "Come along. I have plenty of time to hear it."

Both she and Graham walked the few steps to the door, shoulder to shoulder, but once there she let Graham through first, then stopped in the doorway.

She looked up, searching for something in her father's expression. But she wasn't sure what, just something she needed to see there.

Nothing happened, so very slowly she held out her

hand to him. Her heart was beating so fast, like those stubborn spring birds that pecked at tree trunks, and suddenly she wanted to snatch back her hand. What if he didn't take it?

But he was staring at it. Like he was afraid, which didn't make sense. Her father wasn't afraid of anything. Huge horses. Or the thunder. Or the rain. He wasn't afraid of dying or being lonely. He wouldn't have nightmares or wake up crying. She'd bet he wouldn't even be afraid of those mid-evil knights.

She waited for what seemed like forever with the grandfather clock in the hall ticking and tocking and her hand feeling number and number the longer she stood there.

Finally he reached out and took her hand in his rough and callused one. She let loose the breath she hadn't even known she'd been holding. She felt funny deep inside, like she'd just eaten a big and really good dessert.

His hand was warm around hers; it felt special, holding his hand, almost as fine a feeling as she'd have had if he'd actually done something wonderful like pick her up in his arms and hug her.

They walked out the door together, and down the broad hallway with its long line of sour-faced portraits, the best of Harrington's students over the years.

Kirsty stopped in front of the worst one. "Do you know who that is?"

"Who?"

"Governor Farriday. He looks like he's been sucking on a pickle."

Her father looked at the painting.

"They all look like pickle-suckers," she told him.

He looked down the hallway at the others, then he laughed.

It was the best sound in the whole wide world. She pulled him along with her for a few steps, then he was leading the way and she had to skip a little to keep up with his long strides.

She didn't care. She just held his hand a little tighter and remembered the sound of his laughter.

By the time they caught up with Graham, Kirsty was feeling better. And for the first time in what seemed like forever, she didn't have that uneasy scared feeling that always seemed to be hiding in her shadow like a closet monster, ready to grab her and make her cry.

No, now she and her father and her brother were all walking down the wide stairs, side by side, Graham on their father's left and her on his right.

"I'm still waiting for that long story, Kirsty."

She stopped and stared down at the last two stairs. She hopped forward with her ankles and toes together. If her shoes weren't touching when she landed, her father wouldn't believe her tale. If her shoes were touching, then he would believe her story

She landed, staring intently down at her red leather shoes. They were touching as if they were pasted together. She grinned, then fixed her face in a more serious expression and looked up at her father. "It wasn't our fault at all. The brick, I mean."

He gave her a look filled with suspicion, but that didn't stop her. They were finally in the foyer. She pulled him along toward the huge front doors of Harrington Hall, which seemed to grow larger as they walked closer and closer. Kirsty felt that same anxious bees-buzzing-in-her-stomach kind of feeling she got whenever something special was going to happen, like Christmas or her birthday or a visit from her father.

They walked toward the stack of trunks and bandboxes that held her and her brother's belongings, and she wanted to run out those doors, run really fast, because outside, only a few short steps away, was freedom and home.

But her father stopped and looked down at her, waiting for the explanation she hadn't thought up yet. She took a deep breath, crossed the fingers of her left hand behind her back and looked way up at the most important person in her whole world.

"You see, Father," she told him, tugging on his hand with her free one and finally making him walk through those doors. "Everything happened because of . . . of . . ." She paused, then the excuse came to her like an epif—epit—epifunny. Phooey! She'd missed that spelling word.

They stopped outside on the front portico of Harrington Hall and she felt her father's grip loosen. He was going to pull his hand free, probably so he could cross his arms in that "I'm-waiting-for-an-answer" kind of way he'd been doing.

She didn't look at Graham, who had learned to stand back and let her talk, but squeezed her father's hand really tight, clinging to his thick fingers so he couldn't let go. Then she met his serious look with as stern a one as she could manage, and said very seriously, "Everything happened all because of Chester Farriday . . ."

So soon may I follow
When friendships decay,
And from Love's shining circle
The gems drop away.
When true hearts lie wither'd
And fond ones are flown,
Oh! who would inhabit
This bleak world alone?

Thomas Moore

Take it, William." Amy held out her hand with the emerald ring which felt as if it were burning the word *fool* into her palm.

William's color turned even paler in the spill of moonlight falling on the manicured gardens of the Bayard estate. He looked at her, really looked at her for the first time that evening. "Really, Amy, what sort of nonsense is this?"

He hadn't looked at her . . . all night. She'd noticed that for the first time tonight, then wondered if it had always been like that and she had just been too lost in an imaginary world where she was loved and accepted to see the truth: that the man she thought was in love with her couldn't even bear to look her in the eye. "Take the ring. Please."

He stood there like stone.

"I understand now, William. You can stop pretending. I know."

"What do you know?" His voice held amusement, which was almost more insulting to her than the things she had overheard he and his friends saying: the jokes, the rhymes.

She raised her chin and hoped to God in Heaven that it wasn't quivering. "December is the doom and devastation of the De Pysters. You can marry for money and still have love. Spend her money, spend her body . . ." She could feel her voice growing weaker. "And love every minute of it."

His face colored. He began to stammer and started to step toward her, his hands out in supplication.

"Please. Don't. Don't even try." She held up her hand so he wouldn't touch her and to keep him from seeing the glimmer of tears that flooded into her eyes the moment she had repeated those cruel sentences.

She didn't want to cry in front of him. She didn't. But those words she had repeated hurt. They hurt so much.

A second later she was crying, sobbing hard enough that people began to turn around and look at them. She just stood there, frozen in shame and hurt and unable to will her feet to move, unable to do anything but hold out the engagement ring and sob.

William's expression changed. He wasn't looking to placate her anymore. He looked around quickly and uneasily, his gaze going from face to face as if standing with her was humiliating to him.

His friends, the same people who never welcomed her, prowled closer like jungle cats moving in to view a kill. She was shaking so hard the ring fell from her hand and hit the stone walkway. The sound was small, just a ping, which seemed impossible when the ache she felt was so huge.

William took a step, bent down, and picked up the ring. He looked at it, then began to laugh, laugh loudly, exaggeratedly and more cruelly than he had that afternoon.

"She's breaking our engagement," he told everyone and held up the ring like a trophy to be proud of. "Can you imagine? *She* is breaking *our* engagement." He laughed as if she had done the most amusing thing.

She heard titters, then giggles, and snickers.

"Did you hear that?" William raised his arms out and shouted. "Amy Emerson is breaking an engagement, to me . . ." He thumped his chest with a fist. "A De Pyster."

The laughter grew, both his and theirs; it became sharp and stinging like slaps in the face.

"Looks like the little bourgeois heiress doesn't want to buy her way into society, and after those sharp-eyed lawyers purposely sent her down here to marry her off." He looked at her then with the meanest glare of contempt she had ever witnessed. "They used her money and their loan power to make certain she was accepted." He scanned the crowd again. "See the joke?"

She cried openly, unable not to, and she looked at all those faces, laughing at her as the meaning of his words registered. The lawyers had bought her society entree. "But I didn't know," she whispered half to them and half to herself. She looked at each person, one at a time, at each and every face, unable to believe that human beings could treat another person as they were.

Her blurred gaze flicked up to her William, and the sneer and the contempt on his face showed through clearly, as if she weren't seeing it through a sea of tears. "I thought," she choked over the words, "I thought you loved me."

There was anger in his eyes, but he laughed harder and more cruelly. She turned and ran, ran faster, her shoes tapping across the flagstones in a rhythm that echoed behind her like clapping hands.

She saw nothing in front of her but a blur of shame. Her head down now, she shoved past a small chattering group gathered near the champagne table. Her skirt caught and she heard a tearing sound and felt a pull. She didn't look back, but clutched a handful of silk and lace and jerked it with her as she rushed on.

She heard a shout, then the breaking of glass, but she wouldn't stop. She ran down some stone steps and away, away to the very back of the estate, where a tall stone wall and the darkness were more welcoming than where she had just been.

Her breath catching, she leaned against the wall, her damp cheek pressed against the cold wet ivy. When her chest stopped heaving, she flattened back against the stones and stared up into the night sky through eyes that burned.

Above her were the stars and the moon, those elusive, shining things people were supposed to wish upon. Wishes, hopes, and dreams. What were they really? Just foolish ideas? Like love? Like acceptance? Like kindness?

Those things didn't seem to exist. Or had died like her parents. She couldn't believe that her father had lied when he taught her to believe in them. She kept staring up, searching for answers, for something to cling to.

The scents of roses and honeysuckle were around her, smelling sickeningly sweet. In the distance she could hear the party: the voices that never welcomed her, the music she seldom danced to, the clinking of glass that sounded just like stars falling.

She was nothing to them. An echo in a room full of deaf people. Slowly she sank to the ground as if her legs couldn't bear the weight of her shame. She drew up her knees and buried her head in them, locking her arms around her legs and pulling them tightly against her chest. She rested her cheek on one knee and closed her eyes tightly so no more tears could squeeze through.

With the stars shining brightly overhead, she sat

there on the damp ground in the fall of moonlight and listened to the sounds of laughter, of the chatter and the music all going on without her. She held herself a little bit tighter, like someone who is freezing and can't get warm enough, then she cried. Because her tears were all she had left.

The moon has a face like the clock in the hall;
It shines on thieves on the garden wall.

Robert Louis Stevenson

Georgina rushed down the brick path toward the kitchen, her skirts gripped tightly in her fists, her shoulders back like a conquering general charging toward the enemy lines. The silver lobster and crab trays were picked clean, there were only two servants on the grounds, and the champagne fountain was empty.

That bourgeois Emerson girl, the one that had all the money Georgina should have had, had just made a spectacle of herself by breaking her engagement to William De Pysters.

Georgina hadn't seen the quarrel, and barely knew the girl, but she'd arrived in time to see the aftereffects. The girl had run away somewhere, but not before she'd destroyed a refreshment table and a dozen full bottles of French champagne.

This was the night to make matches, not to break them off. Silly foolish people. She was surrounded by them.

And the silliest one of them all was Phoebe Dearborn. She was all over John Cabot. Georgina's John Cabot. Georgina's rich John Cabot.

"Phoebe Dearborn," she muttered with complete disgust. The woman had a huge fortune all her own. Her father was in banking, shipping, and mining, and if that wasn't rich enough, her maternal grandfather owned half of Portland and a goodly part of Maine and New Hampshire.

Phoebe Dearborn laughed like a braying goat with the hiccups, and whenever she was around a man she fluttered her eyelashes and cooed. It was common knowledge that Phoebe had more faces than the town clock.

Unlike Georgina, she didn't need the Cabot money. Who cared if she could trace her family back to the Dark Ages? Georgina's ancestors had been battling invading barbarians right alongside of them.

Besides, Georgina thought, *she* had snagged John Cabot first. Well, after tonight she will have snagged him.

Georgina walked a little faster, her narrow heeled evening slippers clicking on the bricks like the precise second hand of a Bayard clock. She marched past the high fieldstone fence covered with lush trails of ivy and flaming red bougainvillea, past a wagon and team that she sincerely hoped was filled with more cases of champagne, round the corner of the brick building that housed the kitchens, and right into a man's chest.

A pair of strong hands gripped her by the shoulders and kept her from falling right on her backside. She looked up, way up at the man's face, a face so sharply handsome that gazing at it made her knees suddenly weak and she forgot to breathe.

Behind him the full moon was shoulder high, and its light made his blond hair look golden. He was tall, so very tall that the top of his head almost touched the low eaves of the kitchen, and he had shoulders wide enough to block her view of the building beyond.

But it was his face that left her, Georgina Bayard, a woman with a comment on almost anything, speechless and frozen, standing there and staring at him. He had a chiseled sensual face that made her feel weak and powerless, a face that made her think she was facing something she couldn't handle. She'd seen this kind of face in weak youthful dreams she'd learned to give up years ago.

He wore a pale yellow shirt with an open pointed collar and leather laces instead of mother-of-pearl buttons. Even the local fisherman managed to have shell buttons on their shirts instead of strings.

His tan vest was dull and smudged and made of the kind of soft wrinkled leather that came from weather and wear. He wore it open, as if he had just thrown it on. His dark brown breeches had faded spots from wear and they fit tightly on his long legs. His boots were tall and black, of good leather, but they looked absolutely ancient because of the mud, grass, and nicks.

For one insane moment she wished this man were dressed in white tie and richer than any Cabot, Dearborn, or Winthrop could ever be.

His hands were still firmly gripping her shoulders, which her evening gown bared, a calculated choice since the neckline was elegant but low enough to help pull a proposal from John. She could feel the calluses on this man's palms against her skin.

He had hard hands, the kind that were used to holding leather reins, she thought, then remembered the wagon parked at the back of the kitchens. Those hands were used to handling a team, to unloading wagons. He had the hands of a deliveryman.

"In a hurry there, lass?"

Oh my . . . He had a deep voice, the kind that went right through you, that deep male voice of a girl's

66

wildest dreams. Dreams that had held those last vestiges of innocence. Dreams of recklessness and desire.

If John had a voice like this man's she could forget he was half bald and short. She could close her eyes on her wedding night and just listen to him.

Then it hit her that she must look as stupid as Phoebe Dearborn, standing there and gaping at a delivery man.

"You are in my way." She gave him her most quelling look.

"Aye." He laughed, a rich sound that should have irritated her instead of ringing right through her and making her stupid breath catch in her throat. Too much champagne, she thought. Then she remembered she hadn't had any champagne.

"I'm Georgina Bayard."

He started with the top of her head and gave her a long, slow, bold, and completely insolent looking-over. He said her Christian name as if testing the sound of it on his tongue.

"Miss Bayard," she corrected.

He gave her a wicked grin.

She waved at the wagon she'd passed. "Go unload your delivery wagon." She started to move around him.

He moved with her, arms crossed in a cocksure way that annoyed her to no end.

"I have no time for your play. Move." She glared upward. "Now." Her voice was ice.

He just stood there.

"I said, *move,* you oaf!" She jammed her elbow into his side and hit solid muscle, which she hadn't expected, especially in someone so big. He laughed quietly, which she should have expected, but she didn't care to hear it. She looked up, gave him an overly sweet smile, blinked like Phoebe, and stomped on his instep with her squat heel.

He swore and moved out of her way.

She grabbed her skirts and swished past him, but found herself listening for some response, some cocky word from behind her. All she heard was the distant sound of the party, so she walked on, willing that handsome face of his to disappear completely from her memory, and a minute later, she entered the kitchen doors at full steam.

The door banged against the walls and she stood there, hands on her hips. The servants were standing around talking. *Talking* while her gala was on the brink of failing. She clapped her hands twice and the voices drained away.

"Horace?" she said in a firm and even tone. "Are you my butler or a social secretary?"

The servant had the good sense to flush.

"Is there more champagne?"

"In the icehouse, Miss Bayard."

"Then get it." She gave the closest maid an icy nod. "Emily, the lobster and crab trays are empty. And Muriel," she said to another, "I suggest you get those loaves of bread that were cooling in the pass-through sliced and out to the tables immediately. There's no butter or cheese and the caviar dishes are not full." She scanned the kitchen. "Where is the beef I paid a fortune for?"

Three cooks shifted and grabbed for an oven door.

She sniffed the air for a moment, then spun around to glare at one of those cooks. "Surely those aren't crab cakes I smell burning?"

She let the sudden stillness of the moment work for her, then she clapped her hands once more. "All of you . . . move! *Now!*"

The kitchen was a sudden flurry of motion and commotion. Cooks opened and closed the cast-iron oven doors, silver serving trays clanked against the counters, and servants scattered around the hot room like frightened quail. Within minutes they were barreling out the various kitchen doors with heavy serving trays that held fish dishes and huge hanks of rare beef, sparkling long-stemmed crystal, or chilled bottles of wine balanced on their stiff and uniformed shoulders.

Satisfied, Georgina left the kitchens and took the flagstone path that led back toward the party and to John Cabot, who probably needed to be saved from the bills and coos and dizzying eye flutterings of more-money-than-she-can-count Phoebe.

Georgina turned at the corner of the kitchen building and stopped. It was almost as if she knew what she'd see before she ever turned that corner.

He was still there. Now he leaned against the side of the brick building, one booted ankle crossed over the other. One arm was resting on the open shelf of the serving pass-through while the other held a loaf of warm crusty bread—her guests' warm crusty bread.

He was looking right at her with an expression that said he'd been waiting.

She took a deep breath and planted her hands on her hips. "Still working hard, I see."

He saluted her with what was left of the bread loaf.

"I thought I gave you an order." She used her haughtiest voice.

"Aye, that you did." He took another mouthful and grinned at her while he chewed, appearing for all the world to not care a whit what she said or did, no matter what her tone.

She started to move.

"You give orders well, George."

"Pardon me?"

He nodded at the pass-through. "All you have to do is clap your hands and they all jump to obey you."

"I was referring to that word you used to address me."

"George?"

She shuddered.

He seemed vastly amused and pleased with himself. But she was smart enough to realize if she made an issue out of that horrid name, then he would only use it to irritate her. "I don't see that the manner in which I deal with my servants is any concern of yours."

"Ah, but that's where you're wrong." He finished off the bread, wiped his hands on the front of his shirt, and straightened. "You appear to be a woman who can handle her problems with little opposition."

"Heaven knows, I've had enough practice," she muttered.

"Trouble in paradise?" He glanced around the grounds. "I'd think a place like this would insulate you from trouble."

She just raised her chin and didn't say anything, but some weak part of her wanted to bare her secrets and tell him just how much trouble she was really in.

"I suppose your children obey you as well as the help."

"Not that it should matter to you, or that I should tell you anything about me, but I am not married."

His expression flickered with something ever so briefly. "Your family must be disappointed."

"My family is dead," she shot back. He made her sound like a spinster. "And I'm only twenty-two."

Just the barest of smiles hinted around his mouth, but his eyes still held hers until he looked down and shook his head as if the oaf found her amusing. "Old enough to handle servants. Old enough to handle parties, but not children."

"What do you mean by old enough?"

He gave her a shrug.

"Age doesn't matter unless you are cheese. And I never said that I couldn't handle children." She'd never handled a child in her life, but she wouldn't admit that to him.

His stance was relaxed, nonchalant, but it was his knowing grin, so cocksure and arrogant, that rankled her.

"I can handle anything."

He rubbed his chin thoughtfully. "So, George, you think you can handle children."

"I think I'm handling one now."

He laughed then, and the sound was warm and rich and made her want to laugh with him.

A truly annoying thought.

A second later he had closed the distance between them in two long strides that caught her completely off guard. He moved swiftly and stealthily for so large a man.

"What a waste that you have no husband, George."

He looked as if he wanted to touch her, so she stepped back quickly. "I don't have a husband yet. And my name is not George."

"Yet?" He gazed down at her with amusement. "Are you planning on finding a husband in the next hour?"

"Yes, actually. I am planning on *exactly* that." She grabbed her skirts. "Now if you will just let me by, I'll see if I cannot remedy my marital situation, the one you obviously find so interesting and amusing."

"So you want to be married."

She just raised her chin.

He held her with a look that made her want something she should never want. "Let me pass, please."

Again he didn't move.

"Perhaps you would wish to feel the point of my heel again." She raised her foot and her hem and wiggled the toe of her silk slipper.

He glanced down at her hem after taking what seemed like an hour to rake his gaze down there, then held up his hands in mock surrender and stepped out of her way with overexaggerated gallantry.

She moved swiftly and smoothly away from him, walking with her head high and something inside her hot and simmering. When she was a goodly distance away she called back, "Give me a few minutes and then perhaps my future husband will have you thrown out into the streets right on your thick head."

Feeling completely proud of her sharp-tongued self for a great parting shot, she marched past the rose-bushes, a winner's smile on her lips and her heart beating just a little too fast for her own comfort.

"George!" That deep voice called out to her. "My head isn't the only thing that's thick."

> Never marry for money, ye'll borrow
> it cheaper.
>
> *Old Scottish proverb*

Georgina sat in the corner of her bedroom, plucking rose thorns from her fingers.

"Ouch!" She held up the sharp thorn and scowled at it. She didn't know rose thorns could be that thick.

Immediately she groaned and felt herself flush. She was still embarrassed, mostly because she understood exactly what he'd meant. When you were raised with an older brother, you knew about men and women, about intercourse. If you didn't know about it, you'd never understand what your brother and his friends were talking about, grinning about, or joking about.

She dabbed witch hazel on her skinned palms and tried to picture John Cabot instead of a tall blond man with a face too handsome to be real.

When that didn't work, she tried to imagine the Cabot fortune: piles of money gleaming in the light, golden and heavy, a few thousand gold bricks all lined up like German soldiers, stacks of stock certificates, mortgages, bank notes and bonds, and jewels in blue velvet boxes with the Cabot monogram, diamonds in particular, which were a wonderful investment and all that much better if they were set in platinum and dripping from your ears, neck, fingers, and wrists.

She smiled. *Ah, avarice could bring such splendid thoughts!*

But when she opened her eyes, all she saw was the flowered wallpaper of her bedroom and the way it was starting to show age and turn yellow. Even the patterned carpet that had been woven in Antwerp especially for Grandmother Bayard didn't look rich in a room with old draperies and dingy cushions.

She tried to imagine the room completely redone with watered silk hangings, eighteen-karat gilt frames for the paintings, and French antiques. Just that night she had heard Phoebe talking about a bedroom suite she had seen that had once been used in Versailles.

Georgina would buy it before Phoebe. Yes, one of the first things she would do would be to refurbish all twenty-eight rooms of the house. As Mrs. John Cabot, she would have enough wealth and influence to bribe the importer, enough to buy anything she desired and still never even scratch the surface of the Cabots' golden fortune.

She closed her eyes and concentrated on the images of the new rooms, Phoebe's face, and the vast amounts of Cabot money. What she saw instead was golden hair limned in moonlight and a wicked male smile that made her flush. She snatched up the witch hazel and swabbed her heated face with it, thanking heaven that the path had been so dark in that spot, otherwise he'd have seen her digging her way out of the roses she'd walked into and her humiliation would have been complete.

If she had an ounce of sense, she'd have ignored that classically chiseled face, the man's powerful stance, his amusing banter in that unbelievably stirring voice. She should have had him thrown out. The reason why she hadn't was not something she cared to analyze at that moment.

"Ouch!" She sucked in a breath as she plucked out the last and the sharpest thorn. She blew on her finger, stood quickly, and tossed the witch-hazel cloth on her dressing table.

Leaning down, she peered in the oval mirror. There was no need to pinch her cheeks. They had plenty of color. She settled for tucking a strand of loose black hair back into the French knot at her neck, then she left the room.

Within a matter of minutes she was down the stairs and back in the gardens, but on the other side, following a different secluded path—the path that led to the gazebo and to her goal.

John Cabot was waiting there for her.

This was it!

For some reason she couldn't explain, she slowed her steps, then stopped altogether. She could see the cupola of the gazebo and the whimsical but rusty weather vane that was perched atop it. It had a Bayard clock in the center, but its face was unreadable in the dark.

Oddly, the weather vane was pointing the wrong way. What wind there was had been and still was coming from the west, which meant that vane should have been pointing toward the east.

It seemed today that her life was filled with contradictions and impossibilities; clocks that wouldn't keep time, foolish girls who used the Bayard gala to break engagements instead of bonding in one, servants who didn't do what they were bid, deliverymen with voices that made her arms break out in gooseflesh and who asked her outrageously personal questions that she had actually answered, and now weather vanes that pointed into the wind.

She began to walk again, a little faster, almost as if

she were running away, but the image of that brawny deliveryman went right along with her.

Why couldn't blue blood and all that money have a little brawn and muscle? She supposed wishing for a wealthy man with a fine stature and a handsome face was rather like asking for the moon on a silver platter.

John Cabot was a good five inches shorter than she, and he was already losing his hair. But he had money, all that lovely money.

She turned and looked back at the outline of her home, which was backed by the stars and a blue-black sky. The light from the lanterns waved gently from the soft summer sea breeze, making the house look as if it were alive and breathing.

She stood there for only a second, then she turned back, determined to see this through. Long ago she had decided that the Cabot millions were worth a marriage that might not be the kind in fairy tales, not that she believed that drivel. They were just stories that made people think like fools.

Georgina Bayard was no fool.

She knew what she had to do. She knew a few sweet comments, a long and lingering look, a kiss, and John's wonderfully fat and golden pockets would be hers.

And so would his bald head.

She chewed on her lower lip. Everything would be fine. Everything would. She had already resigned herself to spending a lifetime looking down at her husband, of ignoring his thinning hair and shiny scalp.

So what if he was short and squat and a little dull? For the sake of her home, her name, and her pride, she could live with him for the rest of her life.

And on her wedding night, when the moon was full like tonight, and the stars were almost too bright, so bright you felt as if you could really reach out and touch them, she would look into John Cabot's eyes and say goodbye forever to those last few feelings of innocence and desire that were still lingering deep inside her heart.

Yes, she would. It was all planned out in her mind. On her wedding night, she would just close her eyes and think of redecorating.

So in less time than it took to blink, Georgina's feet moved forward, one step, then another, a survivor heading toward her goal.

As she drew closer she could make out John's silhouette outlined in the yellow glow of the hanging lantern above the gazebo. She took one more step, then stopped and looked down at her dress.

It was midnight blue and she had chosen the silk because it matched her blue eyes, made them look bluer, and her hair even shinier and blacker. Just in case, she pinched her cheeks, then she looked down, gripped the neckline of her gown, and wiggled until her cleavage spilled over and was way overexposed.

No reason to leave everything to chance. She would make her own luck. So she plastered a smile on her face, raised her chin, and tightened her hands into fists, then took one last deep breath.

A second later someone grabbed her from behind.

Stolen sweets are the best.
Colley Cibber

The clock struck, but Calum didn't notice the hour. With the last gong, he removed his spectacles and pinched the bridge of his nose. He realized, with the same sudden awareness he had when waking from a deep sleep, that he had been lost in his work again. He leaned back in his chair and stretched with a low groan from his stiff muscles.

He did this sometimes, lost himself in his work, times like now when he knew that the last ship from Scotland this year was due to dock sometime within the next two weeks. Experience had taught him that the ship could arrive as early as tomorrow.

He took a deep tired breath and rubbed his burning eyes, then scored his fingers through his dark hair and rested his head in his hands for a moment. He needed to be ready. Everything on that ship was his responsibility. He put on his glasses.

He looked around him and realized it was dark outside. The clock above the fireplace read a little after two in the morning. Seven hours he'd been working without a break. When he was immersed in his work, like he was tonight, Calum just lost time.

But time was one of the few things he didn't try to control. To a man who made his life orderly, who lived by routine, and who needed consistency like he did, time was a friend. It gave him a framework in which to work, helped him discover new levels of efficiency, and select methods that made the vastness and demands of his job controllable.

Calum developed systems for everything. He always put his clothes on in a certain order: pants, shirt, belt, socks, shoes, and he laid them out across his bedchamber so he could dress while walking to the dry sink. It saved time.

His bed was huge, but he only slept on one side and laid pillows down the middle so he wouldn't disturb the other side in his sleep. That way he could get up, and only have to tuck in the sheet with the perfect pleated corners on the one side. It took only half the time and allowed him the extra minutes he needed for tasks like shaving. His dark beard was so thick he needed to shave his face twice: each morning and again in the evening.

He understood that sometimes he might get a tad carried away with his desire for a certain regimented routine, but he accepted that about himself. His methods were what made him successful. The same meticulous sense of order that Eachann teased him about, in truth, allowed Calum to focus, and focus intently.

Being organized gave him the freedom to concentrate completely on a task, which in turn allowed him to eke thirty hours from a twenty-four-hour day—to have more time, and time was the basis by which he planned his day, his night, of how he had learned to organize himself and his life. He had been doing it with such efficiency for so long that his routine was as much a part of him as the blood bond he shared with Eachann.

He took a deep breath and stood up, stretching again. His brother hadn't returned.

Calum moved to the window and looked out at the bay. All he saw was a thick white mist that made it look as if the world ended outside his window.

It was that impenetrable wall of fog that engulfed the islands every September. Eachann had claimed the fog would come early this year. And it had.

Calum turned away, thinking that his brother must have decided to stay ashore. He crossed the room and relit the logs in the rock fireplace, then swept up a few of the ashes that had drifted on the hearth.

He started to straighten, then stopped for a moment and polished the brass andirons, moved on to polish a candle branch, and some heavy bookends cast in the shape of lion heads. He set the bookends back and ran the cloth over the leather book bindings, then made certain that each gold-embossed spine was aligned with the next. He turned around and glanced out the window again, thoughtful and feeling edgy.

Eachann had known the weather was about to change. He had even passed up on those blueberry pies so he could get Fergus's women safely back to shore, go to his children's school, and return to the island before the fog rolled in. He'd said as much before he left.

His brother had an uncanny ability to read the weather, something few of those who lived on the islands could do. Most of them, Calum included, lived with the weather in the same way as someone lived with a wild animal made into a pet. They lived with constant unpredictability.

The weather here was an elusive thing. Hell, the fishermen who earned their living from the sea spoke of the moods of the weather, and every islander knew that when you lived on an island, the weather ruled what you could and could not do.

Calum supposed there was some innate thing his brother was born with, an instinct, a special gift that made him see and know what others couldn't. Eachann had a fey touch with animals as well. It served Eachann well with his horses. Calum had seen his brother look into the rolling wild eyes of a frightened horse and calm the rearing beast when nothing or no one else could.

But Eachann's gift wasn't limited to horses. Calum had seen an eagle land on his brother's huge outstretched arm as if the proud elusive bird were an ordinary sparrow lighting on a tree branch. He had seen him look a timber wolf in the eye and send it running away, and he could walk right up to a deer and in no time flat have the animal eating wildflowers from the palm of his huge hand.

A loud crash suddenly rang through the house, followed by the sound of footsteps up the stone stairs. Calum turned just as the door flew open.

Eachann stood there, his sleeping children in his strong arms. A curly blond head, Kirsty's rested against one shoulder and Graham's spiky red head was on the other.

"I need your help," Eachann said.

Calum tried to take Kirsty, but her arms were wrapped so tightly around her father's neck that he had to pull them away first, then he took her, frowning at Eachann.

"I'll explain later. Help me get them in a bed."

"In your section of the house?"

"Hell no." Eachann walked out the door and headed down the west hallway toward the stairs that led to Calum's section of the house.

Their habits and the way the two of them lived were about as alike as the Scottish Highlands and the

81

Sahara Desert. So to keep brotherly peace, they had long ago used the wisdom of Solomon and divided the home into two equal parts.

Right down the middle. Half for Calum, who lived with tidiness, order, and discipline. Half for Eachann, who shoveled out his rooms less often than he mucked out his stable.

"We'll have to put them in one of your rooms."

They went into a small neat room off the hall in the west wing, where they each placed a child in a clean bed. Calum smoothed the covers over little Kirsty, who seemed to have grown a half a foot since he'd last seen her. He folded the sheet with a precise corner and tucked it under the mattress.

She opened her sleepy eyes for a minute and looked at him. "Uncle Calum." Then her drooping lids slipped shut and a small smile curled the corners of her mouth. "We're home," she whispered, and a second later she was fast asleep.

He wondered how his brother would handle the children this time. Eachann had been unable to deal with them after the death of their mother, and even though both Fergus and Calum had tried to help, Eachann took the children to the mainland. When he returned, he said little to Calum, except that they needed to be in school, not running loose on the island.

Before Calum could have another thought, Eachann was out the door and down the stairs two at a time.

At the landing, he stopped and said, "Follow me."

"Why?" Calum called out, but his brother was already down the halls and going out the front doors.

Calum followed him out into the fog, which was so thick he had to stop at the base of the front steps until Eachann's voice drew him toward the road. "Where the hell are we going?"

"You'll see soon enough," came a call through the mist.

Calum followed the sound of Eachann's voice, thinking as he walked almost blindly down the path that his brother's children, especially Kirsty, were very much like their father. Eachann had always been restless and a little wild.

While Calum played by the rules and did things in a safe and logical way, Eachann made his own rules. The brothers seldom agreed on how things should be done. Age, time, and respect had taught them to stand aside and let each other act in his own unique way. Although there were times over the years, if for nothing more than Calum's sanity, when he couldn't help but wish he and Eachann were more alike.

A few moments later their boots made a hollow sound on the planked dock. In a thin wavering spot of mist he caught the looming shadow of Eachann as he hopped on the boat deck before the thick fog closed in again and his shape disappeared. "Come aboard, Calum. I need your help."

"Where the hell are you? I can't see a bloody thing."

"Over here." The sudden yellow glow from an oil lantern burned through the misty fog a few yards away.

"Where is here?" Calum reached for the bulwark and pulled himself on board.

"In the aft, next to the mackerel tank."

Calum felt his way along the deck, muttering to himself, "Mackerel? Since when did Eachann start fishing?"

He joined his brother, who stood there completely silent, but grinning that same wicked grin he got whenever he had bested someone or something, like when Eachann won the caber toss at the annual games or the time he short-sheeted Calum's neat bed.

"I've brought something for you, brother. A gift."

Calum suspected this was another one of Eachann's sick jokes. "A gift?"

"Right in here is the answer to all our troubles of late. Something I decided we do need after all." Eachann leaned down and lifted the latch cover.

There was a muffled noise that sounded like a loud cawing sea gull trapped in the middle of a haystack.

"Look for yourself." Eachann handed him the lantern.

Calum held the lamp low over the holding tank and cast a glance inside. He stared down at what looked like some kind of monster—a huge lump. A wet bundle of rich silk and white skin, of four flailing arms and a kicking foot here and there.

It took a moment to see the lump wasn't a loch monster, but two gagged, sopping wet women dressed in expensive silk evening gowns and wrapped up tightly in an ancient mackerel net. They were wiggling and elbowing one another, each fighting to try to sit upright.

Calum swore graphically and looked at Eachann. "Women? You brought *more* women?"

"Aye." Eachann leaned against the railing with his arms crossed. "Not just more women, but something better." He nodded at the women. "Those are our brides."

To one who, journeying through the night and
    fog,
Is mired neck-deep in an unwelcoming bog,
Experience, like rising of the dawn,
Reveals the path that he should not have gone.

Ambrose Bierce

The brunette came up fighting. The moment she was
released her gag flew left. "You stupid idiot!"

Her fist flew right.

Calum stepped back, even though she was aiming
for Eachann's grinning face.

"Now George . . ." Eachann caught her fist easily
in one hand. "You claimed you wanted a husband."

"Not you, you lummox!" She tried to kick him.

He jerked her against him, then bent, and an
instant later he'd flung her over one shoulder the same
way he would a sack of his horses' oats.

She shrieked like a banshee.

Calum winced. The woman was louder than the
those hellish honking geese that lived by the pond. He
watched Eachann clamp one arm over her struggling
legs. She pinched his back and grabbed at the back of
his shirt. His brother swatted her on the butt. There
was utter silence for one second, then just as Eachann
grinned triumphantly, she arched upward, grabbed
his hair in a fist and yanked, shrieking in outrage.

She scared the hell out of Calum. He suddenly remembered the existence of the other woman and whipped his head back around, half expecting her to be waiting and to come at him screeching and clawing.

She lay there perfectly still, the net tangled in her legs and her hands knotted against her stomach. He couldn't see her face because her long damp blond hair covered it. He took a second to adjust his glasses.

The girl still didn't move.

Calum shifted the lantern closer. "Is she dead?"

His brother didn't answer because he was trying to get the gag back on the shrieking brunette whom he had pinned to his chest with one arm while he struggled with the gag. She stomped on his feet the whole time and threw wild punches that Eachann kept ducking.

"Eachann. This one's not moving."

The brunette turned toward Calum with a furious look. "She's seasick, you moron!"

Eachann stuffed the gag back in her open mouth and pinned her knotted fists behind her with one hand.

Calum stood there like someone watching an ambush from a hillside. He didn't know whether to get involved or stay clear of the whole thing.

Eachann was laughing as he struggled with the woman, which made Calum want to punch him. This wasn't funny. It was reckless and foolish and . . . and was pure trouble.

The blonde moaned.

He spun back around.

"That one's yours," came his brother's voice from behind him.

"The bloody hell she is!" Calum turned again, but his brother had disappeared into the thick mist with the other woman gagged and slung over his shoulder again.

"Eachann!" he shouted. "Dammit! Come back here!"

"Sorry! I've got my hands full with George!" Then Eachann grunted as if he'd taken a hard punch.

"I don't want a wife!" Calum hollered, standing there, a lantern in one hand, while he shook his fist at the empty fog.

The woman moaned again and he spun back. He stared down at her, watching her the way a dog eyed a cornered cat—fully expecting her to strike out at him any second.

But she just lay there, curled into a pitiful ball. She looked as if she weren't capable of moving or screaming or fighting back.

After a minute of nothing but watching her, he shifted and realized that standing there was stupid. She was barely half his size. He waited a second more, then lowered himself into the hold, keeping his eyes and the light from the lantern on her the whole time.

He bent down, quickly pulled the hair back from her face, stared at her, then untied the gag.

All she did was mutter, "Sick . . . so sick. Please . . ."

For the first time in a few years, he wanted to punch Eachann for his foolishness. Stealing women like reivers of old stole cattle, like some feuding clan stole food to eat and women to handfast, like . . . oh hell! Like some sick practical joke.

Yet he knew his wild brother for the defiant and stubborn man that he was. Calum figured that Eachann was half hoping his antics would give credence to all that tall talk the mainlanders made about mad island Scots.

Calum glanced down at the woman.

She looked cold and drained and ill. He cursed and bent down and picked her up. She went completely limp, her arms and legs flopping down like a wilting flower whose petals were unable to withstand the spray of the sea. Her skin so pale it looked like the mist, white and soft and fragile, as if it would vanish into nothingness if the wind touched it.

Something about her seemed familiar. He stared down at her trying to understand what it was. She was helpless. Completely. There was a neediness about her. Like he'd felt in Kirsty tonight. Yet in this young woman the neediness was different. When Kirsty wouldn't let go of Eachann it was as if holding on to him was important. This weak lass curled against him the way a wounded animal cowers against a tree, half in hiding and half for protection.

He didn't know what to do with her, so he held her even tighter against him as he got out of the holding tank. He straightened quickly and moved toward the dock.

"Oh God . . ." She clamped a hand to her head, which lolled over the edge of his shoulder. "Don't move. Please."

He stopped, frozen in his tracks. Minutes ticked by with her saying nothing. He found himself listening to her breathing; it echoed the quiet lapping of the water against the dock pilings. The air was wet with the damp pine and sea taste of island fog.

Her head drifted closer to his neck and he could smell the scent of light perfume like sweet honeysuckle mixed with the sharp tang of the sea. Around them, the mist was freezing and grew thicker and wetter the longer he stood there holding her; it began to seep into his clothes and hers, beading on his forehead and upper lip, and on her hair.

"We cannot stay out here, lass."

All she did was rest wearily against his shoulder as if holding her head up was just too much for her.

"I need to get you somewhere warm and dry."

She never opened her eyes, just murmured, "Slowly. Please walk slowly."

He was extra careful when he stepped down onto the dock. He tried to keep her in the same position without making any quick or jerking motions. He was walking down the dock when she opened her eyes and looked up at him.

"I can't fight you." Her voice was so small he almost thought he had imagined hearing it. Her body was limp again as if she had given up.

But he recognized the look in her eyes. It was fear. Pure unadulterated fear. She actually thought he would harm her. She knew she was powerless to do anything to stop him.

From out of nowhere the sudden need to protect her hit him hard, as if a giant hand had just reached out and slapped him in the face.

He stayed clear of women, except those he could meet on his own terms. The virtuous ones that Fergus brought chased him or scared the bloody hell out of him.

But this woman wasn't chasing him. She was afraid of him. That was a hard thing for him to comprehend. He had never inspired fear in a woman and couldn't imagine it even now.

He kept walking, his conscience and something personal eating at him, some tie or bond or elusive connection that was as strong as the bond he felt with his brother.

To care for a woman? No. He'd long ago vowed that he was happy with things just as they were. No wife. No woman. No confusion. Just his own routine, no one else's.

She was staring up at him.

"I need to get you inside."

She didn't respond, but her body felt suddenly

stiffer in his arms; the fright was still there in her wide eyes. He pulled her a little tighter against him, a small comfort he justified by then ignoring her for a minute or two.

He could feel her watching him. Her breaths were quick and sharp, and he listened to them with the thought that they sounded like a woman in the midst of passion. A strong passion.

He walked on in silence, silence that grew until it was more nerve-racking than noise. He took a deep breath and searched for something to say. "What's your name, lass?"

She didn't respond. Not that he blamed her. But she continued to watch him, closely, seriously.

He could feel her gaze on him almost as if her hand had touched his cheek. He stared straight ahead for a few more steps, then said gruffly, "I won't hurt you."

Again she said nothing, and when he looked at her, her suspicious expression told him she still didn't believe him.

"I give you my word as the MacLachlan of MacLachlan."

She stared at him from curious but wary eyes as he walked along in the wet fog. The only sounds were those of the throbbing surf behind them, the crackle and crunch of his boots on the rocks that were scattered along the path, her short quiet breaths, and some pounding in his ears that felt suspiciously like his heart.

"What is the MacLachlan of MacLachlan?" Her voice was different when it didn't have a moan to it. Quiet, curious, yet bright. Quite a contrast to the she-devil Eachann had slung over his shoulder.

"I am the MacLachlan of MacLachlan. The last laird of the ancient clan of MacLachlan."

"You're Scottish."

"Scots, lass. I'm Scots."

"The disappearing island," she whispered, as if she thought she were in the arms of a ghost.

"You're not believing that rubbish, now are you? The island doesn't disappear. It's only the fog that makes it look so."

"No . . . no," she said, but she didn't sound certain. She was eyeing him again. "You don't sound Scottish." It was almost like she was saying, "You don't look like a ghost."

"I'm Scots, not Scottish."

"You don't sound like a Scot."

"I was born here, on the island, like my father and his father." He turned left, at a spot where the fog thinned past the hemlock tree. Beneath his boots was the sound of gravel that covered the path near the front of the house.

He felt her shiver. "The house is just ahead."

A familiar shadow Calum knew was home loomed before them in the mist, huge and dark and over two stories tall. He slowed as he approached the front steps.

"If you believe you are truly a Scot, then why aren't you living in Scotland?"

He gave a bitter laugh as he opened the front door. "There's a saying that a Scotsman is never at home unless he's abroad." He could see by her eyes that she didn't understand. "Scotland is no longer the home of the Scots, lass."

"Why do you say that?"

"Because to us it's true. Those who are there now are either Sassenach . . . English," he explained, "or men who are more interested in the price of wool than the price of human pride and suffering. Tradition and obligation are not part of them. They might call

themselves Scots, lass, but those men are no Scots."
He carried her inside, then kicked the door shut
behind him with a loud bang.

She didn't flinch at the sound, but seemed intent on
giving him an odd and searching look that said she
had expected him to eat her and was surprised he
hadn't.

"You ask a lot of questions, lass, for someone who
won't tell me her name." He waited, but she said
nothing, just looked away, then her eyes began to
examine the room.

"This is my home, and my father's and his
father's." Odd how his voice sounded like gravel,
rough and angry, yet what he felt was not anger. He
wasn't certain what it was, but he wasn't angry.

She continued to look around them as he crossed
the entry, the sound of his steps echoing up into the
high beam rafters that soared upward over two stories
above them.

He stopped and looked around him. He was proud
of his home; he always had been. His great grandfather had been a large man, like Eachann, and he'd
built the place in the huge proportions and in the
rough Celtic manner of a chieftain's Highland castle.

Yet the whole structure was made from the island's
resources. The slate floors and stone block for walls
were quarried from the pink granite on the island. All
the wood and trim were hemlock, knotted pine, and
maple from the native forests; and fat cobbled gray
stones polished by the motion of the sea had been
made into fireplaces big enough for a clan of Scotsmen to stand inside.

To the MacLachlans who came here, this was a new
castle in a new homeland, built by a proud man, who
had been one of the last Highland warriors. A man
forced to flee his homeland and everything that was

Scots, everything that had, for so many generations, been the MacLachlan of MacLachlan.

His Scots forefather who had lived in four-hundred-year-old castles would laugh and called this house new. But his home meant something more to Calum, and seemed old enough to him, because the stairs had been hollowed by the footsteps of his great-grandfather.

He felt the woman's stare, but he said nothing. She seemed to be studying him as if she were looking for nits. The air was filled with something that made him feel more than awkward, so he turned and walked down a wide paneled hallway with long and proud strides.

A distant female shriek echoed from the east halls, Eachann's wing of the house. Calum stopped.

Something crashed. Glass. There was a loud bang and he thought he heard his brother yelp.

The woman in his arms gave a quiet gasp. He glanced down at her. Her eyes were wide and her full lips had thinned and turned tense.

"He won't harm your friend."

"She's not my friend," she said almost too quickly, like someone who speaks before thinking. But there was no anger or hatred in her voice. In fact, it was oddly without any tone of emotion.

She turned away. "We're from . . . I don't . . ." She was suddenly quiet, and when he looked down at her, she said, "We hardly know each other."

"Neither of you has to worry, lass." From Calum's perspective, Eachann had more to worry about than that wildcat woman did. She was a handful, which he supposed was good revenge. Eachann needed to learn that he couldn't control everything and everyone on one of his whims.

There was another crash, and it crossed Calum's

mind that his brother with the fey powers had finally met the one animal who wouldn't eat from his hand. Hell, from what he'd seen and was hearing, she was more likely to bite the fingers off of it.

He carried the lass into the library where it was clean and warm and familiar. He set her in a large winged chair that stood by the fire and shook out a throw. He stopped and picked a few of the lint balls from it, then laid it over her. While he creased the sides neatly and tucked the ends into the side cushions of the chair pillows, she cocked her head and watched him as if she had never seen such an action.

"What's the matter?" He folded one corner back into a perfectly neat triangle, then pulled it down until the tuck was tight and flat. He squatted down and shoved the edge of the throw neatly beneath the seat cushion.

She blinked, then shook her head. "Nothing."

"Do you not want the covers?"

"I am cold."

"I have something else to warm you up, lass." He poured two whiskeys and handed her one. "Here. Take it."

She didn't move.

"Go on, now. It will settle your stomach and warm you."

She took the glass tentatively, but didn't drink any. Instead she sat quietly pensive, staring at the fire.

Her long hair hung down around her like damp yellow ribbons from a rain-drenched maypole and stuck to her cheeks, which still held no color. The heat from the fire dried the dew that had sprinkled her face and hair.

One small pearl earring dangled from her ear. When she took a breath, it shimmered in the firelight the way a tear does when it's ready to fall. There was a lost look about her, the same sudden lonely and disoriented look of a fragile bird that has just fallen from its nest.

It crossed his mind that she must have family.

God . . . what a thought. He wiped a hand over his face. That was all he needed. Some raging father invading his island to avenge his stolen daughter's honor. Or worse yet, a passel of angry brothers to beat the hell out of him.

He was going to kill Eachann. He was. If brothers showed up, Eachann was going to face them first.

He waited a moment then said, "Lass?"

She turned.

"Your family will be worried."

She looked at him as if she were wondering who he was speaking to, then she turned away with no answer for him.

He gave it another try. "How's your stomach?"

"Fine," she whispered.

He took a long drink, poured another, and when he looked at her again he saw that her color was changing, her cheeks were more pink from the heat. The damp strands of her blond hair were drying and beginning to curl as if suddenly coming back to life. The firelight warmed her face and hair with a golden glow that was the color of early morning sunshine.

He sat there watching, the way he liked to watch a sunrise, with a sense of quiet awe that makes you focus on the smallest detail. Right now he was fascinated by the pulse point in her neck, where the skin was pale and soft. He wondered how her skin would feel against his fingers, and what it would taste like against his mouth. "I wonder how it would smell," he said into his whiskey glass.

She turned just as suddenly. "What did you say?"

He silently cursed his loose tongue. "Nothing." His

tone was much sharper than he'd meant it to be. He knew it the moment he saw her flinch slightly, then turn away again.

He took another stiff drink, then went to the fireplace where he squatted down and jabbed the logs into snapping flames with the poker. Sparks flew all over the hearth and onto his sleeve. He swatted at them, slapping at his shirt sleeves, then scowled down at the ashes scattered all over the place.

He straightened and crossed to the desk almost by rote. A moment later he was bent down sweeping up the hearth with the whisk. When he cleaned up the ashes and burnt splinters of wood, he spotted a trail of wet leaves across the carpet.

He hadn't used the boot jack. What the hell was wrong with him? He never forgot to use the boot jack. He whisked up the leaves into the dustpan, frowning the whole time because he couldn't explain away his curious and odd thoughts of this young woman who meant nothing to him.

"What are you doing?" she asked.

He glanced at her over his shoulder. "Cleaning up the leaves."

"Why?"

"Because I tracked them in."

"Oh." There were a hundred questions in the tone of that one word. She looked around again. "You don't have any help?"

"They've long been in bed."

"Oh."

He rested his elbow on one bent knee. "Why?"

"The house is so clean, that's all. I thought maybe there was a maid. Another woman. Someone . . ." Her voice trailed off.

"There are no women on the island." The instant he'd spoken, he remembered Kirsty, but didn't say anything, just went about his task.

She watched him as if he had grown two moose heads. "What are you doing now?"

He looked down at his hands. He wasn't doing anything odd. He looked up again. "I'm polishing the dustpan."

"You *polish* the dustpan?" she repeated, then blinked twice. After a stretch of puzzled staring, she giggled.

"What's so amusing?"

"You *are* polishing the dustpan."

"Aye."

She giggled again, which should have annoyed him like it did when Eachann laughed at him. But instead he only felt some of his earlier tension drain away. At least she wasn't looking at him as if he was about to have her for breakfast.

He nodded at the glass in her hand. "Drink, lass."

She frowned down at the whisky, then sniffed it.

"It's not poison."

"It smells like it," she muttered.

He gave a small bark of laughter and she looked up, surprised, then after a moment where he couldn't detect a thing from her blank expression, she gave him a small tentative smile.

The room was warm. Too warm. He stopped polishing the dustpan and was frozen there. He wanted to keep her smiling at him because . . . well, he didn't know why. He just did.

He looked away and crossed to the desk in a few rapid and agitated strides. He put away the whisk and dustpan, then closed the drawer harder than he'd intended.

He then ignored her because somehow that made up for the smile he'd given her. He began to straighten the alphabetized piles of papers on his desk. They didn't need straightening, but he did it anyway, tapping the piles on his desktop so every paper would be perfectly aligned. Finally the silence got to him and he cast a quick glance at her.

She was sipping the whiskey and staring into the fire while the light danced on her profile and made it look shadowy. There were no sounds but the crackle of the pine logs and the hollow, almost labored sound of his own deep breaths.

The air filled with tension and awareness. He shoved his spectacles back up his nose and tried to forget she was there looking at him with curiosity as she sat huddled under one curved wing of the chair the way the whooper swans tucked their heads beneath a wing while they napped.

He tried to forget her white skin that looked so soft and her cheeks that had turned pink from the room's warmth. Don't think of her, he told himself. He didn't think. He just watched her long curling hair glow reddish gold in the hot gleam of the firelight.

He realized he couldn't help but think about her. He could feel her presence deep inside of him, as if she were a part of him that he'd never known existed.

The clock struck three with loud and sudden gongs that made them both start. Simultaneously they both turned to look at the clock, realized what they'd done, whipped back around, and sat in awkward silence again. He ran a hand through his hair, then sat on a corner of his desk, staring at the mantel. He felt even more tense and somehow suddenly weak, as if the small blond woman was draining him of something vital.

The clock face came into focus and he remembered the time. That was the problem. He was just plain tired. He could feel the strain of the day like one felt a bruise. It was almost as if each hour had battered him as it past by.

No wonder his mind was playing tricks on him and his chest was tight and the room became warm when the lass looked at him. Exhaustion could do that, he rationalized.

He could imagine how she must feel, thanks to the antics of his wild brother. She stared at him with that same cautious look in her eyes, but just a moment before her eyelids had slipped down twice and she had stifled a yawn.

He stepped around the desk and walked toward her. He stopped and extended his hand. "It's late."

She must not have seen him because she almost jumped out of her skin. "What?"

"The time."

She frowned at the clock.

"We need to go upstairs now."

"Why?" There were those eyes again. Wary. Wide.

"Because, lass, it's time we went to bed."

You ought never take anything that don't belong
to you—if you cannot carry it off.

Mark Twain

Georgina didn't stop to watch the vase fly past the
oaf's head and shatter against a wall. She was too busy
grabbing something else to throw.

The closest thing was a pillow.

No pain, she thought with disgust and tossed it
aside.

"You missed, George. Next time you might want to
try throwing with your eyes open."

Her gaze lit on a brass bowl filled with apples. She
glanced up when he moved toward her, still grinning
as if ruining her life were funny.

She picked up an apple, looked straight at him, and
threw it. "You've ruined everything!"

He sidestepped. "Much closer. But your aim is off
by a good two feet."

She let the next one fly; it smacked against the wall
with a *splat!*

He shook his fat head.

"You don't care do you?" She heaved another one
at him. "You don't care that you have ruined my life!"

He dodged the apple, then began to applaud. "Very close. I felt the wind on that one. Now if you'll just take aim and concentrate . . ."

She wanted to go at him herself, to scream or yell or beat his chest with her fists until he understood what he had done to her. But she stood there, impotently looking at him, aware that her chest was heaving with each breath she took, that her emotions were lying so near the surface that she was ready to crack.

"Tell me how I've ruined your life."

She looked him square in the eye and sought a calming breath or two. "There was a man waiting for me in the gazebo."

"All alone with a man, George?"

"I was alone with you."

"Aye." He smiled slowly.

"Besides this was a perfectly proper meeting."

"In a gazebo near the back of the garden at night." His look was too knowing, his voice too smug.

"He was going to propose." Her voice sounded defensive, even to her, so she stood a little straighter. "He was going to marry me."

He shrugged. "Marriage isn't a problem for me. Actually, it's the best solution." He leaned back against the edge of a chair and crossed his ankles in the aggravating and lazy way he had. "I'll marry you."

"Oh? Be still my heart."

He laughed again.

"I want to marry John Cabot."

At that he roared with laughter, so she flung another apple at him.

The devil snatched it right out of the air. "Ah . . . I see." He nodded, holding the apple up to the light and appearing to examine it. "You are in love with him."

"Yes!" she lied.

He lowered his gaze slowly, which was just as

annoying as everything else he did, then he gave her a long penetrating look that said he didn't believe her.

She raised her chin a notch. "Madly in love. Madly. Absolutely. I think of him night and day. He's my life. My future. My . . ." She waved a hand around. "John Cabot is everything I could ever want in a husband."

He tossed the apple like a ball, then polished it on his shirtfront, ignoring her. He took a bite and chewed obnoxiously, then swallowed. He just stood there eating the apple as if he were waiting for her to throw another one and knew she would miss him by a mile.

After a tense few seconds, he said, "You want to know what I think, George?"

"No, but I'm certain you'll tell me."

He grinned. "Perhaps not."

She grabbed another apple and stood there just like he did, trying to give him the same look of nonchalance he gave her.

"I think you don't need to pull down your bodice to attract a man."

She stood there, realizing what he just said and what he had seen in the dark of the garden. She wished the floor would just open up and swallow her.

"Now I have to admit it was quite a sight . . ." He gave her a slow hot smile. "And still is, but I had already decided I wanted you before you pulled your dress down almost to your waist."

I will not let him goad me. I will not, she thought, resisting the urge to yank her dress neckline up around her throat, which she was certain was flushed as red as her flaming face felt.

The seconds slowly dragged by. After a minute or so she looked at the apple, taking her own turn at drawing out the time before she said, "So that's what you think?"

He crossed his arms, daring her to throw again. "Aye. That's what I think."

"Well then." She tossed the apple lightly in the air, as if she were gauging its weight. She studied his head for another exaggerated moment, then gave him her sweetest smile. "I guess I'll have to throw the next one right where you think."

He laughed. "You couldn't hit my head if I stood still as a stone, George." He crossed those hammy arms of his again.

A second later the apple hit him right between the legs.

"I didn't say anything about your head."

He bent double and shouted five truly vile curses all in one incredibly inventive sentence.

She raced for the door.

Just as she reached for the handle, the door burst open and slammed against a wall.

Amy Emerson stood in the doorway, wrapped in a red plaid blanket and brandishing a shiny pistol. She looked at Georgina in surprise, then her gaze shot to where the lummox was doubled over.

"Here!" She pulled her other hand from the blanket and handed Georgina a thick coil of braided drapery cord. "Tie him up!"

He straightened and stood gaping at them, then his eyes narrowed. He was no longer amused. "Where's Calum?"

"Your brother?" Amy waved the pistol as if he'd asked a foolish question. "Don't worry. There's only a little blood."

"Blood?" His voice was lethal and he took a step.

Amy used two hands to raise the gun and aim it straight at him. "Don't take another step."

He froze, his now hardened gaze flicked from the gun to her face, then back to the gun, which was pointed at his chest.

"Your brother only has a small cut."

"A cut?" Where'd you get a knife?"

Amy frowned at him. "I didn't have a knife." She looked at Georgina. "Did I say I had a knife?"

Georgina shook her head.

Amy looked back at Eachann MacLachlan. "I didn't say I had a knife. I think you're trying to confuse me."

Eachann spoke through gritted teeth. "You said he was bleeding from a cut."

"Oh . . . that was from the whisky glass."

"My brother cut his hand on a whisky glass?"

"No. His head."

Eachann was the one who looked confused. "He cut his head on a whisky glass?"

"Just a small glass. It only made a little cut about, say . . ." Amy held up her fingers to show how much and looked at Georgina. "How big would you say that is?"

"About a half of an inch," Georgina answered, then added, "hardly deadly."

"That's true." She looked at him and repeated, "Hardly deadly. He'll be fine." Amy paused, her expression thoughtful. "The knot on his forehead was a little bigger though. But don't worry, he was coming to as I was tying him up. I'm certain his mind wasn't befuddled or anything because he looked like he wanted to clean up all the broken glass."

The oaf groaned and shook his head.

"Sit down, please." Amy pointed the pistol at him and waved it around.

He held one hand up. "For crissake! Stop waving that gun around! It could go off!"

She waved it some more. "Well, if you don't want me to wave the gun," she said reasonably, "then you need to sit down."

He moved toward the closest chair so quickly

Georgina almost laughed. He was scowling the whole time.

The chair was a huge monstrosity filled with crumpled pieces of paper, wadded up shirts, some crusty dishes, and a huge pile of walnut shells. He bent slightly and with one huge arm, swiped everything off onto the floor.

He turned, eyeing them from a face that was not the least pleased. He sat down rather slowly, wincing at one point. He gave Georgina a look of retribution that could have cooked her.

"What's wrong with him?" Amy whispered, keeping the pistol pointed at him.

"Nothing," Georgina said brightly as she unrolled the braided cord. "He's just been thinking too hard."

He swore under his breath.

Georgina didn't smile, but shifted so she stood beside him and wouldn't block the aim of Amy's gun, for safety's sake. She could see from the sharp way he watched them that he was waiting for one of them to make a mistake. "Stick out your hands."

He turned his head slowly and looked up at her. His look promised dire revenge.

But she ignored him and twisted the tie around his wrists. "Now your big feet, please."

He didn't move.

She squatted down and pulled the drapery tie downward with a firm jerk that made him inhale sharply, then looped it around his ankles a few times. Kneeling at his beat-up boots, she gave him another sugary smile, then tied the knots even tighter.

"You'll regret that, George," he murmured through gritted teeth.

"Oh, I think not." She reached out and patted his cheek, then reached across him on purpose and grabbed another apple. She leaned back on her heels and held the apple up between their faces.

His eyes narrowed and he opened his mouth to speak.

She stuck the apple right inside, then feigned surprise. "Oh dear, were you going to say something? Nothing of importance, I'm certain."

His neck was slowly turning red, and redder.

She looked him square in his angry eyes and said, "Angry, Mr. MacLachlan? What a shame. Your mother should have taught you not to take things that aren't yours."

She stood, brushed her hands together, and looked up at Amy. "Ready?"

Amy nodded, then her gaze searched the room and stopped on the far wall. "Grab that other blanket. You might need it."

Georgina crossed the room, stepping over squashed apples and clutter she had hardly noticed before. The room was a mess. She pulled another red woolen blanket off a wooden peg on the wall, wrapped it around her shoulders, and spun around.

"Let's go," Amy said, still waving the gun at him as she turned and went to the doorway.

Georgina crossed the room and gave the oaf one last look, a triumphant one that said she had won this time, before she closed the doors behind them.

Amy picked up a basket covered with a cloth. "Follow me."

A few minutes later they were standing on the outside steps. Amy didn't move, but looked around her, frowning. She chewed on her lower lip, then looked at Georgina. "Where do we go now?"

All Georgina could see was white mist. "The fog looks even thicker than before. These islands have treacherous cliffs. If we aren't careful we could walk off one."

"The lantern is still on the deck of the boat. Calum set it down before he carried me here."

"Let's go then." Georgina pulled Amy down two steps.

Suddenly Amy stopped and her head shot up. "What was that noise?"

"What?" Georgina looked around but saw only fog and the dark shadow of the house behind them.

"I thought I heard something squeak, like a hinge."

They both stared at the front door.

"It's still closed." Georgina turned back to her. "It was probably some animal, a squirrel or a bird. Sound carries in the fog, especially at night." She grabbed Amy's arm again. "Come this way."

They went down two more steps.

A loud crash came from behind them, scaring Amy so badly she dropped the pistol and grabbed Georgina's arm with both hands.

Georgina gasped, then spun around, half expecting the oaf to somehow be standing there.

"What was that?" Amy whispered, releasing her grip a little.

Georgina pried Amy's fingers from her arm and walked up one step. Her evening slipper crunched on something that cracked under her weight. She bent down where a china washbowl lay in shattered pieces on the stone landing.

Georgina looked at the upper story, but she couldn't see anything, only fog and the dark shadow of the outline of the house looming high above them.

Amy had picked up the gun and now was peering over her shoulder at the steps. "How did that get there?"

"I don't know. I can't see up there, but let's get out of here. Quickly." They turned and took off down the steps just as the matching pitcher fell from the foggy sky and cracked apart right where they had been standing.

Georgina half dragged a gasping Amy along with her.

"Did you see that?" Amy whispered in a terrified voice.

"Forget about it! We need to get that lantern. *Now!*"

They took off running and disappeared into the dense fog. The only sounds with them were the gravel crunching loudly under their fleeing feet, their static breaths, and the faint rumble of the sea against some distant rocky shore, so they never heard the upstairs window squeak closed.

Always acknowledge a fault frankly. This will
throw those in authority off their guard and give
you a chance to commit more.

Mark Twain

Calum pulled his wrists upward with a hard yank and
the drapery ties fell away. He untied his feet and stood
up, then searched the floor for his glasses. They were
lying near the shattered whisky glass. He hooked the
spectacles over his ears and shoved them up the
bridge of his nose, then ran through the doors. He
made for the east wing, blotting the small stream of
blood on his forehead with a neatly folded handkerchief as he ran.

Out of the corner of his eye he caught a flash of
movement and stopped. He looked up the stairs.

Near the stair landing, Kirsty's small and curly
blond head poked out from behind a thick newel post.

"What are you doing up?"

"Someone stole the MacLachlan plaids, Uncle
Calum. I saw them." Her voice lowered to an excited
whisper. "Are they thieves?"

"Get yourself back in bed, lassie."

"Why aren't we sleeping in our beds?"

"The rooms aren't ready. Now get yourself in bed."

"Where's Father?"

"He's busy. Go to bed."

"Why?"

"This is not your worry."

She planted her hands on her small hips, raised her small chin, and frowned down at him. "I'm a Mac-Lachlan too."

Aye, he thought. Pure, stubborn Scot. "And are you forgetting who's your laird, my MacLachlan lassie? Surely you wouldn't be so foolish as to disobey an order from the laird of your clan?"

She seemed to think about that, then eyed him for a moment, appearing to weigh the consequences of her decision. She slowly turned and brought herself back up the stairs like someone dragging a boulder. Halfway up she paused, then looked down at him with almost a too-serious look for a child. "You're right, Uncle Calum. I should be in bed." She raised her chin, took a deep breath that puffed her small chest out and held enough drama for the stage, and she marched up the stairs, then disappeared around the corner.

He heard the upstairs door click shut and ran down to his brother's rooms. He threw open the door.

Eachann sat in a huge chair surrounded by a few months' worth of his usual clutter. He was hunched over, his hands bound to his feet, and there was an apple stuck in his mouth.

Calum didn't say the first thing that came to him when he realized his brother had an apple in his mouth while trussed up and sitting in his pigsty of a room. Although, as he crossed the room, he thought it was enough to make him believe that God had a keen wit about Him.

Calum pried the apple out of his brother's mouth. Eachann grunted, then worked the numbness out of his jaw while Calum bent down and untied his hands and feet.

"Are you hurt?" Calum pulled free one of what looked to him like thirty or more tight knots.

"No." Eachann stared at Calum's forehead. "Are you?"

"It's nothing." Calum untied another knot, then stared at the rest of them. He held them up and asked, "She wanted to make certain you didn't get away, didn't she?" There looked to be twenty odd knots left.

"How'd you get free?"

"The blond lass only tied one knot." Calum pulled the ties loose. "And a bow." He looked at Eachann and shook his head.

Eachann stood quickly, rubbing his wrists and scowling at the door. "Did you hear that?"

Calum turned around. "What?"

"I thought I heard something."

Calum froze and listened. "I don't hear anything."

Eachann held up a hand. "Quiet."

They both stood there, but there was no sound.

"I guess it was nothing." Then Eachann frowned and added, "I thought I heard the front doors close just a moment ago."

"I doubt those two women would be foolish enough to come back."

Eachann crossed the room and pulled a gun from a rack on the wall. He tossed it to Calum. "Here. Take this and I'll get some lanterns."

"A gun?" Calum stared at it, then looked up at Eachann. "Are you daft? I'll not be shooting any poor scared women, even if one of them did crack me over the head with a whisky glass."

Eachann was fumbling though a closet and he stopped and looked at him. "We can't go out there unarmed. Your bride took a pistol with her." He turned back and began to jerk things from inside.

"She won't shoot us. And she's not my bride. I have no plans to marry anyone, which you and I will settle between us later."

"There's nothing to settle. Your bride—"

"She's not my bride."

"A woman who tied you up with a bow is carrying a loaded gun, which should be enough reason for us to be armed, but she's also frightened and somewhere out there in the fog."

Calum supposed he had a point.

"Here." Eachann shoved a lantern into his chest. "Take this and let's go." He crossed the room with long determined strides. "We need to find them before they walk off a cliff and we have no wives."

"I'll not be marrying anyone. Eachann? Eachann!" But Calum was talking to an empty doorway.

The front door slammed shut with a loud thud.

Calum shook his head and moments later he crossed through the same doorway with heavy steps and a strong feeling of impending doom.

Two old crows sat on a fence rail
Talking of effect and cause,
Of weeds and flowers,
And nature's laws.
One of them muttered, one of them stuttered,
Each of them thought far more than he uttered.

Vachel Lindsay

Do you think this place is safe?" Amy looked around the dark and dank cave while Georgina set the lantern on a nearby rock ledge.

"Safer than being locked in a room with the oaf and his brother."

The more Amy looked around, the less safe she felt. However this dark wet cave was better than trying to find their way in the dense fog. "I suppose you're right."

She scanned the low rocky roof of the cave where the mist from outside hovered like smoke in the low dark crevices. Behind her was the constant dripping of water as it plopped into a small pool under the rocks.

Out of the corner of her eye, Amy caught a small flash of shadow. Her breath caught in her chest, made it feel tight. She whipped her head around. The shadows were nothing too ominous; they were only the black sea crabs that scudded to hide in between the wet rocks. She exhaled, but for a few lingering seconds her heart still felt as if it had a butterfly trapped inside of it.

In the distance she could hear the surf; it sounded angry. But inside the sea just lapped quietly into the shallow cave, the way the ocean drifted on the shoreline on a lazy summer afternoon. The mist outside was so thick and white that it blocked any view. It was almost as if the black and empty world ended right there, at the very entrance to this cave.

She looked at Georgina. She looked so calm. Her appearance was the only thing that was unruffled about her. Her dress was a mess, like Amy's and her long black hair had fallen from its intricate evening knot and was a tangled mass of snarled and heavy curls that fell clear to her waist.

She remembered the first time she'd seen Georgina Bayard, standing in a circle of people who seemed to fade into their surroundings once you noticed her. She wasn't tall; she didn't stand out that way. But she had a look about her that drew your attention. It wasn't just because she usually looked as if she knew some special secret no one else did. For some reason you realized she was unique the first moment you saw her.

When Georgina spoke, her voice was firm and frank. Most people listened intently to whatever she said because her tone, her expression, her stance, everything was so very self-assured.

But then she was a striking woman. She had the most perfect face and figure Amy had ever seen. Her hair was jet black and her skin was the same white glow cast by a full moon. She had high defined cheekbones and full rosy lips, the kind some women painted on with light pink rouge. And she had the widest pale crystal blue eyes you'd ever seen. Her eyes were so light a color that they were the first thing you noticed when you looked at her face. Amy often wondered if that was because Georgina had a direct way of looking right through you, as if she could pinpoint your most vulnerable secret with those clear eyes should she deign to do so.

But there was a frankness and honesty about her sharp blunt way of speaking and her penetrating looks that Amy had found curiously out of place in a social group that hid their real personas beneath false smiles, cool demeanor, and an air of snobbish indifference. You only had to look at Georgina for a minute or two and you could see her strength. No one who knew Georgina Bayard doubted that if she wanted something, she would find a way to get it. Period.

But now, here inside this cave, Georgina just watched the dark water until she must have felt Amy's stare, because she looked up. After a moment she said, "I wonder what's happening at home."

"I expect by now they've gotten together a search party."

Georgina laughed. "You're joking."

"No."

"First they would have to notice we're missing."

"You don't think they'd notice if their hostess was gone?" Amy knew no one would be looking for her. Certainly not William.

"Who knows." Georgina shrugged. "Maybe if the food ran out. And if they did notice, would anyone care?" She gave a short laugh. "They certainly swilled enough champagne for no one to care about much of anything." Her look was as droll as her words.

"But they'd have to notice that you weren't there. They'll contact someone."

"Even if they did notice, which I doubt since there was plenty of champagne, how would they find us? There are hundreds of islands off the coast." Georgina dropped a rock in the water where it made circles that faded as quickly as Amy's hope of being rescued.

She realized then that she was fooling herself again, pretending those people would care. Georgina was right.

"We're stuck here until we can find a way to escape." Georgina was quiet for a moment, her face creased with thoughts only she knew. She turned and glowered at the cave entrance. "I can't believe the fog picked tonight of all nights to roll in. It's not even September yet."

Amy stared at the dark cave entrance. Her father always told her that everything happened for a reason. She wondered what reason there was for this predicament. But the longer she sat there, the more she felt it—that same chess-pawn feeling she had when she did something that wasn't her own idea.

"You look about ready to faint. Tell me you're not going to." Georgina was staring at her with an annoyed look. "That's all we need."

"No." Amy glanced down at her hands, uncomfortable and feeling as if Georgina could see those spooky thoughts inside Amy's head. When she looked up at her again, Georgina was still staring at her.

"There's a reason we're here," Amy blurted out.

"Of course there's a reason. We're here because of the fog."

"No. I meant there's a reason we're on the island."

"There's a reason, all right," Georgina said with disgust. "We're here because some lummox with more arrogance than wit kidnapped us." She threw another rock so hard it skipped across the surface of the cave's pool the same way the fat sea pigeons made splashes when they played in the sea.

But to Amy there was nothing playful about the situation. To her it had become eerie and frightening and all too real. "No, you don't understand. I can feel it. There's a reason that things happen."

"You mean as in fate or destiny?" Georgina did laugh; it had a hollow sound. She tossed a handful of small granite stones that caught specks of lantern light and looked like tiny fireflies. "I believe people make their own destiny."

Amy wondered if Georgina really believed that, since she hadn't looked her in the eye when she'd said it. Her father had told her once that people who spoke the truth looked you in the eye. Odd that she would remember that now when it did her no good. She certainly wished she would have remembered that piece of advice when she'd met William.

She was quiet for a moment, trying to think of how to express in words exactly what she was feeling. She looked up at Georgina. "There are people who believe there is a higher plan. That everything happens for a reason."

Georgina just stared back.

"Like . . . well . . ." She searched her mind for an example. "There's a reason that the moon rises at night."

"Perhaps the moon rises at night because if it rose in the day then it would be called the sun."

"You are so cynical."

"Thank you." Georgina gave her a wide smile that was too exaggerated to be anything but sardonic.

"You don't think there *is* a reason the stars shine?"

"I can't think of anything else stars are good for. Shining will do. Keeps the night from being too boring, I suppose."

"I used to believe that stars were something to wish on." Amy's voice sounded the way she was feeling. Ashamed.

"I'd say that kind of thinking was your first mistake." There was cool amusement in Georgina voice that said she thought Amy was as foolish as she felt.

"I suppose you're right."

"Naturally." Georgina oozed confidence.

Amy felt suddenly smaller and weaker because after today she had little confidence in her own beliefs.

"Well, I know one thing. I wish there would be a reason for the fog to lift so we could get off this stupid island. I have to get home. And soon."

And here I am with no reason to go home, Amy thought. All that was waiting for her was a group of strangers sitting like gods in some granite building in Manhattan. She could just picture her executors huddled around a big expensive table while they devised ways to use her wealth to bribe someone else to take her off their hands.

It was clear to Amy that she had nothing to go home to, nothing that mattered to her anyway. She had wealth. But money wasn't important to her. Her homes were really just expensive empty rooms with expensive empty fireplaces in expensive empty houses. Shells that held everything money could buy except the one thing she really wanted: to be part of a loving family again.

She swallowed because she knew she would cry again if she didn't, then she looked around the cave. It was dark and clammy and smelled as if the sea had been locked inside those rock walls since before the beginning of time. That briny odor of the ocean filled the damp cave air the way smoke chokes a chimney. She could hear the water breaking on the ledges in the distance. Those waves sounded as far away and out of touch with the world as she was.

She wondered if Georgina Bayard ever felt isolated and lost. Probably not. She didn't think Georgina would let herself be afraid of anything, especially being alone. Amy turned and watched her, half out of curiosity and half because she thought she might learn a way to be stronger.

Georgina was staring at the wall of rock across from them, her thoughts seeming very far away while she absently tossed a small handful of rocks that plopped in the water and sank.

"What do you think would make him do something like that?"

"Who? And what?" Georgina turned and looked at her.

"Kidnap us. Why do you think a man like Eachann MacLachlan would just snatch us as if we would be willing to do whatever he and his brother wanted?"

"Extreme arrogance."

Arrogance was one of the words Amy thought of when she remembered Georgina Bayard's set of friends, people who were accepted like William and the others. They were arrogant and cold.

Amy felt Georgina staring at her and looked up.

"What did you mean when you said a 'man like Eachann MacLachlan'?"

"A handsome man."

The look Georgina gave her was thoughtful. "You think he's handsome?"

"Don't you?"

"I hadn't noticed," Georgina answered so fast even Amy didn't believe her. She was probably just too proud to admit that Eachann was extremely handsome. He had those kind of green eyes that could look at you and melt your bones. Men like him always put Amy off a little. She didn't know how to talk to them because she was too busy just staring at their incredible faces.

Now the other brother, Calum, was different. He was handsome too. In fact, she actually preferred his dark looks and more serious manner. She never felt as if he were laughing at her.

For a few foolish minutes she had almost begun to like him. Imagine, a man who tucks blankets around you and polishes the dustpan.

Then he'd gone and ruined the whole thing by trying to take her to his bed. She supposed the brothers were just brutes at heart. Which made her a little sad and pensive. She looked at Georgina. "There has to be a reason for someone to willingly hurt another person."

"People care about what they want for themselves. They don't care if someone else gets hurt. I learned that a long time ago." For the briefest of moments Georgina wore an odd, almost wistful expression, then she caught Amy looking at her and her lips thinned into that hard and determined line that seemed to dare you not to question her. She looked away and wiped her palms on her water-stained skirt as if she needed to keep her hands busy.

Amy wondered what or who had taught Georgina Bayard to look out for herself alone. Or were people just born selfish?

Georgina nodded at the basket sitting between them. "What's in that thing?" She shifted closer, wiggling slightly till she appeared to find a comfortable position.

Amy peeled back a corner of the nubby cloth that covered it and took out a doughnut. She held it up. "Food."

Georgina tore back the cloth and looked inside. "Oh my God . . . pies."

Amy took a large bite of the doughnut and watched Georgina. From the way her eyes lit up, you'd have thought those pies were made of hundred-dollar gold pieces. She lifted out a whole pie and held it beneath her nose before she smelled it and groaned like someone who hadn't eaten since birth.

"Where did you find this heavenly food?"

Amy swallowed a heavy wad of sweet doughnut and shrugged. "The basket was in the kitchen. I stumbled across it when I was trying to find you."

Meanwhile Georgina had set the pie in her lap and was rummaging inside the basket, her head so close that her black hair caught on the willow-twig handle. But that didn't stop her. She just jerked her hair out of the way, leaving a thin strand of coal-black hair springing from the basket weave as she searched for something.

A second later she pulled out a knife and fork. She looked at them both for an instant, then tossed the knife back in the basket. In less time than it took Amy to swallow again, Georgina was eating plump forkfuls right from the center of the pie.

"Hmmmm. I adore blueberry pie." She crammed another huge bite into her mouth and chewed with her eyes closed.

Amy finished off one doughnut and grabbed another.

Georgina opened her eyes and looked at Amy. She gulped down another mouthful, then asked, "What is that? Bread?"

"Doughnuts," Amy said with her mouth full.

Georgina nodded and they ate in companionable silence.

Amy was on her fifth doughnut when Georgina finally stopped shoveling pie into her mouth and stared at her. Amy stopped chewing and swallowed. "What's wrong?" She knew she had eaten five whole doughnuts—she always ate when she was nervous—but Georgina had eaten almost all of a huge pie.

"Nothing." Georgina quickly took another mouthful and dropped her gaze, jabbing the fork into the pie crust and watching it crumble.

Amy dropped a half-eaten doughnut in her lap and was silent.

Georgina glanced up. "What's the matter?"

"I think you were thinking of something."

Shrugging, Georgina looked away. "Just thinking, nothing important."

"Thinking about what?"

She was very still, then she fixed Amy with a square look. "Why did you come to help me escape?"

"Why?" Amy frowned. "What do you mean 'why?' What else would I do?"

"Save yourself."

"And leave you there?" She almost laughed, until she realized Georgina was perfectly serious. "I couldn't do that . . . leave you alone. We were kidnapped together."

"I've never been friendly or even kind to you, yet you came to help me. I don't understand you."

"Human kindness is nothing to understand." When Georgina didn't respond, Amy said, "If you saw someone who was in trouble, say, about to step in front of a carriage, you'd warn them or help somehow, perhaps try to pull them back to safety."

Georgina ate some more pie, then looked up at Amy and gave her a wicked smile. "If it was Phoebe Dearborn," she said swallowing, "I'd certainly give her a little help."

"There, you see? You would have done the same thing I did."

"Actually I didn't mean help in exactly that way."

"I don't understand."

"I meant that I'd help her along."

Amy gaped at her.

Georgina nodded. "I love to give her a little push."

"You'd push your friend in front of a moving carriage?" Amy was silent, then she began to laugh. "No, you wouldn't. You're just teasing me."

Georgina jabbed the fork into the pie crust. "I hate Phoebe Dearborn."

Amy was still laughing. "Even so, you wouldn't harm her."

"Well," Georgina admitted. "I supposed not, but it would be tempting." Her tone said that she would love the freedom to do something dire to Phoebe Dearborn.

"If you had escaped first. I know that you would have come to help me."

"Would I?" Georgina tapped the fork against her chin. Her face was honestly thoughtful. "I don't know if I would have."

"I think you try to be cold and hard because you think you have to be."

Georgina laughed sarcastically. "You don't know me at all." She dropped the pie tin on the rock next to her and tossed the fork inside. Her voice grew steely and her expression narrowed. "I will do whatever I have to do to survive and to win." She leaned over and stuck her hands in the water, then dried them furiously on her petticoat.

Amy looked down at the half-eaten doughnut in her hand. "I couldn't be happy if I had to hurt another person to get what I wanted."

"How quaint and idealistic."

Amy just shrugged, because she felt quaint when she was with Georgina. A plain pine rocker sitting next to a Chippendale chair made of rare ebony.

"You say you wouldn't hurt someone."

"Not purposely."

Georgina watched her with a knowing look. "Then tell me something."

"What?"

"Why did you crack the oaf's brother with a whisky glass?"

"I didn't want to!" Amy lowered her voice and

stared at her lap. "I was scared. He said he was going to take me to bed. I couldn't let him do that. I had to do something."

"I see." Georgina nodded. "I'll give you that excuse. It was you or him." She paused. "And I suppose you pointed that gun at the oaf because it was him or us. But . . ." The word just hung there.

"But what?"

"Why did you humiliate William De Pysters in front of everyone at the gala?"

"I didn't humiliate him. I gave him his ring back because he lied to me." When Georgina didn't say anything, Amy added, "He didn't love me."

"You thought he loved you?" Georgina shook her head. "Love and marriage don't go together. Believe me. Why would someone marry for love? It's just a useless emotion, a figment of the imagination.

"Name, wealth, and bloodlines are what matters. Even beauty doesn't really hurt or help you. Although I suppose a man can come around a little quicker if you give him a little encouragement—low-cut necklines, a kiss that's long enough to light a little passion, a feminine gesture like a finger to his lips or a hand on his chest.

"I've seen those things bring a man to his knees, but only if you have the right name or enough money. Certainly an emotional attachment like love—which I don't believe exists anyway—has no place in any social marriage."

Amy raised her chin. "My parents loved each other."

"Really? How amusing."

Amy looked down at her hands, then after a second she said quietly, "It was wonderful."

"Well, you go on and believe that if you want. But you are only looking to get hurt. Love doesn't mean a pot of beans to me. I will marry John Cabot and the only thing I'll love is all that glorious Cabot money."

"But what about him? If you plan to marry him then you must care for him. Just a little."

Georgina's expression grew fierce and stubborn. She shook her head. "No. Have you met him? Do you know who he is?"

"Yes." Amy was quiet. John Cabot looked a little like a mole she'd seen poke his head out of a hole in the garden on her estate. "He must have some fine qualities."

Georgina looked at her as if she had just said something truly stupid.

"A sense of humor?"

Georgina shook her head.

"Kindness?"

"Kind people are not rich."

"My father was kind and rich."

Georgina shrugged as if she didn't believe her and never would.

"What you say sounds so cold and hard. I can't be like that."

"If you want to survive in this world, you'll learn to be hard. It's the only way to protect yourself." She looked up again. "William couldn't have hurt you, Amy, if you hadn't been thinking of hearts and flowers and other silly love fantasies. William had the name; you had the money."

Her words cut right through Amy. She was a person, not just a dollar figure. Didn't people matter to anyone anymore?

"You did a foolish thing."

"If it's foolish to want your husband to love you for the person you are and cherish you and to hold you in his heart, to need you in his life, then call me a fool." Amy looked away because she had to. "William made a private and painful moment into a scene, just like he made cruel jests about me. The least a woman can ask for is that a man respect her."

She turned back, hoping her eyes weren't as moist as they felt. She raised her chin a notch, knowing Georgina had even more pride than she did. "I don't believe you would marry a man who thought of you as a joke."

Georgina wasn't looking at her, but she took a moment and seemed to think about Amy's words. "If the man had enough money I would."

"You would not."

"I would." She paused. "Then I'd spend the rest of my life getting even. I'd make his life miserable." Her eyes lit with sharp flashes of quick thoughts and narrowed as if she were actually living out the fantasy.

"But what about your life? That would be a miserable way to live, especially in a marriage."

"With a rich man? I don't think so."

"What kind of life is that?" Amy muttered.

"Busy." Georgina grinned. "Busy spending." Her voice sounded flippant, almost too flippant. But her expression looked for all the world as if she truly didn't care.

Amy sat there for a moment and watched her with a confused sense of awe and pity. She was a strong woman, driven and quick-thinking and seemingly certain of her path in life, so determined that she acted as if she would fight to make certain everything went her own way. Yet even with someone as brittle and determined as Georgina Bayard appeared, Amy wondered if she was really that strong on the inside.

Amy stared at the cave entrance, lost in her thoughts, her eyes seeing nothing because her imagination was doing her seeing for her. In her mind's eye she pictured two men standing side by side. The words *Destiny* and *Fate* were where their faces should have been. The mist swirled all around and a huge ship with the name *Escape* painted on its bow was floating behind them, the boarding ramp just a few feet away.

Fate was tall and blond, with huge arms and muscular legs. Destiny was just a smidgen shorter and had black hair. Spectacles dangled from one of his ears and he had a whisk broom and dustpan clutched protectively to his broad chest.

Both men moved in unison toward the cave entrance, walking slowly, as if time were beginning to stop, the way people always moved in daydreams. Amy could see herself standing there, unable to escape, even though her mind was telling her to run. She couldn't will herself to move.

But Georgina Bayard moved. She ran around Amy and punched Fate right in his square jaw. Destiny took one horror-filled look at Georgina's raised-and-shaking fist and he just melted back into the mist.

Amy blinked, turned, and looked at Georgina who was just sitting next to her. She wasn't staring at Amy, like Amy thought she might be. Instead, the other woman was looking down at the water.

Her expression changed suddenly, her dark slash of brows frowning together for a brief instant before she looked up. "I think the tide is rising. Look." She pointed at the water, which had risen and was only about an inch from the rock shelf where they sat.

"It *is* getting higher. What should we do?"

"Leave." Georgina started to move.

Amy got to her knees and dusted off her skirt, which seemed a futile effort since her clothing was tattered like rags. She shook her head, looked up, then froze. A second later she jabbed an elbow into Georgina's ribs.

"Ouch!" Georgina flinched and scowled at her. "What did you do that for?"

Amy nodded at the mouth of the cave and she heard Georgina, who was on all fours, inhale sharply.

Standing at the entrance to the cave with eerie lantern light cast over her was a little girl with curly golden hair. She was dressed in a white high-necked nightgown with lace at the hem where her pink bare toes peeked out and curled over the edge of a flat rock. She looked like an angel who had appeared out of the mist.

For just a second Amy blinked, thinking what she saw was just a vision. But the angel child was all too real.

The look on the child's face, however, was anything but angelic. She scowled at them as if she faced the devil and his entire horned and cloven army. Then very slowly the child raised her small hands and aimed a large quivering pistol right at them.

I'm not denying that women are foolish. God
Almighty made them to match the men.

George Eliot

The woman is a perfect match for you."

"I don't need a woman." Calum scowled at
Eachann while they worked their way through the
thick forest near the cove. He stopped to bat a low
branch out of his way, then had to swipe a shower of
dew and pine needles off his face and head. He glared
at Eachann's broad back while he picked his shirt
clean.

Eachann turned to face him. "Not even a woman
who is a victim?" He clapped Calum on the shoulder
and got that goading grin on his face. "What happened to you, brother? And here I thought you
wanted to single-handedly save the world from injustice."

Calum's nerves were worn thin and he told
Eachann in a foul but explicit term what he could go
do. But his brother wore an expression he knew only
too well.

Stubborn. Pig-headed. Too damn smart. Every trait

that got Eachann in trouble, which usually meant Calum was in trouble right along with him. Like now.

"This woman is just what you need."

"How would you know what I need?"

Eachann laughed. "I know better than anyone else."

"You're beginning to sound like Fergus."

Eachann stood in the center of the woods, looking as keenly attentive as a staghound waiting for the wind to bring the scent of game. Calum moved to join him and his boots sunk deeply into thick mud. He looked up. The mist hovered in the trees above them as if the thick spruce branches were arms ready to drop the heavy fog right on their heads.

Scowling, he stood there and impatiently picked pine tar from his hair. The stuff was like molasses. He looked down at his hands, then tried to wipe them clean with his handkerchief. It stuck to the tar on his palm. He shook it a few times and watched the white handkerchief wave from his palm like a flag of surrender.

Now Eachann was walking around the clearing, obviously looking for signs of the women. After a few steps he paused and shook his head. "They're not here either."

"Why are we standing around? Instinct is no way to find anyone. We need to comb the area from the house in a methodical way. Use thorough patterns so we cover every inch of ground. There have to be footprints somewhere around here."

Eachann spun around and began to walk back toward the quay as if he hadn't heard a word Calum had said. So Calum shouted after him. "We'll never find them this way. They could be anywhere." Calum tried to pull his boots from the sucking mud. There was a loud slurping pop. "Hell and blast!" He glanced up at Eachann's back. "You should have left things as they were. This is the most foolish trick you've ever pulled!"

Eachann just kept walking, but his voice traveled back. "I'd be willing to wager half my stable that had you been where I was, and had you seen what I saw, you'd have rescued the lass faster than I did."

Calum jammed his handkerchief into a pocket and went after him. "It would serve you right to lose those horses of yours. I just might take that wager."

"No. You won't." Eachann's tone was certain.

"Aye, I will."

The stable was Eachann's territory, and to Calum's never-ending surprise it was usually clean. But it was in sore need of some organization: a well-planned workspace, a sense of order, and everything stored in its proper place. There were plenty of times when his hands itched not with pine tar, but with the need to fix up Eachann's workplace.

The bags of feed could be in one area and stacked neatly, perhaps according to the date purchased. The tack could use some polishing—Eachann wasn't good with those kinds of details—and Calum could hang proper-sized hooks for bridles and halters that were in easy reach, aligned and placed in the order of frequency of use.

"If you touch my stable I'll blacken your eye. I know you, Calum." Eachann faced him. "The first thing you'd do is board the horses in their stalls by name. Alphabetically. Then you'd plan a feeding, training, and breeding schedule. Next you'd probably make one of those blasted charts for the organized placement of all the tackle and gear."

Eachann was right. Calum had just been plotting his chart. But he would be damned if he would admit it. Organizing Eachann's stable was a frequent fantasy of Calum's, mostly out of a notion of self-defense. The last time he was there, he had walked around a corner and tripped over the handle of a muck shovel.

Eachann eyed him for a moment. "Wipe that scowl off your face, brother. You've lost your sense of humor. You never used to be so blasted bedeviled about everything."

"I like my life calm and organized."

"Aye. Boring."

"I like my boring life. And you'd be getting piss-tired if those women were turned loose on you. Every time I turn around someone is sticking some woman under my nose."

Eachann began walking again, but not before Calum heard him mutter just how he'd like to have that black-haired she-devil under more than just his nose.

He'd like to plant his fist under Eachann's nose. He took a few more steps. The only place Calum wanted those women was off of his island. Now.

After a few minutes of walking in and out of the perimeter of the cove, Eachann said, "You do have to admit the lass I brought you is better-looking than any woman Fergus ever found. She's a pretty little thing, even if she does cry too much."

"She didn't cry," Calum said. His tone was defensive. Where did that come from? He ground to a stop, frowning and suddenly uncomfortable.

But try as he might, he couldn't make himself angry at her. When he thought of her image, he remembered what he'd seen in her eyes, a look that struck him where he was most vulnerable. She needed saving.

Calum glanced up. He'd lost Eachann to the mist again. "Slow down, dammit! I can't find you in this fog."

"I'm over here," Eachann called out.

Calum strode toward his brother's voice and grumbled, "I still can't believe you resorted to kidnapping."

"It's in the blood. You know as well as I do that many a MacLachlan has helped himself to a bride."

"That was two hundred years ago. In Scotland."

Eachann shrugged. "I did it for your own good."

"My good?" Even Calum had to laugh at that lie. "Oh, I see. Right now there are two women wandering this island because you were only thinking of me?"

Eachann didn't respond, which meant Calum was right and his brother was too stubborn to agree.

Calum bent down and held the lantern close to the sand. He scanned the ground but still saw no footprints, just the skinny three-pronged impressions of seagulls and sandpipers and the smooth polished rocks tossed up by the sea. He was beginning to think their search here was futile. He straightened and faced Eachann. "I think we should split up."

"Fine. You go in the opposite direction I am."

Calum turned to walk the other way and ground to a halt. The opposite direction was the sea.

He spun back and caught up with Eachann who was smirking. "You can go straight to hell. You think this is all a joke. Their families are probably ready to storm the island and hang us by our necks . . . or something worse."

"Aye, and the gravestone could read: 'Here lie the brothers MacLachlan. They were well-hung.'"

"Is nothing serious to you?"

"They have no families, Calum."

"How do you know?"

"George volunteered the information." There was a note of amusement in Eachann's voice, as if he was the only one who knew the joke. He glanced at Calum and added, "Don't worry. I asked a friendly little redhaired maid about your lass."

Calum thought about that. "If you took the time to ask about their families then that means you had this planned."

"No. I didn't have this planned. I found myself in a difficult situation once I was ashore. It didn't take me long to figure out I needed a woman."

"Couldn't you just visit Justine's and pay for one for a few hours?"

"I didn't need a woman for her body." Eachann turned and went back toward the west end of the cove. "Besides, I didn't have any plans to nab one for you until I saw the blonde and realized she was just what you did need, even if she is a little mild and meek."

Calum tromped along behind him. "Considering what happened to her, I'd say she was showing more mettle than most women."

"You think so? Didn't seem like much of a fighter to me. Now, George, there's a woman that puts up a good fight. Must have some good Scots blood in her somewhere. Not like your bride."

"There's nothing wrong with my—damn. . . . She's not my bride. I am *not* marrying anyone."

"Fine. I'll take her back."

"Good."

"I'll just dump her right back into the hands of that fellow who hurt her."

Calum stopped. "Someone hurt her?"

"Aye." Eachann kept walking down the beach. "Some horse's ass humiliated the poor lass."

"How?"

"I found both women at a society party."

"What the hell were you doing at a society party?"

"Just passing through."

Calum knew that was another lie. His look must have said so because when he caught up, Eachann added, "Well, passing through long enough to see your lass—"

"She's not—"

"Okay, okay . . ." Eachann raised a hand. "I was there long enough to see the lass break her engagement. Her future husband didn't much like it. When he saw he couldn't change her mind he announced to everyone within shouting distance that she wasn't good enough to carry the name of his blue-blooded family. He belittled her in front of everyone. She ran off crying and hid in the back of the garden."

So that was the reason the lass seemed so broken. She was wounded. He followed Eachann down the beach in silence, thinking that his brother had just made things worse for the girl when he kidnapped her. The damn impulsive fool. He should have left her to her tears.

"I saw her bent over and crying. She looked so beaten down I thought of you. She was rescue bait." He looked up. "Stop glowering and admit it. You do have this driving need to save every downtrodden and unfortunate soul on the face of the earth."

Rescue bait? Calum supposed in a way Eachann was right. But Calum didn't care if his brother poked fun at him. Like most brothers, they had grown up needling each other. Eachann would goad him about his neatness the same way Calum needled him back about his sloth. Of late the source for Eachann's needling had been Calum's work.

But Calum believed what he did; it gave him satisfaction and a purpose he hadn't had before he'd discovered something worthwhile to do.

He'd heard about the clearances in Scotland, most of the Scots here had. They felt rage at the cruel injustice of throwing people off the land they and their families had occupied for hundreds of years.

The new lairds of Scotland had been slowly driving the Highlanders from their homes. It seemed there was more profit in grazing sheep than supporting clan families. Now there were more Scots in North America than there were left in Highlands.

But until he saw the immigrants with his own eyes, the horror of their situation hadn't hit him. Most immigrated here with the promise of a fresh start. But the lairds lied to them more often than not.

Once here the Highlanders wandered the streets with nothing, not even a command of English. Most only spoke Gaelic. For too long before Calum knew of them, many had starved or frozen to death trying to get to the open lands of Canada's upper provinces.

"Hell, Calum, you've managed to turn injustice into a profession."

It was just like Eachann to change the subject, especially now when they were arguing. Calum knew his brother saw his idealism as a joke. But he knew Eachann wasn't as disinterested in Calum's work as he sounded.

When they were younger, Eachann had helped him with the Scots who came on those ships, like the ship he expected to arrive anytime. Eachann met his wife, Sibeal, while he had been helping Calum settle families displaced by the clearances.

Since Eachann had lost her, he had changed. There was more of an edge to his brother, a cruel and cynical side to him and his jokes. As time passed Eachann had done more foolish and impulsive things, like he'd done tonight and that day when he'd taken his children away.

Of the two of them, Eachann had always been the brother who was slow to anger but quick to act, too often acting without much forethought. After Sibeal died, Eachann became selfish and disinterested in anything except his horses. Those animals were like a refuge to him. So much so, he had all but abandoned his children.

At first Calum thought it was only grief that would pass. But with time Eachann hadn't grown closer to Kirsty and Graham. Instead he let them do as they wished. When they grew wild and whiny and demanded his attention, he had just upped and taken them to the mainland where he put them away in a boarding school.

For months afterward, Eachann was seldom around the house. He was moody and he had stopped helping Calum altogether. He had stopped doing anything but raise and break and ride his horses, as if doing so were his only purpose. There was more and more that his brother sloughed off, until there was little in life that Eachann appeared to care about.

In fact, when Calum thought about it, he realized that Eachann had shown little interest in anything over the last two years. Until now.

His brother stopped in front of him and was searching around them. Calum held the lantern high as Eachann cursed and muttered, "Damn creatures could get themselves killed."

For the first time in ages Eachann's voice wasn't caustic or amused, but filled with a sincere emotion.

Calum stood there thinking about that for a long time. He could let his brother get away with his actions like before, when he lost Sibeal. Or this time he could try to get Eachann to talk.

Calum stood there a moment longer, then reached out and placed a hand on Eachann's broad shoulder. He could feel the tenseness. Very quietly and seriously he asked, "Why did you really do this?"

Eachann turned and gave Calum a snide look that melted away when he must have seen how concerned Calum was. Eachann took a deep breath, then looked around as if he were searching for the right words.

"Why did I do this?" he responded quietly. He looked up at Calum. "The truth?"

"Aye." He nodded. "The truth."

Eachann's expression became empty, a look that Calum remembered seeing before. It was the same look he'd worn years ago when their father died and they both knew they were alone, the same look he had when they'd found his wife Sibeal dead.

His brother took another breath and stared down at the ground. Tension was in the air, the kind of tension that felt alive and made the air suddenly thick and heavy.

Eachann looked up, his eyes not reflecting laughter or cynicism or icy disdain. Instead they were full of something that looked just like plain old fear. They both stood there in the fog, studying each other unguarded.

"Because of Kirsty and Graham." There was pain in Eachann's voice when he said his children's names.

Calum didn't criticize. All he could say was "Explain."

But before either of them could move, before he could even take a breath or reach out a hand again, a shot rang out.

The Proverb says that providence protects children and idiots. I know it because I have tested it.

Mark Twain

The gun went off with a flash of light and a loud crack. Sudden and powerful recoil knocked the child off the rock and right into the sea.

Before the gunshot could echo around the walls of the cave, Georgina was in the water. She swam deeper, then pressed her hands against an underwater rock ledge beneath the cave entrance. She felt her way around it.

On the other side of the rocks the water was cooler and looked dense and black. She swam downward in a spiral circle. Searching. Out of the corner of her eye, a flash of white flicked just below her.

She flipped and kicked down toward it, grabbing blindly. Her hands found nothing. She reached out again and again, frantically.

Her hand brushed against fabric. Her fist closed over it. The child's nightgown.

Georgina kicked upward, pulling the girl with her. She could see the surface hovering above them. A small area shone silver-gold in the weak glow of the distant lantern light and waved eerily above the rock ledge, just a few feet away, maybe only one, two, three more strong kicks upward.

Her chest was aching with tight air; it felt as if it would burst. She kicked up again and again, one . . . two . . . three . . . and more times. The pain in her chest scared her, it swelled so severely. Time had seemed to stop.

She tore at her full petticoat until she had ripped it off and it drifted down and away. She held the child with one arm and reached toward the surface. She kicked again, hard and powerfully.

She broke through the surface and gasped. Cold damp air cooled her mouth, throat, and chest. Water slapped at her face. She jerked the child up, slid her hands under girl's limp arms, and pulled her head out of the water.

Georgina waited to hear the child gasp.

There was nothing. The little girl's eyes were closed. Her lips were closed. She was grayish and didn't move.

"Breathe! Come on. . . ." Georgina nudged her small chin up. "Breathe!" she shouted into the child's ear. "I said breathe!"

The girl choked and began to struggle, kicking and slapping at the water and Georgina while she coughed up water and air.

"Stop it!" Georgina held her tighter. "Hold still or you'll drown us both!"

The girl gasped twice, then began to struggle and kick, shaking her head from side to side and saying, "Let me go! Let me go!" She kicked Georgina in the stomach and tried to move away.

Georgina hissed. "Stop it!"

Finally the girl stilled, staring up at her with frightened eyes.

"I'm not going to hurt you. But if you don't hold still, you'll drown both of us."

The child stared at her for a long tense moment.

"Do you understand?"

The girl nodded.

Georgina glanced around to get her bearings. The fog hovered right above them. She could see the rocks to her left, but they were more distant. The water was moving faster. It felt colder on her legs and the current was stronger.

She could hear the sea rushing against the island's rocks. The sound grew louder. Closer. The current was carrying them away from rocks and the cave.

Georgina clamped her arm over the child's bony chest so she was pinned against her body. Then she began to swim, taking one-armed strokes that were deep but difficult. It was like swimming through mud.

When the stitch in her side became so sharp that breathing was hard, she paused and treaded water to rest. She stared blankly at the water and the white fog surrounding them.

This seemed so futile. And she was tired. The child coughed and Georgina looked down at her. She knew she needed to keep the girl's head above water.

And my own.

She almost laughed out loud. Keeping her head above water . . .

"Seems that's all I've done lately," she muttered.

She felt the girl's stare and looked down at her. This was Georgina's own little snippet of irony. No one else but her bankers would understand.

So she began to swim again in the same hard-fought, side-arm strokes. Her breath grew short and sharp. It felt as if the tide and current were giant hands trying to hold her back and keep her from reaching the shore.

To get her bearings she glanced left, right, then back over her shoulder. A faint glow of yellow light spilled through the mouth of the cave, making it look for one crazy moment like a cynical smile. She stared at it, knowing that smile would slowly and eerily disappear as the tide filled the cave.

The fog rolled up and down with the sea like shades on a window. One moment she could catch a snatch of black rocky coastline. The next moment there was nothing but a cocoon of mist.

She didn't swim on. She knew to wait until the fog lifted high enough for her to see the cave. Then she could gain some perspective. And when that mist finally did lift a bit, the light from the cave had grown smaller; the smile was narrow now and upside down like a frown.

Amy had to be inside the cave. The lantern was still there. But the tide was rising and it would trap her. She took a deep breath and shouted, "Amy!"

There was no answer.

"Amy!"

Still nothing.

"Amy!"

The air sounded as if it carried a distant voice. Or she thought it did.

"Amy!" she screamed as loudly as she could.

The sound came again. But it wasn't Amy.

It was a man's voice.

"Father!" the child screamed and began to struggle in her arms again.

Georgina fought to hold the girl, but she heard a deep and familiar voice. "Kirsty?"

Oh God . . . no, she thought. Not him.

"Kirsty!" he shouted.

"Here, Father! We're here!"

She heard him swear, the same word he'd used

when she kicked him. Georgina looked down. This little girl was the oaf's daughter?

There was the sound of a splash, and instinctively she turned toward it. A foolish mistake.

Turn away from him, not toward him!

But before she could move or even breathe, a man's muscled arm closed around her and the girl, almost lifting them from the water with one swift motion. Without a word, he swam back through the currents, carrying them along with an almost supernatural power.

They hit the shore so quickly Georgina was stunned. She couldn't decide if they were really that close to shore or if he actually swam that well. She struggled to stand but couldn't because he held her too tightly; his arm was clamped around her waist.

He never said a word, but every time she tried to move he tightened his grip on her and pinned both her and the child closer to his chest. He moved sluggishly up a steep dune, then dropped them in the damp sand, falling to his knees next to her.

She held the little girl, who was strangely silent and still as she lay sprawled on Georgina's body.

For a few moments no one spoke. The only sound was the rush of their breathing. His. Hers. The child's.

Georgina started to move, but he planted a hand in the sand above her shoulder and straddled her hips with his hard knees. He moved too quickly for a man who had swum so hard. Her arms and legs felt as limp as the soaked ribbons on her gown.

She met his hard look. "Amy's still inside a cave." Odd how her voice was smaller and breathy. Weak. It didn't sound like her.

He didn't respond.

She cleared her throat. "The tide's coming in."

"Calum!" was all he said.

Someone loomed over them.

The oaf looked up. "The other one's stuck in a sea cave."

"Which cave? Where?" It was the brother's panicked voice.

She pointed where the fog floated slightly, showing the thin slice of light that was left. Her hand was shaking.

"The caves to the south," Eachann answered him. "It must be the one near the point. Hurry, Calum. The tide's rising."

A second later Calum MacLachlan was gone and all she heard was the sound of someone running down the beach.

She was racked with a sudden chill, as if someone had just thrown water on her. She was soaked and half spent, a small child lying so still on her and Eachann MacLachlan kneeling over them. He was braced on his forearms. Cold water dripped from his hair onto her neck and shoulders.

Plop. Plop. Drips that were like numbers counting down toward something ominous—perhaps the moment the world would come crashing down on her.

Georgina raised her chin to meet the look she expected to see. It took every ounce of strength she had left to hold her chin up and not shake. Her body seemed on the verge of shattering. She could feel the shakes coming as she looked at him.

But he wasn't looking at her. His gaze was fixed on his daughter, his expression so hard it looked ready to crack.

"What in the hell have you been doing?"

The girl was still as a stone.

"Kirsty?"

"Me?" the child asked in a hoarse tone.

"Aye."

She looked away and mumbled something about

plaids and thieves and guns and saving relics like medieval knights had.

It was utter nonsense.

But the oaf was distracted. Her perfect chance.

Cautiously, Georgina started to slide back and out from under both of them. But her feet felt oddly numb. She tried again.

His hand shot out and clamped onto her arm.

She stared down at his hand. It was so large he almost held her entire upper arm in that one tight grip. Her breath was a lump in her throat when she glanced back at him.

"Don't move." He pinned his daughter with another cold look. "I want the truth, not one of your stories, Kirsty."

The girl's teeth began to chatter and she was shaking the way Georgina wanted to.

All of them were soaked and surrounded by cold damp fog and even colder wet sand.

The oaf seemed oblivious to it.

Georgina's mind flashed back in time to the chilling image of another little girl sitting on a sand dune shaking from fear and exertion.

No one had noticed her either.

Something snapped inside of her and she pulled the little girl so close against her that the child's wet head slipped snugly beneath Georgina's chin. "For God's sake, lecture her later!"

He gave her a sharp look.

"Get the poor child inside before she freezes to death."

The child tilted her head for a moment and stared up at her, still shaking stiffly with those cold and shimmying kinds of shakes that your body won't let you control. Georgina knew then because she was shaking with them too.

But she was silent. She met Eachann's hard look with one of her own.

His hand fell away. His gaze flicked from her to his daughter. He muttered another curse, then grabbed something that was lying in the sand and wrapped it around them.

It was his coat. Before she could blink he was standing above them. A second later he scooped them up in his arms and carried them off through the mist.

> Be respectful of your superiors,
> if you have any.
>
> *Mark Twain*

Kirsty scowled at the black-haired woman huddled in a scratchy blanket like hers and sitting near her on the wool rug. The two of them were locked in the bathing room with a toasty fire burning in the corner woodstove.

The woman had been staring at her hands, which were knotted into tight fists and pressed against her belly as if she were angry. If Kirsty had liked her, she might have said the woman was very pretty, maybe even beautiful.

The lady looked up as if she somehow knew she was thinking about her.

Kirsty gave her a fierce stare. She decided the lady's long wet hair was really a bunch of curly black snakes that would bite you if you got too close. Her skin was white. Didn't ghosts have white skin? They must have white skin because they were really dead and so they had no blood left inside of them.

This woman had snaky hair and dead-ghost skin

147

and . . . and wicked kelpie eyes that were looking at her right now.

Kirsty tried to look at the woman the same way she looked at her classmates when they made her feel she wasn't good enough to play with them. She sat a little straighter and said, "I don't like you."

"Good. I'm not particularly fond of you either." She slapped her hair out of her face and it whipped back behind her. Her hair was so long the tips of it brushed the rug.

She ignored Kirsty and looked around the bathing room, frowning. She stared at the tank and tub for a long time, then she looked around some more. After a moment she muttered, "No windows."

Kirsty watched her cautiously. If she was looking for windows that meant she was going to steal something else or she was going to try to get away. "Father locked the door and now you can't get out."

"Thank you for that brilliant piece of knowledge. I doubt I could have figured it out on my own, windows being so hard to distinguish."

"What's *distinguish?*"

"Something your father isn't."

Kirsty didn't like it when grownups did that, made funny remarks that they knew she didn't understand. But she wouldn't let the lady know it. She pulled her blanket tighter around herself and stared at her because she wanted to make her feel uneasy too.

The woman gave her the same look, and hers worked better because Kirsty felt as if she could see every next thought inside her head. Kirsty tried to think of everything ugly . . . snakes and spiders and Miss Harrington's ruler.

But the lady wasn't paying attention to her anymore. Instead she talked to herself and muttered something about kidnapping.

Kirsty stuck her chin up in the air. "My father would never let you kidnap Graham and me."

"Kidnap you?" She burst out laughing. "Now that's rich."

"My father is the bravest and strongest man in the whole world."

The woman stopped laughing. She was quiet for a second. She stared at Kirsty as if she wanted to say something very badly. But she didn't speak, just looked like she was concentrating really hard, the way Kirsty had to do during arithmetic lessons.

The lock clicked suddenly and they both turned toward the door at the same time. Her father filled the doorway like those paintings in Harrington Hall filled their big frames.

"Well, well . . ." the woman said in a snotty voice. "Look at this. Samson's here."

Kirsty looked back at the lady again, wondering if she was making fun of her. But the lady was glaring at her father with one of those prickly looks people got when they wanted to let you know they'd get even. The same nasty look Chester Farriday gave her when he pulled his dumb old head from the mop bucket.

Her father stood there with dry clothes over his arm while he stared at the woman. He didn't look angry, but she had his full attention, something that Kirsty had to work so hard for.

"She's a thief," Kirsty reminded him.

Her father's gaze flicked to her. "She saved your foolish little life."

"I can swim." She *could* swim.

He looked as if he wanted to argue but said nothing. Instead he tossed her dry nightclothes. She watched him while she quickly changed clothes. He closed the door, walked over, and stood above the snake-haired woman, who had to crane her neck back to look all the way up at her father. He was so very tall.

"I told you to get out of those wet clothes, George."

The lady pulled the blanket tighter around her and her jaw got really tight. "No."

They looked at each other for the longest time. Kirsty sat there watching them, looking from one to the other. The air grew really funny, like it did before a lightning storm when it was perfectly quiet and all the birds had suddenly gone away.

She didn't like the way her father looked at this George woman. She didn't know why. All she knew was she wanted him to stop because she was getting one of those strong feelings she got inside her sometimes. It was like her heart hurt or some important part of her was growing really small and soon there wouldn't be anything left. She used to get that feeling just before she began to do something really dumb, like cry.

"So you want to stay in those soaked clothes and freeze to death." He wore a strange smile, the kind Graham had when he knew a secret and hadn't told her.

"I'm perfectly fine."

He pulled his gaze away from the snake woman and looked at Kirsty. "Go to bed. And stay there."

Kirsty didn't move, but watched her father turn away from her again. He leaned down and picked up the woman by her waist so she was standing really close to him. He said something to her in a low voice that no matter how hard she tried Kirsty couldn't hear.

No one seemed to notice when she stood and moved closer to them. She moved quietly until she was so close to them that the woman's torn dress dripped cold water onto her bare feet.

Her ghost skin had turned bright pink, and she said, "I wouldn't try to do that if I were you."

"Is that a challenge, George?"

Kirsty tugged on her father's shirtsleeve while she looked up at them. "Do what?"

They both turned toward her.

"I told you to go to bed."

"I'm not tired."

Her father let the woman go for a second and ran a hand through his hair. He looked at her and then at the woman. "Get out of those wet clothes and put this on." He handed the woman some clothes. On top was something green and shiny and familiar.

"No! That was Mama's!" Kirsty yanked the dress out of the woman's hands and held it tightly against her so no one could take it away.

Her father looked at her as if she had socked him.

"It was Mama's," she said, and to her horror she could feel herself start to cry. The tears just rose up from her chest to stick in her throat like thick choking mud stuck to your feet.

"It's only a dress," he said. "What does it matter?"

Kirsty didn't answer him. She just looked down at the dress, which was dotted with small dark wet spots from her tears.

"Now that was brilliant, MacOaf," the lady muttered.

"How was I supposed to know she would do this?"

"You wouldn't know. Obviously that kind of knowledge would involve thinking."

Her father swore under his breath, then looked at Kirsty, frowning fiercely. "Are you crying?"

She stared up at him through blurred eyes that couldn't really see anything but her dumb old tears.

"You are crying," he said, as if she had disappointed him.

She spun around them, and ran out the door, dragging the dress with her as she ran down the hall.

She didn't stop until she was inside the dark bedroom with Graham. She closed the door and leaned against it, her breath catching for a second.

Graham was still asleep. She could tell because he hadn't moved. When her eyes adjusted to the dark she could see his even breathing.

Her brother never cried for their mother or their father. Graham never had nightmares and went to sleep just because he was told to.

She stood with her back pressed hard against the door and she looked around the dark room. It was so very quiet, the way the air was before those cold strong storms that came sometimes.

There was nothing to be afraid of. No monsters lived in the tall closet with the mirrored doors. No snakes or alligators were hiding under the bed so they could bite her toes.

But still she was afraid. She crossed the bare floor quickly, just in case, then she crawled on the bed. She lay her head down on a feather pillow that was cold with the chill of the room. She didn't use the sheets and blankets to cover her. Instead she wrapped her mother's pretty green dress over her.

If she tried really, really hard she could remember her mother. She could see her dark red hair and hear her laugh. As she lay there very still and quietly, she began to smell her mother's scent, so faint and far away at first, the way it was sometimes when she tried to picture her mother's face. Like she almost had to chase after the image to remember.

But the smell of her mother was there, just like all those memories of when they were happy and were still there. Somewhere. Or was she losing those too? It was then, with the faintest scent of lavender around her, that Kirsty cried herself to sleep.

"Guess who holds thee?"—"Death," I said. But
    there
The silver answer rang—"Not Death, but Love."
                                        Elizabeth Barrett Browning

Amy was going to die.

Once the little girl with the gun had appeared,
everything happened so fast. The gun went off; Amy
went in the water. When she resurfaced both the girl
and Georgina were gone. It was as if the sea had just
reached out and swept them away.

Her parents must have told her a thousand times
when she was growing up: if you're lost, stay in one
place so someone can find you. But she never had
been lost or separated from them. Till now.

So she had stayed in one place for the longest time,
watching the cave fill up while she waited to be found.
Now she realized that the only thing that had found
her was the rising tide.

She spotted a single starfish on the wall behind the
lantern. It clung there the same way she clung to the
rock ledge. Alone. Even the black crabs were long
gone. Water glistened from the cave wall in front of
her like mirrors reflecting a kaleidoscope of what her
short life had been.

She wondered if drowning was an easy way to die. If it was instant. Did people really sink to the bottom? Would she look up and see a dark cloaked figure floating toward her? She couldn't quite conjure up a mental image of Death approaching her with a sickle gripped tightly in one white hand and the last breath of her life held in the other. Was dying alone the best way? Or the worst way?

If Georgina were still there she wouldn't be alone. But Georgina wasn't here. Amy felt certain that Georgina wouldn't abandon her, no matter how brittle she tried to be. Amy trusted her.

Besides she had heard Georgina call her name. She could be lost out there somewhere. She could die too. But the Georgina Bayard she knew wouldn't let a little thing like the Atlantic Ocean defeat her.

Amy looked out at the sea, wondering if she had any of Georgina's nerve within her. She wished she was a better swimmer. She took a deep breath and tried to climb out of the water. Her heavy skirt and the constant cramp in her side stopped her. No matter how many times she tried to pull herself up, she just couldn't find the strength.

She suddenly regretted all those doughnuts she'd eaten. They sat in her stomach like a tub of mud and made her side ache terribly whenever she even tried to swim a stroke.

She gripped the jagged and slippery edge of the rock ledge and looked out at the cave entrance. The water was so high she could only see a sliver of mist; it floated like sea smoke.

The lantern sat on the ledge near her hands and still flickered weakly. One more inch of water and the wick would be out.

She propped an elbow on the rock, rested her head on it for a moment or two, and tried to calm herself.

Her heart was thudding fast. Her breaths were shallow and hurried. She was just plain scared.

She bit her lip hard and slowly tried to pull herself along the rock toward the entrance, afraid to let go. Afraid not to.

Calum MacLachlan swam through the cave entrance a second later, a lonely figure making steady, methodical strokes that cut through the water easily. One more stroke and his head came up and turned toward the light while he treaded water.

His spectacles were gone and his black hair was slicked back like a sea lion's. Light from the fading, sputtering lantern cast the sharp angles of his cheeks and strong jaw into hollow shadows. Water clung to a deep smudge of a thick beard stubble that made his jaw and cheeks look like they were dusted with coal.

Amy looked into that darkly handsome face of his and felt a nervous mixture of fear and thanksgiving. How strange he was to her, this man who had kept hollering to his brother that he didn't want her. Yet he had fully expected her to go willingly into his bed. She had been scared of him then.

She was scared of him now. Until he moved closer with an intense look of relief that surprised and confused her. Before she could speak he was next to her in the water. One large hand reached out and cupped her jaw and cheek as tenderly as any lover's touch she could ever dream up.

"You're okay." For a moment she wondered if she had imagined the wealth of emotion she'd heard in his voice. In those two words.

It had been so long since she had heard that kindness and protectiveness in a man's voice that she couldn't respond. She thought of her father, the only man she had known who had loved her for herself. It was a difficult memory for her and thinking about him had brought tears to her eyes.

Calum MacLachlan mistook those tears for fright.

"I know you hit me with the glass because you were frightened. Don't be. I won't hurt you, lass. I give you my word."

She stared at him.

The look he gave her fell over her like magic. "I'd sooner cut out my own heart."

That was the last thing she'd expected to hear from him. Common sense told her she should be quivering with fear. His arm slid firmly around her and he pulled her to his chest, which was warm and real and made her feel safe.

"Will you trust me?"

She looked at his face, really looked at it, and saw nothing there to be afraid of. His expression was full of only honest concern for her.

He was waiting for an answer.

She nodded, and none too soon either, because just a moment later a shallow wave drifted in and the lantern went out.

It was suddenly black. She inhaled sharply; it sounded loud inside the dark hollowness of the cave.

"I have you, lass. I'm going to turn away. Put your arms around my neck. Let my back support you. All you have to do is hold on. Do you understand?"

"Yes." She locked her hands around his neck. He touched her fingers for a second, gave them a reassuring pat, then he swam out of the cave.

A few strokes and she took a breath of cold foggy air, then lay her head on his shoulder in exhausted relief while he continued to swim, and that was how Calum MacLachlan saved her life.

Advice would always be more acceptable if it didn't conflict with our plans.

New England proverb

Georgina was still locked in the bathing room. She prowled the room the way a caged animal did. Animals had a natural instinct to keep moving, so when the opportunity came they could act in an instant. She would be ready if the moment came when she could escape.

So she was thinking and walking, because there was nothing else left to do. She thought about John Cabot, about her home, and all her plans. Her stomach wound into a tight knot.

One rash and stupid act by the MacOaf and she was on the verge of losing everything. He'd taken everything she had been fighting to save and put it just out of her reach. She punched a fist into her other hand as she walked. She had to get back. She had to.

If she could return before too much time had passed, she could make an excuse about her disappearance.

What kind of excuse? She paced again, thinking of

lies. She stopped and struck a pose she thought she liked. She cast a quick glance in the mirror on a wall.

Too stiff.

She rolled her shoulders back and raised her chin to an elegant and confident level.

Much better. "Why, John, dear!" she said with a swipe of a raised and elegantly graceful hand—the same gesture used to greet guests you wanted to impress. "You won't believe what happened!"

She froze in that stance for a moment before her posture crumpled. Then what could she say? She wandered around the room in a circle, thinking.

What to say? What to say? God knows she could not tell the truth. She could just see his face. "Well, John, dear, you see this enormous Scot came and snatched me away, then locked me in his home."

She'd have no reputation left. Her reputation was all she had. John Cabot would never marry her if he knew she'd been kidnapped. That would be just too scandalous.

She had to escape, come up with some excuse. Perhaps she could tell him she had gone after Amy Emerson. Yes, that would work.

Two women alone. That took care of a chaperon. She nodded. Then she could come up with something heroic to work on John's sympathy. She would have to repair the damage to his ego. After all, she hadn't shown up to meet him. Heroism was good for sympathy. Sacrifice and all that sappy rot would certainly work. He was, after all, a man. Men respected heroism.

Within a few minutes she had her plan, complete with the sympathy element. She rubbed her hands together, then crossed over to the woodstove in the corner of the room and warmed her hands and feet.

The room had slick slate floors that were icy when

you didn't walk on the rug. She looked around her. The room was surprisingly large and convenient.

There was plumbed water and taps. A surprise. She'd thought of these coastal islands as backward, places that only had one-room fishermen's shacks filled with dead fish and dust. Outhouses and earth toilets. Rickety moorings and wrecked pieces of ships.

A large copper water vat stood in the corner near the stove, and pipes snaked out if it and ran to the sink set in a knotted pine cabinet and onto the huge porcelain-lined tub.

There was a linen closet she had first thought was a door to an adjoining room. Inside the closet were thick bathing towels stacked in a neat orderly fashion, every one aligned with the next.

Considering what she had seen of the house, which wasn't much, she'd thought the place was a huge sty. But this room was spotless. The house seemed to be a strange mix of mess and order.

But right now, to her, it was just a prison. She felt too blasted helpless, unable to do anything but pace the room and think. She wanted to act, not think. She wanted to get away. She wanted to get home.

She stared at the locked door for a long time, then searched the room for something to jimmy the lock. As she looked around she caught a reflection of herself. The image was enough to make her cry—if she were one to cry. She wasn't.

She jerked a hairpin from her hair and spent the next half hour bending it and twisting it and trying to make it work like a key. Finally she placed a hand on her back and straightened stiffly. She glared at the door, then at her reflection before she jammed the pin back into her hair where it was about as useful as an empty purse.

She stood there trying to think of something to do.

She was cold. And she should just take a bath. It would certainly warm her up.

But with her luck, MacOaf would come strolling in. She eyed those water pipes to see if she could loosen one and conk him on his fat head. But after a few futile tries there was no way to get any section of the pipe loose.

Exhausted and angry, she gave up and just sank to floor. She sat there, her chin resting in one hand while she mentally called down inventive curses on Eachann MacLachlan's arrogant, handsome, and overly large head.

She had just wished that all his great-grandchildren would be horned when she got bored and started counting her bruises.

Twenty-seven on one leg alone.

With a groan from her tired and sore muscles, she creaked upright, pretending she didn't have too many bruises to count. She crossed the room.

At the sink, she turned on a spigot and bent down, using her hand to help her drink. She finished, wiped her mouth, then reached out to turn off the faucet. And froze.

A second later she was laughing with wicked glee.

> Love starts when another person's needs become
> more important than your own.
>
> *Anonymous*

Somewhere high up in Heaven there had to be a big golden book that explained why people fell in love for no intelligent reason. Amy knew this had to be, because by the time Calum had her safely on shore, her broken heart wasn't broken anymore.

She could feel his look and glanced up.

"Are you warm enough? It's not much farther."

"Yes. I'm fine." And she was. He'd bundled her up in his dry coat, donned his spectacles, and swung her into his arms before she even had a chance to take a step. It was terribly romantic.

He stared down at her. "What's wrong?"

"Nothing," she told him, knowing she couldn't tell him what she was feeling. So she just looked away.

When she looked back, he was watching her so pointedly and as if he couldn't help himself. She wanted to reach and touch his cheek to soften his expression. He was so serious. He was so intense. She wondered what his laughter would sound like.

Neither of them spoke as he carried her toward the

house. The silence was almost worse than her confused feelings about this man; it hung about them the same way the fog did—you were aware of it, but just plowed on through anyway and hoped it wouldn't last.

She knew the instant he wasn't looking at her anymore. It was such an odd thing that she could feel his gaze on her every time. As surely as if he had touched her. She watched him openly, trying to understand exactly who this man was.

She cocked her head slightly. "Your glasses are fogged up."

"Aye, lass. But they'll have to stay foggy. My hands are full right now."

She felt her own flush. He carried her up the hillside without a complaint or a labored breath.

She reached up and removed his spectacles. His steps slowed to the barest of movement, just distant crunches on the gravel of the path.

Amy used the wet skirt of her gown to polish his lenses. Very carefully, she reached up and set the glasses on his straight nose, then hooked the wire stems back over his ears.

"There," she said matter-of-factly and she smiled.

He pinned her with a look as confused as she had felt just a few seconds before.

He almost ran with her up the steps, went inside and kicked the door closed. He stood in the giant entry with all the wood-paneled walls soaring up above them like the ancient island pines from which they were made.

He muttered in frustration.

"What's the matter?"

He gave her a long stare, then admitted, "I still don't know your name."

Before she had her reasons for not telling him. But she wasn't afraid of him anymore.

He was waiting for her and said quietly, "Haven't I just earned the right to know your name?"

She smiled. "Thank you for rescuing me."

He just waited.

"Amy. My name is Amy."

He stood there as if he needed to absorb the sound of it, then he started suddenly like someone who just realized where he was. He cleared his throat gruffly, then juggled her slightly to adjust her weight in his arms.

She winced.

He froze. "Did I hurt you?"

She shook her head. "It's only a cramp in my side. From the water, I think. Just as soon as I'm warm, I'll be fine."

"Well then, Amy-my-lass, let's get you settled in by a warm fire."

Her name sounded like a melody when he said it that way. He carried her into the same room he took her to before.

"There you are." Eachann MacLachlan crossed the room like a man possessed. "Where are the keys to your supply house?"

Calum frowned. "Right where I always keep them. In the top drawer of the desk."

"The desk is locked."

Calum set Amy down in the chair. "You're alone?"

"Kirsty is in bed. George is locked in the bathing room where she can't cause me any more trouble. She needs dry clothes."

"So does Amy." Calum unlocked a drawer, then looked at her.

"Who?"

"Amy. This is Amy."

"Oh." Eachann took the key, then started to leave, but stopped short of the door. "Is there enough clothing in storage?"

Calum flipped open a green ledger book and used a finger to scan it. He looked up. "There's plenty and the next ship is the last one this year. We can restock."

"Good." Eachann turned to leave.

"Eachann?"

"Aye?"

"The women's clothing is in the trunks nearest the front," Calum told him. "They're labeled according to content and size." He paused and took a breath, and then both brothers spoke at the same time.

"There's a chart on the wall above them."

Calum snapped his mouth shut and looked at Amy. His face colored slightly. His brother had embarrassed him. She felt a sudden sense of anger when she looked at the man who had kidnapped her.

Eachann MacLachlan had a knowing expression. "Are they stacked alphabetically . . . drawers above petticoats and shirts?" He leaned indolently against the doorjamb and waited for his brother to respond.

Just then Amy felt something fall in her wet hair. She slapped a hand on her head, then frowned. There was nothing there. Then something flicked on her bodice. She looked down, but still saw nothing.

She swiped at her hair and dress, wondering if there could be bugs on her from the cave. She took one last swipe then looked up at the men.

Calum held his hand out in front of him, palm side up. He was watching water drip into it.

Meanwhile, Eachann stared up at the ceiling with a perfectly stunned look. "Dammit to hell! I'm going to wring her blue-blooded neck!"

A second later he was gone, leaving Calum and Amy staring up at the ceiling where a growing stain of water dripped and plopped all over them.

Some kiss hot
Some kiss cold,
Some don't kiss at all,
Until they're told.

Anonymous

The oaf opened the door. Georgina was waiting. She smacked him hard in the face with a sopping wet towel. The water rushed out the door, and so did she.

She ran down the hall, where the water was seeping out behind her; it hid her wet footprints. She passed three doors and went around a small turn, ran down another hallway and another short turn. She jerked open the first door and disappeared inside.

The room was huge and dimly lit by smoldering logs in a fireplace big enough to stand in. Unfortunately, she couldn't hide in it. She knew she had only a few minutes.

He would have to check the rooms she passed; that gave her time. She scanned the bedroom quickly, listening with half an ear for Eachann MacLachlan's footsteps.

There were two doors across from a massive dark carved wooden bed. She went for the door farthest from the entry. Inside was a long tunnel-like closet with a mishmash of men's clothing hung along a big wooden clothing rod. Boots and leather shoes were strewn all over the floor along with a saddle, a couple of crops, and some things that were completely unidentifiable.

She closed the door and moved deeper into the dark closet. It was like walking through a train wreck. She stepped on a spur with her bare foot and stumbled. She bit back an oath and grabbed a handful of clothes to keep from falling.

Her shoulder hit the wall with a thud.

Oh God . . . what if he'd heard her?

She swiftly and quietly moved into the depths of the closet, picking her way through while her heart thudded in her ears. She edged between two camel-backed trunks and felt the sweep of silk and woolen dresses that were hung on the back section of the rod. She dug around behind them, hoping for a cabinet or storage nook. But there was nothing but wall.

There had to be some place in here to hide, some place where he couldn't find her by just pushing aside the clothes. She reached out, feeling her way in the dark and trying to keep from stumbling again over what she couldn't see.

Her hand hit the end wall. The closet was a dead end.

She turned and made her way through the mess again.

There was a noise, as if a nearby door had just closed. Her breath stopped.

Hide! Quickly!

The trunks were too obvious. Panicking, she looked up, shoved some dresses together, and grabbed the wooden rod.

A couple of minutes later she was standing on the wooden rod, her damp skirt wrung out and tucked up tightly between her legs. She had her hands braced on the ceiling.

The door opened. He moved inside slowly. His head first.

She felt like a moron. Why hadn't she grabbed something to hit him with? There was enough litter and junk lying all over the floor. She let her angst go because it was too late now.

Instead she concentrated on being quiet. Quiet as a mouse. She held her breath inside her chest so long that she was almost afraid that exhaling would give her away. She watched his every movement, even grew irritated that his breathing looked easy. Not tense like hers.

Just as she'd figured, he did look in the trunks. He turned then and moved back toward the door. She prayed her skirt wouldn't pick that moment to drip on him; it didn't.

The door closed. She exhaled then, very quietly still because he was just outside the door. She didn't move until she heard an odd sound.

She listened keenly and realized the odd noise was the sound of his sodden boots squishing across the bedroom floor. She almost wished she could have floated on the ceiling and watched him in that flooded room.

She knew he must be searching the bedroom and she waited, perched tensely on the wooden clothes rod. Finally she heard the squishing again and the bedroom door clicked closed.

With a deep breath she sagged back against the wall, then swung down from the rod. Still being cautious, she only opened the door a small crack. She didn't trust him.

She listened, but heard nothing, so she opened the door and looked out quickly. She made straight for the door, thinking if she could get back downstairs, then she could get away.

Her hand closed over the cool brass doorknob. She turned it slowly.

He could be in the hall.

The doorknob stuck. She frowned down at it, then slowly turned it the other way. Nothing.

She jiggled it as she turned it toward the right, then left again. She stared down at the brass placket with a sudden feeling of sinking dread.

"Looking for this, George?"

She inhaled sharply, then her shoulders sagged and her hand just fell away from the door handle. She needed a moment and shoved a tangle of snarled hair back from her face before she turned around.

Eachann MacLachlan leaned against a bedpost, his wet boots tossed to one side. One hairy male foot crossed the other while he watched her with that arrogant and sardonic expression she really hated.

In one hand he was holding up the key. She looked from the key to his face. Even in the dim firelight she could see a bright red slap mark from the towel on one cheek and part of his jaw. For the briefest of instants, a small humane part of her was aware of how that must have hurt.

But her sense returned. He didn't need her pity. He needed a good thrashing for what he had done to her. She gave him a look as haughty as she could drum up.

They both just stood there.

Finally he pushed away from the bed and walked slowly toward her. "You're causing a lot of unnecessary trouble for yourself."

"I've caused trouble?"

"Aye." He was barely a foot away.

"Me?" she almost shrieked the word.

"You're lucky I'm a patient man."

She saw red. She drew back her hand in a fist and

threw a hard punch right for his cocky face. He caught her fist the way he'd caught the apple. His huge hand just snatched it in a snap.

He held it tightly, just as his dark green eyes held hers with an unfamiliar gleam. He pulled her against him with a hard jerk. One hand pinned her fist behind her back and the other hand slid to her neck and gripped it.

She never took her eyes off him. Something in his look mocked her. She wanted him to see her anger, to feel the heat of it the way she did.

Her blood felt like it was burning through her body. Her emotional control was stretched so thin it felt as if it would snap any moment.

She tried to kick him.

He stepped back just as her knee came up. "Stop fighting me. You won't win."

"I won't give in."

"Neither will I." His words were a challenge, but the look he had was what kept her silent. It was unsettling because it no longer mocked her. It was different. Raw and intense.

His gaze flicked to her mouth. The hand that held her neck tightened. She could feel pressure from his thumb. Then he lowered his head.

"Don't."

His mouth stopped just barely an inch from hers. His breath was hot and brushed her lips. He didn't move again. But he didn't blink either. The longer he looked at her, the harder it was for her to breathe, to keep her own eyes equally hard. For a brief moment she felt a flash of sympathy for rabbits and foxes and whatever other game was destined to be hunted and trapped.

"You don't want this." His statement was really a question.

It took her a moment to find her voice, at least to

find a voice she was certain wouldn't give away her fear. When she spoke her tone was clear. "No."

She waited for him. He would do it. She was certain he would kiss her anyway. This was a man who took whatever he wanted.

The next thing she knew he had swept her up into his arms. He carried her to the unmade bed. A terrible panic seized her. The room swam for a dizzying moment; it was such a foreign and helpless feeling that she couldn't stop the small sound of fear that escaped her lips.

He dropped her on the bed so hard she bounced. Stunned, she looked up at him.

He stood there looming over her with a stance and look like that of Lucifer. She was acutely aware that he was powerful enough to do whatever he wanted to her. He knew it too; she could read that awareness in his eyes.

"Go to sleep, George," He jerked a blanket over her.

She watched him waiting for his next move. She didn't believe he would leave her alone. But she remembered she wasn't alone. Amy.

She sat up. "What about Amy?"

He looked back at her. "Calum rescued her."

"Where is she?"

"She's with him. Just like you're with me."

At the foot of the bed he grabbed his boots and shoved his feet into them, then crossed the room and unlocked the door. He turned in the doorway, one hand firmly gripping the edge of the door. "Don't try anything else foolish. There's no way out of here."

> I like men to behave like men.
> I like them strong and childish.
>
> *Francoise Sagan*

There was a way out.

Georgina tugged hard on the last tight knot in her makeshift rope. She had used his shirts. She stood and walked across the room to a window.

After eyeing the rocky ground below, she looked back at the length of the rope. She really couldn't tell if it was long enough. She needed to test it so she went to the window and pulled up hard on the sash.

The window was heavy and swollen from the moist air. She raised it and it squeaked loudly. She stopped. She had to make certain no one heard her.

Once it was open she leaned outside and fed down the line of shirts. The end stopped just short of the ground.

She gave a wicked laugh. "Go to sleep? Hunh!" She laughed again. "Not me, MacOaf."

She was still muttering happily when she sat down by the headboard of the huge bed and tied the remaining end around one of the heavily carved feet. She used at least seven good and tight double knots.

She stood, dusted off her hands, and ran back to the window where she judged the length again.

Perhaps one more shirt. She drew up the link of shirts and coiled it on the floor.

A moment later she stood inside the closet, examining the clothes. She'd used every last one of his shirts, so she thumbed through the remaining things and took a pair of buckskin leather riding breeches. They worked wonderfully.

Daylight was coming and the mist outside was growing lighter. But she was ready. She picked up a heavy coat she was stealing and wrapped some spare clothes inside, tying the arms of the jacket together with a firm knot.

For just the briefest span of seconds she thought of the little girl, Kirsty. Georgina was certain the skirt and shirtwaist she was wearing and the dress for Amy she'd rolled inside the heavy jacket were her mother's clothes.

She had no choice. Besides there were plenty of things left for the child. She tossed the bundled clothing outside before she crawled onto the window ledge and sat there with her feet dangling in the damp air.

It was certainly a long way down. She took a deep breath and turned around. She gripped the shirts tightly in both hands, then she lowered herself out the upper window.

She moved carefully, hand over hand. Twice she scraped the side of the house and the rocks scratched her knuckles and forearms.

The rope became wilder the farther down she got. It tended to swing back and forth. To keep from banging against the house every half foot or so, she had to struggle and kick her legs wildly and clamp the rope between her thighs.

She looked down. She was just about halfway. So

she paused for a moment, took a deep breath, then she slid the next hand down a few inches.

Not more than an instant later she heard a sharp whistle.

She froze.

"Great legs, George." Eachann was standing beneath her, right next to the side of the house. He had one boot resting on a large rock and an elbow propped on his bent knee while he grinned up at her.

She hung there, her legs wrapped tightly around his shirts and her hands gripping them so hard her arms had begun to quiver.

"Do that little thing again where you wiggle your butt and let my shirts slide between your drawers."

Her hands slipped and she struggled, kicking out her legs to try to grasp a steady hold again.

He was crowing the whole time. "Thanks, George. That last eyeful was even better." He paused. "You know, I'll never look at these shirts in the same way again." Then he gave an obnoxious and wicked bark of laughter.

She struggled and fumed and flushed angrily, trying to keep her legs together and to not slide down any farther.

Time ticked by with nothing but stubborn silence.

He stretched and gave a mock yawn, then said, "Not in a hurry anymore? Well, that's fine, George. I'm in no hurry."

Her arms were killing her.

His arms were crossed again in that annoying way he had, as if all he had to do was wait and the world would come to him.

She didn't budge, just glared down at him. Then her hands slipped again and she groaned, hanging there stubbornly.

"George." He held out his arms. "Just let go. I'll catch you."

She looked up at the window above her. Gritting her teeth, she started to climb back up, but she could only go about a foot because she had almost no feeling left in her arms and hands.

"You are stubborn."

She knew she didn't have the strength to go back up. But to admit that to him would be worse than sawing off her own feet.

He gave an exaggerated sigh. "Well, then. I have no choice." He reached out and tugged on the shirts. "The way I see it, the odds are three to one it will hold both of us. Let's test it."

"Wait! It can't possibly hold both of us!"

"I thought I warned you about doing anything else foolish. You don't listen very well." He grabbed the shirts and jerked them so tautly that Georgina slid down two feet all at once.

She shrieked.

His hands slid slowly up her calves.

She kicked her legs out at him, but missed. Her hands slipped. She fell the rest of the way. Her bottom smacked him right in the chest and they both tumbled to the ground.

Stunned and shocked, she lay there sprawled all over him.

She was mortified.

He was laughing.

> 'Tis always morning somewhere.
>
> *Henry Wadsworth Longfellow*

It was almost morning and Calum wasn't laughing. He was standing in the library before an open window. He dumped out a bucket half filled with water. It was just one of many scattered randomly around the room. He set the bucket down and went to get another. He walked past the chair where Amy was curled up and sound asleep. She'd been asleep since the ceiling had stopped leaking. About a half an hour ago.

He stopped to watch her for what must have been the tenth time. He didn't know why he felt compelled to look at her. He just did.

A log snapped loudly in the fireplace. He remembered himself and turned away. It wasn't easy.

He grabbed two more buckets, crossed the room, and dumped them out. He closed the window and turned the latch, but he didn't move.

He rubbed a hand over his tired eyes, then shoved his hands in his pockets and stared outside in an attempt to prove to himself he could look at something else.

It had been one hell of a night. Thank God it was almost over. Outside, the color of the fog was changing. The sun was coming up; it turned the dark gray curtain of mist into a bright white one.

This was the kind of fog that rolled in and walled off the islands, made them seem like small independent countries. Most mainlanders thought of the islands as places where you were lonely and trapped. Prisons.

Islanders seemed like foreigners to those who lived on the mainland where they could move about from town to town or city to city with something they mistook for freedom.

But Calum had Highland blood flowing through his veins. He liked the aloneness. The isolation. He had freedom here, where he could do as he wished. He was free to hunt or ride, run or walk about all that was his own.

To him it wasn't a prison, but a refuge.

But he suddenly felt confused and uncomfortable in his own home; it was like waking up to find that his skin didn't fit. He tried to sort out his feelings and found himself looking at Amy again.

She was still sound asleep in that chair.

Sometime in the past few years he had gotten to the point where he stopped looking at women unless they annoyed him. He had grown cold and afraid of them. He didn't even know when it had happened.

But she didn't annoy him. She fascinated him. She even made him forget that he didn't particularly like women.

The door burst open and banged hard against the wall. Calum winced. His brother's favorite entrance.

He turned and, sure enough, Eachann strode into the room with the shrew slung over his shoulder.

You could have heard her in Boston.

Calum's feelings about women returned with a vengeance. He walked over and closed the doors again.

Eachann dumped the shrew in an empty chair and braced his hands on the arms, pinning her there.

"Let me up, MacOaf."

"Your friend is all safe and sound. She's right over there, George."

The shrew raised her chin. "She's only an acquaintance." She turned toward Amy. "Not—" She stopped and suddenly whipped her head around.

Calum realized she was glaring at him.

"What did you do to her?"

He looked at Amy, then back to the shrew named George. "Nothing."

"I know differently." She tried to get up. "Let me up."

"No." Eachann wouldn't move.

She looked back at Calum. "I know you threatened to hurt her."

"I've never hurt a woman in my life."

"That's a lie! When we were in the cave, she told me what you tried to do."

"If my brother was going to hurt her, George, he wouldn't have rescued her."

"Ha!"

Calum was more confused than ever. The lass was still sound asleep. He wasn't surprised. She had to be exhausted. He tried to remember what he'd said or done that would make her tell this woman something so ridiculous. As he remembered it, he'd been trying to take away her fear, not add to it.

He could feel George watching him. It made him nervous, which made it hard for him to think. He paced a moment, staring at the wet carpet.

Earlier Amy had been afraid of him, afraid enough

to knock him daft with a whisky glass. But he didn't think she was afraid of him anymore. He shoved his glasses back up his nose and turned. "What did she tell you?"

"She said you were going to ravish her."

"Ravish her?" Calum stood there dumbfounded. He thought back. What the hell had he said to her?

"Calum?" Eachann roared with laughter.

"Amy wouldn't lie to me."

"Calum wouldn't ravish a woman," Eachann told her.

"I thought she was tired so I said it was time to go to bed."

The shrew's chin came up. "See."

"I didn't mean together." Calum ran a hand through his hair. "I meant to go to sleep. Alone."

"I don't believe you." She glanced at Amy. "She's not even moving. What have you done to her?"

"Nothing. The poor lass is exhausted. Let her up, Eachann. She's not going to believe me until she sees for herself."

Eachann straightened and stepped back. The shrew shot upright. She marched over to Amy and knelt down beside her. "Amy. Wake up."

The lass didn't move.

"Amy." She picked up her hand and rubbed and shook it. "Amy. Wake up."

Amy opened her eyes and stared at them from empty dazed eyes.

"Are you all right?"

"Umm-hmmm." Amy wiggled in the chair, then winced. "I'm just so tired and sore."

"Calum wouldn't hurt her. I told you that."

"And I'm supposed to believe you? Sorry, MacOaf, but you have no credibility."

Calum looked back and forth from one to the other. He was getting dizzy.

"My brother saved her life."

"And you ruined mine!"

"You think not marrying Tom Cabbage will ruin your life, George?"

"His name is John Cabot."

Calum had never seen anything like this.

George stood up and jammed her fists on her hips. "You kidnap us and keep us prisoners and I'm supposed to believe you won't hurt us?"

She had a point.

Eachann was almost nose to nose with the woman. "I had my reasons."

His brother was so damn stubborn. Calum had heard enough. He'd let them fight it out. He crossed over to Amy's chair and scooped her up in his arms. "I'm not going to hurt you or Amy. But I think she needs to be sleeping in a bed." He gave George a pointed look. "In a bed *alone*."

"Oh my God. . . ." was all George said.

He looked at her, but she wasn't looking at him.

He heard Eachann mutter a curse.

Calum followed her look of horror to Amy's chair. The whole right side was stained with blood.

If you fall, pick something up while you're down there.

New England Proverb

Georgina was wrapping a bandage on the flesh wound in Amy's side. The bullet had sliced an angry path through the skin beneath her ribs. The gash was deep and ran in a jagged bloody streak about six inches long.

Georgina looked up at Calum MacLachlan, who was holding Amy up so she could finish.

His face was white. She almost felt sorry for him.

"I didn't know she was hurt." His voice was filled with angst. "There wasn't any blood before."

Georgina tied off the ends of the bandage. "You can lay her back down now."

He was so gentle with Amy. It was almost as if he thought she was so fragile she would break in two. His concern was honest and open, so much so that she wanted to put his mind at ease.

"The cold water probably slowed her bleeding. Once you got her inside and by that fire it must have started again."

Calum's expression was still so guilt-ridden. "She

never said a word. She just said she had a cramp in her side."

"She probably didn't even know she'd been hit. Didn't you say she told you she'd fallen in when the gun went off?"

"Aye, that's what she said. She was more worried about you and Kirsty."

That was the Amy she'd come to know inside that cave. The same Amy who wouldn't have left Georgina behind. The one who shared her food and part of herself. The little fool who believed in destiny and wishes on stars, in love and friendship.

Georgina looked down at her and wondered how people could be so very different. Amy did look fragile. She hadn't awakened the whole time Georgina was cleaning and wrapping the wound.

Her face was still very pale. She brushed back some curly hair that had fallen over Amy's face, then pulled the blanket back over her. She started to fold it back.

Calum reached for the covers. "I'll do it." Then he folded the wool blankets back with precise neat folds and began to pleat and tightly tuck in the sides.

Eachann opened the door and came inside. "How bad is it?"

Calum looked at his brother with an odd look that Georgina couldn't read. He jerked the coverlet tightly over the foot of the bed and neatly tucked it under the mattress. "It's a flesh wound. She's lucky."

He straightened and confronted Eachann. "What are you going to do about Kirsty and Graham?"

"What do you mean what am I going to do about them?"

"Think. They're children. Do you want Kirsty to know what happened?"

"No. I guess not. I'll call Fergus. He can take them to the cottage at Eagle Point for a few days."

Georgina looked up. "Where's that?"

"On the other side of the island," Calum answered distractedly.

Eachann looked relieved. He nodded at Amy. "They can stay there at least until she's better."

Calum pinned him with a long serious stare. "Those children shouldn't know about any of this. When the fog lifts, Eachann, you have to take the women back."

"I don't have to do anything." Eachann was scowling.

Calum didn't say anything, but the tension in the room grew thicker and heavier.

Finally Eachann broke eye contact and turned to leave. "I'll call Fergus." He started to close the door, then he paused and looked at his brother. "I don't want to be chasing after her again. Lock them inside."

Georgina gave him her coldest look. "Do you think I would just leave her like this?"

"Yes," he said without hesitation, and he closed the door.

Georgina sat there quietly, then looked up at Calum. "Will you really take us back home?"

"I can't do anything until the weather clears."

Georgina breathed a relieved sigh. She believed this MacLachlan. He was honest. "Thank God. It should clear in another day or so."

"I wouldn't count on it. There have been times when the fog has lasted for a month."

"A month? I can't be gone a month!"

Calum opened the door. "I can't change the weather. We'll just have to wait." When he left, he locked the door.

A month? She couldn't be gone a whole month. There was no excuse for her disappearing for a month. A week would be a difficult-enough lie.

How could this have happened? How?

The deep blare of a horn came from outside; it

sounded like a moose call. She crossed over to the window and opened it.

Eachann stood on the grounds below, blowing some kind of huge animal horn with tassels hanging off of it. While he blew it three more times, she heard the front door close and Calum walked over and stood directly behind his brother.

Eachann dropped the horn from his mouth and Calum tapped him on the shoulder.

Eachann turned around.

His brother punched him so hard he knocked him flat on his back.

Georgina's mouth fell open. She hadn't seen that coming.

One look at Eachann lying there with a stunned look on his face said he hadn't seen it coming either.

She felt the sudden urge to applaud.

He rubbed his jaw. "What the hell did you do that for?"

"That was for being so damn stupid!"

Eachann swore, then jumped to his feet too swiftly for someone of his size. He held his hands up in front of him. "I'm not going fight with you, Calum."

"Good." Calum hit him again anyway. Harder than before. "That one was for Amy."

"Goddammit! I didn't shoot her!"

"No . . . you just kidnapped her."

Eachann lay there longer this time. He wiped the blood from his lip and scowled down at his hand.

"Get up so I can hit you again."

Georgina gripped the window ledge tightly and leaned out. "Calum! Please . . . wait!"

Both men looked up at her.

"Can I be next?"

Eachann glared up at her with narrowed eyes, as if he couldn't wait to get his hands on her. He stood again, wiping his lip.

But he only got as far as his feet.

Calum used his left fist this time.

Ouch! Georgina flinched. She'd bet that one *really* hurt. He'd hit him with an uppercut right to the jaw.

Eachann didn't get up at all.

"Nevermind!" she called down to Calum. "You're doing just fine." She closed the window with a firm and satisfied snap, then went back to sit with Amy.

Providence always makes it a point to find out what you are after, so as to see that you don't get it.

Mark Twain

Kirsty couldn't hear through the door. She blamed her great-great-grandfather. He had built doors all through the house that were way too thick. If the doors had been this solid at Harrington Hall, she would have never heard anything.

How was she going to learn what her father wanted if she couldn't spy on him? It was *vexatious*—another spelling word. Worse yet, there was no keyhole to spy through.

Who had ever heard of a door with no keyhole?

Finally she cupped her hand in the shape of a moonsnail and then pressed it *and* her ear against the door. If she listened really hard she thought she could hear Uncle Calum's voice. The voice faded and she turned her head and tried the other ear.

"Och! 'Tis that a nosy little beastie I see with her ear pressed to the door?"

Kirsty shot up faster than Graham could spit. "Fergus!"

He lifted her high above him. "What's this here? I

caught myself a brownie sneaking around to steal a body's dreams."

"Everyone knows that brownies don't steal dreams."

"They dinna?"

"No." She brought her face really close to his. She raised her fingers like claws and wiggled them in between their noses. "Brownies sneak into your bed at night and put warts on your nose."

He laughed loud and heartily. "Are ye going tae put warts on my nose?"

She crossed her arms and gave him a firm nod. "I'm not a brownie!"

"Let me see . . ." He brought her so close to his gruff old face that their noses touched. He had fog and dew in his long white hair and his beard, and it peppered his weathered and wrinkled face like raindrops.

Fergus MacLachlan had a face that looked just like plum duff with an acorn thrown in. His nose was plump and round and his eyes were bright green; they sparkled beneath eyebrows that looked like fluffy inchworms. His cheeks were red and rosy like the sweet candied cherries some of the girls at school got from their parents as rewards or just because they missed them.

He squinted up at her. "Och! Ye're right. I can see now. Ye're no brownie."

"I told you so."

"'Tis a wee beastie I see."

"I'm not a beastie! I'm Kirsty."

"Ye canna be Kirsty. Why she was awee one, only this high. Ye canna be my Kirsty."

"I am Kirsty!"

He set her down and poked more fun at her by pretending he didn't believe her and making a big to-do. He walked around her while he rubbed his bearded chin thoughtfully. He bent down and squinted at her.

Fergus refused to wear spectacles. He claimed he could see just fine without wearing round windows on his nose that made him look like a "silly auld fool." He said if the good Lord wanted him to wear glasses he'd have been born with them. Even her mama had never been able to sweet-talk him into wearing them.

She laughed, planted her fists on her hips, and turned with him. "I grew three whole inches."

"Aye, lassie, I can see ye've grown."

"And I'm home now, Fergus. I'm home."

He stopped his fooling and scooped her up in another bear hug.

"Aye," he said gruffly. "Ye're home, lassie." He swung her on his broad shoulders and carried her down the hallway.

She bounced along on his shoulders and pretended she was one of those mid-evil knights riding a desk-tree charger. After a moment she patted Fergus on the head. "Where are we going?"

"I need to fetch Graham."

"Why?"

"Because I've a surprise fer ye both."

"A surprise?"

"Aye."

"What kind of surprise?"

"Weel now . . . if I tell ye, then it wouldna be a surprise now, would it?"

"Please, Fergus . . . please tell me before you tell Graham. I want to be first."

"I'm taking ye both to Eagle Point."

"On the other side of the island?"

"Aye."

"Why?"

"Och! Ye dinna want to go with me, lassie? Ye dinna want me to tell ye stories about the great Scots and teach you to catch a trout with yer hands?" He opened a door. "Duck down now, lassie."

She bent down low on his shoulders while he carried her inside their room where Graham was sitting on the bed and pulling on his stockings and shoes.

"Fergus!" Graham shot off the bed and ran toward them, then tripped over his laces and fell flat on the floor.

Fergus stood over him and chuckled. "A smart mon ties his shoes before he runs in them, laddie."

"Graham's not smart," Kirsty said petulantly.

"I am too! I am smart! I know what five times five is and that spiders only live for one year and lobsters aren't red until you cook them."

Fergus looked at Graham. "All that, laddie? All that is inside this wee head?"

Kirsty tugged on Fergus's ear. "Let me down."

He squatted down and she jumped off his shoulders and landed with her arms out and her ankles pressed together for good luck.

"His head is overstuffed now, Fergus. There won't be any room left for him to learn anything."

Graham scowled at her. "Troll."

"Baby."

"Fishface."

"Skunkbreath." She didn't care what he called her. She knew something he didn't. She looked up at Fergus and said, "His head's so full you can't teach him anything else. You'll have to leave him behind."

Graham grabbed Fergus's big hand. "Where are you going?"

She lifted her chin. "To Eagle Point. Fergus is going to teach me how to catch trout."

"I wanna go too."

"Then pack yer things, laddie."

Graham ran to pack while Fergus teased him about growing too fast like he had teased her.

Kirsty didn't want to leave. They just got home last night. Why did they have to leave so soon?

She walked sluggishly over to the bed and dragged a valise out from underneath. She plopped the valise on the mattress and opened it.

Mama's green dress was still curled near her pillow in an empty shapeless ball.

All of a sudden she felt as if she were going to cry again. She turned her back on Graham and Fergus and she took some deep breaths. Part of her wondered if she had made her father angry when she cried last night and when she wouldn't let the snake-lady wear the dress.

She stared at her toes and wished she could be so very different. She wished she didn't feel so confused all the time. She wished she didn't cry . . . ever. She wished she could be like the little girls at school who had two parents who visited them and brought them gifts and told them they missed them.

The only time her father came to the school was when they were bad. Being good never got Kirsty what she wanted. Being good wouldn't bring her mama back or make her father want to be with her.

"Pack up yer things, lassie. See, like Graham here is. If ye dinna hurry up he's going tae be done first."

Kirsty spun around and packed her things and the green dress. She packed really fast, shoving anything handy into the valise.

She beat Graham. Which really hadn't been hard. Whenever he had turned his back, she unpacked some of his clothes and put them back inside the drawers. He was so smart he never noticed.

A little while later, when she was perched on a hard wooden wagon seat heading off to the opposite end of the island with Fergus and Graham, she looked back at her home. She could barely see it because of all the fog. It was just a huge shadow that looked dark and empty and cold.

But she watched it anyway, watched it melt away like a daydream. She played that game where you had to keep your eyes on something or else it might disappear for real. She looked long and hard until she couldn't even see the high pointed roof anymore.

Finally she turned back around and stared at the horses' tails. She chewed on her lip. When she thought she might cry she pinched herself. A big hollow feeling settled in her stomach and she sat there, feeling sick inside because she had no idea what it was she had done to make her father send them away again.

He gazed and gazed and gazed and gazed
Amazed, amazed, amazed, amazed.
                                    Robert Browning

Calum opened the door as quietly as he could. Amy's eyes were still closed. It looked as if she hadn't moved an inch. He wondered if a shallow wound like that could be more serious on a woman, especially a small vulnerable woman like Amy.

George looked up from her bedside vigil.

"She's still asleep?" he asked.

She nodded.

He walked across the room to the bed and stood there for an awkward moment. His gaze went from Amy to this black-haired woman named George. Such an odd name for a woman. George. Who would name a girl George?

He had to admit she had good looks. She was the kind of woman who would turn most men's heads. But looks didn't catch his attention. Manner did.

She had frightened him at first. She was someone he wanted to stay as far away from as possible. But it seemed she was only shrewish with Eachann. She had been civil to him, which was a surprise.

191

He couldn't fault her for the way she'd been acting. She wasn't here by her own doing. Eachann deserved more than a few punches.

But aside from the circumstances, George had won his favor when she insisted on sitting at Amy's side for the last few hours.

Calum shoved his hands in his pockets and just stood there, feeling dumb and big and clumsy. He didn't know what to say to her.

She looked up at him with a question in her eyes, then she laughed. "I promise I won't bite."

Even he had to chuckle. He waited until they both stopped laughing and the silence was heavy again. "How did you get a name like George?"

"You don't like my name?"

He swore to himself. Now he'd stepped in it. He could feel himself flush.

She gave a small laugh. "I'm sorry. I shouldn't have done that. The name George is your brother's idea of fun. My name is Georgina, Georgina Bayard."

"Bayard?" He thought about that. "Like the clocks?"

"One and the same."

He shoved his hands in his pockets. "I'm sorry Eachann did this."

"So am I." She stared at the window. "I'm more sorry than you can possibly know." There was a bleak and distant look on her face.

"He hasn't been himself since his wife died."

She didn't say anything for a long time, appeared to be chewing over what he'd said. She looked at him again. "When did she die?"

"About three years ago. She loved to sail. We still don't know what exactly happened. Eachann was the one who found the boat on some rocks. She washed ashore two days later."

She shook her head and looked away. "How horrible."

"She was alone that day. In a way I suppose there was some luck involved. Sometimes she took the children with her."

"Children? There's more than one?"

"Aye. You met Kirsty."

"Yes." She looked at Amy. "We met."

"Her brother Graham is a year older."

She didn't say anything.

Calum tried to find the right words to explain to this woman that his brother wasn't always so rash in his actions. "Eachann doesn't always think about the consequences of what he chooses to do. He's not a bad man. Just a lost one."

She was stoically silent.

He would see she looked worn out. He wondered if she had slept at all. He knew she hadn't eaten. "I'll stay with Amy. Go down to the kitchen. David will give you something to eat."

"You don't think I'll try to run away?"

His look was clear and direct. "No."

Georgina gave a small nod, then asked, "Who's David?"

"A cousin. He does a little bit of everything, including all the cooking."

"How many people live on the island?"

"Kirsty and Graham. Some cousins—Fergus, David and Will, Eachann and myself."

"That's all?"

"That's all."

"No women?"

"Not since Sibeal died. Other than Kirsty."

Georgina stood up stiffly. She sucked in a breath and rubbed her lower back. "I think I've been sitting in one spot too long."

"Go on, now. Get yourself some food. The kitchen is downstairs on the back side of the house."

She looked at Amy again. "She hasn't moved."

Calum nodded, his attention already on Amy. Somewhere in the back of his mind he heard the bedroom door close. He was careful when he sat down. He leaned back against the footboard of the bed and rested an ankle on his knee.

Amy just lay there completely unaware of what she was doing to him. His insides were twisted into tense knots. She unsettled him, confused him, made him aware of feelings he didn't know he had.

He had the most profound sense of impending doom, as if his life would never be the same again. It was like he was living a nightmare or a dream or someone else's life.

There was nothing he could do about it, because the confusion came from her. He couldn't wake up from this or walk away from it.

He looked down at her pale face. She had ivory skin and he remembered there was a slight pink flush on her cheekbones when she wasn't ill. Her hair was thick and curly. Georgina must have brushed it because it was spread out on her pillow like sunshine.

He took in her features: the small heart-shaped face, a narrow nose that turned up a little at the end, a strong chin. She had thin brows and he could see the small blue veins in her eyelids. Her cheekbones were high and her face was full and fresh, more youthful than most.

He reached out and just touched her cheek. It was warm, not as cold as it looked. He ran his fingertips over it aware that she was soft and real. She was no dream.

Time went by. He had no idea how much time and he didn't care. He just waited there, wanting to be with her, needing to watch her sleep because he was afraid if he didn't that she might not wake up at all.

It was a fool's thought, romantic drivel like poetry and melodramatic plays he'd seen and thought were stupid. He never thought they were very realistic because he had never experienced romance.

But now he couldn't seem to control what was inside his head. It was almost as if part of her was flowing into him, taking over his head, his thoughts.

He had thought himself immune to women. None of them touched him, deep inside. None struck a fire in him. No woman interested him enough to make him want to learn about her, to understand how she thought.

He didn't see her in the same way he saw other women. He didn't see her the way he saw the female immigrants he helped. She was different. When he looked at Amy, he didn't only see her with his eyes. He saw her with his heart.

Something that scared the hell out of him.

His pulse pounded like the distant surf when she touched him. He picked up her hand. His pulse pounded like the distant surf when he touched her too. His heart was beating like waves in his ears. Why was this woman able to make him forget he didn't particularly like women? What was it about her?

He examined her hand, almost as if by doing so he thought he could find the answer. But there was no answer there.

He turned over her hand and ran a finger along her palm, following the line of life that wound its way across it. He opened his own hand and looked at his palm. He placed it beside hers.

His hand was big and blunt; hers was small and elegant. Her nails were shaped like half-moons; his were square, like the sails on a ship. Calluses from hard work had bubbled on his hands. Her palm was soft and pale and looked new compared to his. His skin was so much darker than hers, as different as their moods.

He put her hand down and straightened the covers, even though they didn't need straightening. There was a peace about her, which he found ironic.

When he looked at her, when he was with her, or when he thought of her, peace was not what he felt. He experienced a storm of feelings, strong and full and consuming.

It was something he didn't want to put a name to even though he thought he knew what it was. Something he had thought he was beyond feeling.

But he wasn't. When he looked at Amy, what he felt was as old as time. What Calum felt was intense. It wasn't love. No, not love. It was passion.

> Always act like a winner,
> even if you're losing.
>   *Anonymous*

Georgina found the kitchen with little trouble. She might be stuck on an island where none of her escape plans worked, but her nose still worked. She followed it until she stood before a set of large paneled doors.

She pushed them open, descended the two steps down into a large room with a wide window along one wall. The wall to her right was all rock and had another one of those huge fireplaces.

She turned at the bottom of the steps and froze.

Eachann MacLachlan was sitting at a massive pine table in the center of the room. His big feet were propped on the corner of the table and his chair was pushed back and teetering on two legs. He had something that looked like a towel pressed against his face, so all she could see was his stubborn jaw.

"Hi, George."

The man had an uncanny ability to know where she was at every moment. It was unsettling. He had never even looked at her.

"There went my appetite," she muttered. She took a deep breath and crossed the room to stand at the opposite end of the table. She gripped the back of a pine chair.

"Sit down and eat," he told her. He still hadn't looked at her.

There were two places set at the table: his and the seat next to him. She released the chair and crossed over to the spare place, gathered up the plate and utensils, then turned to go back to the end seat.

His chair legs slammed to the floor at the same moment he grabbed her arm. "Sit here." His voice was muffled; it came from behind the towel.

She looked down at him. He took away the towel and she stared down at his swollen face.

She almost flinched. Almost, not quite.

He looked like the very devil. One eyelid was turning bright purple and swollen shut. There was a jagged and brownish-red cut on his lower lip—a lip that was twice its normal size. He had a round ugly bruise at the base of his chin that seemed to grow as she stood there. She could almost see the outline of his brother's knuckles.

"Sit down."

She sat.

"David!" he called out. A door behind him opened and a man came inside carrying a heavy tin pail. He was tall, like Eachann and his brother, but rail thin and bony as a herring. He had bright red-orange hair that came to his shoulders; it was the same color as a new penny.

As he moved closer to Eachann, she could see that his face was a wash of freckles. He had a long and pointed chin with a knob on the end that was about the size of an egg, and when he looked at her and grinned, all she saw was teeth.

He set the pail down with a thump. "These rocks came from the spring. They're colder than the other ones."

Eachann opened the wet towel and dumped some smooth stones on the table. He bent over the pail, pulled out more rocks, and wrapped them in the towel. He glanced up at David who was staring at her. "Thanks. This is George."

"Georgina Bayard," she corrected in the lightest tone she could come up with, considering she felt an intense desire to add to Eachann's bruises.

David looked at her. "Like the clocks."

She nodded.

"Clocks?" Eachann set the towel back on his swollen eye and then looked from David to her.

"Aye," David said.

She looked at the oaf. "You'd have to be able to read to understand."

David laughed and gave Georgina a quick wink before he turned around and went over to a range that was set into the far wall.

"Well, I guess you told me." Eachann stared at her from his good eye.

He stared at her on purpose, just to annoy her, so she made a point of ignoring him.

David set a bowl of steaming rolls on the table, a crock of butter, then added a plate of eggs, bacon and sausage and a slab of ham, potatoes, apple sauce, fresh blueberries, and a large pitcher of milk.

She realized she was still clutching the plate to her chest. She set it down.

It clanked loudly.

She did her best to continue to ignore Eachann while she ate. She was on her second helping of ham when he reached out and stabbed a sausage.

"Too bad you lost your appetite."

She just gave him a cool stare and cut the ham with a vicious stroke of her knife. She jabbed it into the meat, then looked up and gave him a sweet smile.

He bit off a chunk of sausage and chewed while he grinned at her.

The silence was awkward. The only sounds in the room were made by David, who stood at a worktable, a flour-dusted apron tied around his waist while he punched a huge glob of white dough. The man just didn't look like a cook.

But the food was wonderful.

"So, David." Eachann broke the silence. "What do you think of George?"

David looked up and grinned. "She's a bonny one."

"You think so?" He made a big deal about eyeing her as if he were trying to see her in a new light. He stabbed another sausage and ate it. "She's a desperate woman, though."

"Desperate to get away from you," she muttered.

"Desperate to get married."

She looked right through him and took a bite of eggs, pretending she wasn't listening to him talk about her as if she weren't there.

"She wants to marry John Cadaver."

She choked on her eggs.

He patted her back solicitously and handed her a cup of milk.

David was looking from Eachann to her with an odd expression.

"Cabot," she said through gritted teeth. "His name is John Cabot."

"That's right. I keep forgetting the fellow's name."

"I'd like to forget yours."

He saluted her with his fork.

David punched the dough a few more times, then covered it with a damp towel. He looked at her, then at Eachann, and shook his head a few times before he left the room through another door. She could hear his shoes clumping down some wooden stairs.

She ignored the MacOaf and looked out the window. The fog hugged the hillside. She wondered if the stuff would ever lift. It was like a curtain that closed them off from the world. Her world. The world she had to get back to.

"Worried you're not going to get home, George?"

The man could read her mind.

"I'll get home."

He laughed. "That's what I like about you. You're more stubborn than I am."

"A barn-soured mule isn't as stubborn as you are. I can hardly believe you are real."

"Come upstairs with me for about an hour and I'll show you how real I am."

"I really hate you."

He laughed.

"I can't believe you are a father."

He stopped laughing.

"You go around ruining people's lives. Why can't you just raise your children and leave innocent people alone?"

He was angry now. She could see it and she was glad.

"I don't know anything about children." His tone was gruff.

"You don't know or you don't care to know?"

"I don't have to know. That's why I snatched you."

Her fork froze in midair. "What did you just say?"

"I said that was why I snatched you. I needed someone to look after my children."

"You kidnapped me to *watch* your children?" she said, trying to absorb it. She recalled snatches of their conversation in her garden. His comments about handling children. He had been interviewing her for the job!

She stood very slowly and planted her hands on the table. "You ruined my life because you couldn't just hire a nursemaid?"

He didn't say a word.

"My God. . . . You are an idiot. That is the most selfish, stupid, arrogant, and completely asinine thing I have ever heard!"

"Not really," he said in a lazy tone that annoyed her. It implied she was too stupid to understand his reasoning. "You claimed you wanted a husband. I needed a mother for my children. Seems simple enough."

"I don't want to marry you! I want to marry John Cabot! He's rich, you fool!"

"I have enough money to support you, George. And you don't even have to pull your dress to your waist to wrangle an offer out of me. I told you before. I can marry you."

"You can go to hell."

He dropped the towel on the table with an angry thud and he stood, towering over her. "Aye, and you can go right on your back on that table."

She wasn't afraid of him. "That's your way of doing everything, isn't it? If you can't get what you want, you just take it. I wonder if you know how very much I despise you."

He didn't say anything. But seconds later he grabbed her so quickly she never saw it coming. His mouth was on hers before she could take a breath.

He groaned painfully, pulled back and swore. She shoved him away from her and wiped her mouth. She didn't care that he'd stopped, that he'd hurt himself. He'd humiliated her.

They just glared at each other. The air between them turned wicked. He took a step toward her.

She grabbed the nearest thing: her fork.

She waved it in front of his bruised face. "Stay back."

His gaze flicked from her to the fork and back to her again.

"You touch me. You come near me, and hell and all its tortures will be heaven compared to one minute with me and this fork."

She backed away from him. Then she was running up the stairs and away as quickly as she could.

Eachann dumped the rocks out on the table. He spent a minute or two filling the towel with fresh cool rocks, then he stuck it back on his face, scowling at the world in general.

David closed the door to the cellar with a hard slam that made Eachann turn around, the towel still pressed to one side of his face.

David just stared at him, dumbfounded. "Did I hear that right?"

"What?"

"On her back on the table?"

"It would be a good place for her."

David gave a short laugh. "You're a fool."

Eachann's expression grew belligerent. "She's causing trouble."

"The trouble isn't her. The trouble is you. You're confused."

"I can't wait to hear why," he muttered.

"You're treating the wrong ache."

Eachann scowled at him from his one good eye.

"That cold towel shouldn't be on your swollen face. You ought to put it between your legs."

> I wonder what fool it was that first
> invented kissing.
>
> *Jonathan Swift*

Amy awoke to the sound of pacing. She blinked a few times because everything was a bright blur.

The first thing she recognized was Calum. He walked from the bureau to the window, then back to the bureau, back to the window, then back to the bureau. He never looked at her because he was staring at the floor as he walked, his hands shoved into his pockets.

It was like watching a metronome.

He stopped at the window and removed his spectacles. He began polishing them with the curtain. He held the glasses up to the light, then polished them some more.

After hooking the stems over his ears, he used a finger to shove them into place on the bridge of his nose. His hands went back into his pockets and he just stared outside.

The windowpanes were as foggy on the inside as the air was outside. A drop of moisture dripped down the glass. Calum reached out and caught it with a finger, lifted it into the misty daylight and seemed fascinated with the way it ran around his finger.

For some reason Amy couldn't explain, she wanted to watch him waste time a little longer. He began to draw vertical lines in the window mist. Then he did horizontal ones. He filled in the squares with little markings she couldn't make out.

She wondered if he was even aware of what he was doing. He seemed so far away, so preoccupied, as if his head were in some different place, a place that must have been bleak and dismal if she were to go by his expression.

She wanted to go touch him. He looked like he needed touching. She knew what it was like to feel lost in your own skin. And that was how he looked. Lost inside.

She got up carefully, and as silently as a mouse she padded over to where he stood. He was leaning against the window frame with one broad shoulder while he wrote intently on the glass.

She reached out and gently placed her hand on his shoulder. He almost jumped out of his skin.

He hollered so loudly he scared her half to death and she screamed.

"Amy?" His hands closed over her shoulders.

A second later he was holding her so closely that her palms were flat against his chest. She looked up at him.

His face was unreadable. His eyes were dark and watchful.

She reached up and touched his jaw. It was rough and prickly with black whiskers that shadowed the hollows of his cheeks and grew so thickly on his chin.

He still stared down at her. His gaze seemed to soak her up; it went from her eyes, to her nose, and then he stared at her mouth for the longest time.

There was a flash of naked longing in those dark eyes of his. She doubted he even knew it was there.

But she did and she lifted her face toward his.

His lips touched hers, just barely, lightly, as if he had to test the feel of them, as if she would crack in two if he kissed her too hard.

As kisses went, it wasn't a long one or a passionate one. It wasn't practiced. He didn't rub his lips on hers really hard like William did.

It was just a gentle intimate touch of their lips.

Calum broke off the kiss and looked down at her, his expression suddenly confused and almost angry-looking.

She placed her fingertips to his lips. "You kissed me."

"Aye." His voice was little more than a rasp, as if admitting what he had done was difficult for him.

"Are you angry?"

"No. But I should not have done that, Amy-my-lass."

She liked it when he called her that. It sounded special and different, something that was only for her. "Why shouldn't you have kissed me? I was willing."

He didn't answer.

"Oh." She looked away, stared down at her bare toes. "You didn't like it."

"I like it too much."

She smiled and looked up at him again, moving her mouth toward his. "Good. Let's do it again."

He didn't look like he wanted to do it again. He looked like he wanted to shrink into the ground.

She realized what she had said. It was like being with William again. She wished the floor would just open up and swallow her. Suddenly she felt as gauche as William and his cruel friends had thought her to be.

She could feel Calum's gaze on her, so she turned away. "I'm sorry. I understand. I make those kinds of mistakes all the time. I . . . I." Her voice cracked. She was going to cry.

He swore under his breath, then ran a hand through his hair. He turned back to her. "Amy."

She stayed where she was.

He reached up and took off his glasses and tucked them in his pocket. He placed his hands on her shoulders and turned her around. He kissed her again, harder this time and longer before he pulled back. "Open your mouth."

She blinked up at him. "What?"

"I said 'Open your mouth'."

"Why?"

"So I can kiss you."

"You just kissed me."

"I know."

"My mouth wasn't open then."

"I know."

"Then why do I have to open my mouth?"

"Because I'm going to put my tongue inside."

She stared at him, then burst out laughing. "That's really funny, Calum. Really funny." She began to giggle. She looked up at his face. He'd kept it so serious and that made her laugh even more. "You know, I think that is the funniest thing I've ever heard. I mean just think about how stupid and silly that is." She shook her head and repeated, "Put your tongue in my mouth." She broke into another fit of giggles.

She patted him on his cheek. "I'm glad you can make me laugh. And you can stop trying to look so serious. It worked."

"But Amy—"

The door opened and Georgina came inside.

"You're up!"

Amy nodded. With a moment of regret she felt Calum's hands slip away from her shoulders.

Georgina came toward her. "How is your side?"

"It hurts. Why?"

"A gunshot should hurt."

"A gunshot?" She blinked, then placed her hand on her ribs. It wasn't as sore as her side felt last night. It had been a sharp pain, like a cramp that was constant. This was just a dull aching like when you pulled a muscle or ran into something really hard.

Georgina just stared at her as if she couldn't believe what she was hearing.

Amy looked to Calum. His face was suddenly flushed. He fumbled with his spectacles for a moment.

Georgina placed her hands on her hips like a mother hen. She gave Calum a look that said she thought he was an idiot. "You didn't tell her?"

"There wasn't time."

"How can you not have time to tell her what happened? It's not that difficult. She wakes up and you say four words. 'Amy. You were shot.'"

When he didn't respond she turned back to Amy. "You're wearing a bandage."

Amy felt sheepish.

"You didn't feel anything?"

"Well, yes, but not in my side." As soon as she said it, she thought she heard Calum bite back a small groan.

They all stood there in rather telling silence.

Finally Georgina shook her head and started to guide Amy back to the bed. "You shouldn't be up."

"I'm okay. Really. I am."

"No, I want to check and see if you are still bleeding and then you need something to eat."

"I'll leave you two alone." Calum moved to the

door so swiftly you'd have thought he was being chased by the hounds of hell.

But when he opened the door, he paused and looked back at Amy with the oddest expression.

She smiled and gave him a little wave of her fingers.

He stood there as if he wanted to say something serious and important.

She waited, but a second later he just turned and left.

Nothing that is can pause or stay;
The moon will wax, the moon will wane.
The mist and clouds will turn to rain,
The rain to mist and cloud again,
Tomorrow will be today.

Henry Wadsworth Longfellow

The fog stuck around for two full weeks.

During that time, Georgina Bayard had thought up, practiced, and discarded over a hundred truly hard-to-swallow excuses to give John Cabot about where she had been.

Eachann MacLachlan's face had healed, but his obnoxious personality had only gotten worse. Amy Emerson learned that people did kiss with their tongues. And Calum MacLachlan had developed a new chart: one to graph and do analysis on the course of seduction.

When the fog finally left the Maine coast, it did so quickly. It was almost as if someone had snapped their fingers and *poof!* it was gone as suddenly as the Emerson heiress.

Along with the clear blue sky and the ocean breeze came news to Arrant Island that *The New Hebrides* had landed in Bath with the last shipload of Scots immigrants. Calum spent the morning loading the supplies on the coaster. Eachann was at his stables.

Amy moped around the house and Georgina lolled away the morning in the bathtub.

Georgina stood by the tub and dried herself off. She wrapped a thick towel around her, while she tried to decide what to wear.

She had two choices of clothing: both of them bad. She wasn't sure which one made her look less like a dairy maid.

She held up the skirt and shirtwaist. They were brown. Ugly dirt brown. She held the dress up and stood back and looked in the mirror. My God . . . who could wear this color? It was a shade somewhere between barn straw and pea soup, and when she held it up to her face it turned her skin sallow and yellowish gray. Even her eyes didn't look like they had color. The dress turned them from blue to dull gray.

By process of elimination—a short process—she wore the shirtwaist and skirt. She brushed her hair until it was slick and shiny and the same glossy black color of a brand cabriolet, the kind with carmine trim and silver moldings. The perfect carriage. She would have John buy one just to carry her to her wedding.

She braided her hair and then twisted it up, pinched her cheeks and bit her lips. She was ready. She left the bathing room and walked down the hallway.

From behind one bedroom door she could hear Amy crying. She knocked on it firmly, then just opened it without an invitation. Amy was lying across her bed with her face buried in her arms. She was sobbing for all she was worth.

"For heaven's sake, Amy, you'll make your skin blotchy and your nose bright red."

"I don't care," Amy whined into the mattress.

"Well I do. Get up."

Amy rolled over and rested one arm dramatically over her eyes. "I have nothing to get up for."

That million or so dollars in the bank would get me up. Georgina stood there.

After a moment of silence Amy peeked out from under her arm. She stared at her for the longest time, then said, "You look pretty."

Georgina patted the tight twist in the back of her hair. "Yes, well, as good as one can look wearing clothing the color of barn fodder." She dug into the pocket of her ugly skirt and pulled out a clean nose rag. "Here, dry your eyes. We're going home. Thank God. There's no reason to cry."

"There is for me."

Good grief. The woman has a bank full of money and she doesn't even want to go home to it.

Georgina would go home and roll in it or spend an hour with her little blue bank book pressed to her heart. She scowled down at Amy. She'd been sulking ever since she got up and saw the sunshine. "Stop feeling sorry for yourself."

"I don't want to go back."

"Why?"

"Because there's nothing to go back to."

"How many homes do you have?"

She sighed as if it were such a burden. "Seven."

Georgina rolled her eyes. "Seems to me one of those might be preferable to this."

Amy was stubbornly quiet.

Apparently not. Georgina tried another tactic. "What about your executors? By now they'll be frantically trying to locate you."

"Yes, they probably will. But not because I matter. They'll just bribe someone else to take me off their hands. I don't care if they ever find me." Amy's expression was mulish, a look Georgina certainly knew well. "I don't want to go home. My homes are cold and empty. I don't want those attorneys to handle my life anymore."

"Look, Amy, you'll be fine. I have a splendid idea. After I marry John Cabot, I'll make it a point to introduce you to someone who won't marry you for your money."

"I don't want to marry some rich man."

"Think about this. If you marry someone who has more money than you, then you won't have to worry about someone marrying you for your money."

Amy's face grew very distant.

Georgina waited, then asked, "Are you listening to me?"

Amy glanced up at her. "I was just thinking. If someone doesn't know I have any money, then they can't marry me for it, can they?"

Georgina had a sinking feeling. "No, but why would you want to marry someone poor?"

"I didn't say someone poor. I just don't want money to get in the way."

"Get in the way?" Georgina began to laugh. "I wish."

Amy sat stiff as a pine tree. "The executors control what I do, but if I could give you my money I would."

Georgina stopped laughing. "You really mean that. You would give it to me, wouldn't you?"

Amy nodded. "But they'd never let me even try." She took a deep breath, looked Georgina straight in the eye and said, "I've made a decision. If I'm going to marry anyone, I want to marry Calum."

Now Georgina wanted to cry. She plopped down on the bed next to Amy. "I was afraid of this. This is not a smart decision for you." When Amy said nothing she asked, "How does he feel?"

"I don't know how he feels." Amy had a lost look, but then she brightened. "He likes to kiss me."

"If kisses meant a life-long committment there would be no such thing as a spinster." Georgina thought about Amy's situation for a second, then asked, "Are you certain this is what you want?"

Amy nodded.

"Absolutely certain?"

"Absolutely."

"Then you'll just have to get him to bring it up. The trick is to make him think it was his idea." Georgina pulled her knees up on the bed, linked her hands over them, and got comfortable, figuring this kind of lesson could take a while. She looked at Amy and said, "Let me tell you all about men."

Amy leaned closer, ready to listen. Her expression was intent enough Georgina figured, she really did want Calum MacLachlan. She began her sage woman-to-woman advice with the world the way she saw it.

"First of all, you must understand men."

Amy groaned like someone had twisted her fingers off.

"Don't get all worried." Georgina raised a hand. "They aren't that complicated."

"They seem complicated to me."

"They aren't. Here's a perfect example." Georgina gave her an easy smile. "How many men chase after homely women?"

"None."

"Unfortunately that's right. Men want a girl to have beauty instead of brains."

"Why?"

"It's really quite simple." Georgina gave an airy wave of her hand. "You see, men see much better than they think."

Happy hearts and happy faces
Happy play in grassy places—
That was how in ancient ages
Children grew to kings and sages.
                    Robert Louis Stevenson

Bright September sunshine had the same effect on Kirsty and Graham that the full moon had on wild banshees. They screamed and hollered and chased things through the damp grass. They ran after marsh moths and bumblebees. They sped past the wild grapes that grew up a gray stone wall, over a small rock bridge, and up a grassy hillside where the golden-rod blazed and the blueberry plants were already turning as red as firehouse paint.

At the edge of the woods, they hid in the elderberry bushes beneath the bough of a fat crab-apple tree, disappearing into the low branches like sparrows with their tails flicking.

"Now be very, very quiet, Graham, or I'll have to pinch you again." Kirsty pulled her knees tightly against her chest and locked her hands around them while she listened for Fergus.

"Do you think he's lost?" Graham whispered.

"Shhh!" Kirsty shoved her fingers in front of his face and made pinching gestures.

His golden eyes grew wide. He clamped a grubby hand over his mouth and watched her like a dog that had something treed.

On the days when the fog was thick and wet and cold and they had to stay inside, Fergus set them near a toasty fire and told them of Scotland, of the Highlands and the places where their ancestors grew up and fought, lived and died.

He taught them so many things, better things than they learned at Harrington Hall. He taught them that the seventh child of a seventh child has the sight, that the Devil Himself once kept school in Scotland and taught the lairds and the chieftains to fight.

From Fergus they heard tales of the Picts and the Celtic tribes that painted their faces blue before they went into battle; and they found out that any Scot worth his salt knew the MacCodrums were descended from seals.

There were lessons like: how to find a kelpie. Kirsty and Graham learned you have to be clever and look in cool streams and rivers; you have to remember that kelpies like to take on the shape of a beautiful horse. They found out that ghosts and witches, goblins and beasties can be warded off with even the smallest piece of rowan bark.

So when Graham had walked around waving a chunk of tree bark in front of his face whenever he saw Kirsty, she had gotten even by pinching him when he least expected it.

She figured she had trained him well over the days when they'd had to stay indoors, because now he couldn't tell when she would really pinch him and when she wouldn't.

Fergus came tramping up the hillside trail. He stopped at the crest. Kirsty and Graham were huddled so close together they were like pages in a book.

Kirsty could see Fergus's big feet. Once when she

had asked him why his feet were so big, he had said they were big so he could scare off the wee fairies that came to steal the tongues of little lassies who asked too many questions.

She peered up from beneath the twisted brambles and branches. With his long white hair and his big shoulders, Fergus looked like a giant against the big blue sky. He was almost as big as her father.

"Och! Come out with ye. I canna see ye wee rascals, but I ken ye're in there."

Silly old Graham started to move, so Kirsty socked him in the arm and raised a finger to her lips. She gave him her most ferocious frown.

Boys were so dumb!

Fergus was bluffing. He didn't know where they were. Next time she would hide alone. No silly old boys, not even her silly old brother.

"Ouch!" Kirsty's mouth dropped open. She scowled at Graham. "You pinched me!"

He crossed his arms just like Fergus and their father did, then he gave her a belligerent look and a nod. "Aye."

"You can't pinch *me.*"

"I just did."

Two huge and tanned hands parted the bushes. Fergus squinted down at them. "Come out now, ye two. Quit yer arguing."

Graham crawled out before she could, another first. But she was still trying to understand how she had gotten pinched. What was the matter with Graham? If she couldn't bully him anymore, who was left to bully?

Did boys suddenly grow brains? She didn't think so. Most of the boys she knew acted like they didn't have a brain in their heads.

She got on her hands and knees and crawled out of the bushes, straightened, and dusted herself off.

"Weel, there ye be, lassie. Let's get going, now."
Fergus patted her head like you would an old dog, and
he turned and walked down the path.

Graham ran ahead of him so he could be first to
"roll down the hill like a boulder." As if she wanted to
roll down the hillside.

Instead she skipped along and caught up with
Fergus. "Are we going back home? Did Father finally
send for us?"

She knew the answer when Fergus didn't look at
her, but stared straight ahead.

"No, lassie."

"Why can't we go home?"

"I told ye, yer father's got business to do."

She slowed her steps and lagged along behind him.
He stopped and turned. He held out his hammy hand.
"Come along, lass."

She took two steps and slid her hand into his big
one. "Where are we going?"

"To tickle a trout."

"How do you tickle a trout?"

"I'll be showing ye, lassie."

"Where are the trout?"

"Up ahead. Near the bridge. Trout like to hide in
the rocks. We have tae lure them out."

She walked along with him. "Fergus?"

"Aye?"

"Why do trout have rainbows in their skins?"

He stopped suddenly and planted his hands on his
hips. "Are ye going tae be talking me ear off again?"

"No. I just wondered." She swatted a bumblebee,
then stared at it for a long time.

Fergus stopped near the bridge over the stream and
said to her. "Why are ye stopping?"

"I was just wondering." She caught up with him.
"Why do they call them *bumblebees?* If you listen

really close and you can hear a bee hum. They don't bumble. Shouldn't they be called *humblebees?*"

Fergus just laughed and pulled both Graham and her into the stream. He taught them how to lock their fingers together and set them in the cold water, down just a few inches beneath the glassy surface.

He taught them to be very, very still—Graham failed at that—and showed them what every Scot knew was true: if you were gentle, if you were very still, if you had the wit and blood of the Highlands, then the fish would just settle right into your open palms and let you tickle them with one bent finger until they were senseless and ready to become your tasty dinner.

Kirsty had more questions. Lots more questions. Sometimes she felt as if she were just one big question. So often no one could answer her questions. They just ignored her or made a joke as if her questions didn't matter, but it mattered to her.

Even Fergus who had so many fine tales to tell, who knew how to tickle trout, could speak Gaelic and make a fire without a flint, couldn't answer all her questions.

So she settled in and learned to tickle trout and tested new ways to intimidate her brother, but she never learned the things she really wanted to learn: like why do mothers die and why did her father not want them around?

Time is
   Too slow for those who Wait
Too swift for those who Fear,
   Too long for those who Grieve
Too short for those who Rejoice;
   But for those who Love,
      Time is
      Eternity

Anonymous

Amy stood on the deck of the coaster and watched the hills of Portland come into view, large gray humps of the real world that grew larger and clearer the closer they sailed to the mainland. The sea had been fairly calm and blue as they passed five or six other islands heading toward shore. To her it all passed too quickly, for before long the chalky weathered wharf with its busy side docks was standing before them.

Huddled in moorings around the west curve of the bay were fishing smacks and dories, coasters and sloops. Wooden lobster traps were stacked like teetering blocks along the sides of the clapboard wharf shacks, where spouts of steam and smoke drifted up into the blue sky from small rusty pipes that stuck out of the shingled shack roofs like pointing fingers.

Delivery wagons and teams were lined up along the busy street. Some were already loading barrels of fish oil, pine clapboards, and oak staves, all products from the nearby islands. Icemen dragged big blocks of shimmering ice speckled with straw into the wharf shacks where fresh seafood was weighed, cleaned, and sold.

Amy just stood there, a little undone, because she couldn't believe they were in Portland already. It seemed to her as if they had just left the island.

Georgina stopped her constant pacing of the deck and came to stand next to her. "Well, that certainly took long enough." She slapped some hair out of her face as if time were all too annoying to her. "I didn't think we'd ever get here." She scanned the dockside, her hands tapping impatiently on the rail. After a moment she glanced at Amy. "Will you be all right?"

"Yes."

They didn't speak for a bit, but both just watched the bustling dock, each lost in thoughts of their own.

Amy turned to her. "I wish you good luck in your marriage, Georgina. I hope John Cabot will be everything you want."

"He is. Have you changed your mind?"

Amy shook her head. "I know what I want."

Georgina nodded. "Then I hope you get it. Just don't forget my advice."

Amy smiled. "You don't have to worry. I'll not soon forget."

Georgina offered her hand and they said goodbye.

Both brothers were busy tying down and she and Georgina had to stand there an awkward moment longer. She felt impotent, numb, and nervous. She didn't know if she could be like Georgina, who had just marched over to Eachann and was harping at him about taking so long.

Those two were a queer set of rivals. Georgina stood there with her chin as high as someone who had no concept of fear at all. Her hands were planted on her hips and one foot tapped impatiently on the deck.

The more Georgina talked, the slower Eachann worked. She wondered if in her fit Georgina even noticed. Eventually he moseyed over to the side, with Georgina marching on his heels. He jumped onto the dock with long-legged ease and started walking away.

"Don't you walk away from me!" Georgina called out. "MacOaf!"

Amy winced. Georgina was fearless. Or tactless. Or maybe both.

He turned so slowly it was like watching a week pass. He stood there eyeing Georgina from a face that was unreadable.

She stuck out her hand like a queen and said, "I need help down."

Some of the men alongside the dock were leaning against the shacks, intently watching them. A few lobstermen had frozen in their moored dories, and a group of dock workers stopped talking and turned toward the coaster.

Eachann never said a word, but he walked back and stood there, looking at her hand for the longest time.

You could have cut the air with a knife. His stony gaze flicked from her hand to her face. Amy watched him take Georgina's hand.

Amy could see it coming. But Georgina didn't; she appeared too busy trying to look down her nose at him.

In less time than it took to blink, Eachann dipped his wide shoulder and flung Georgina right over it, clamping his arm around the backs of her legs.

She shrieked like mad, but Eachann ignored her and just strode casually down the dock to the cheers and catcalls of the fishermen. He gave them a salute and set Georgina down in the street the same way you would drop a load of rocks.

"It's like watching two angry mules harnessed together."

Amy turned at the sound of Calum's voice.

His black hair was ruffled from the voyage and he

had shed his coat and rolled up the sleeves of his shirt to work the sails. His forearms were tanned and lined with snake-like muscles; his hands were strong and capable of working the sails. It seemed hard to believe those were the same hands that had touched her cheek so tenderly.

She raised her gaze to his jaw, which was shadowed like always, but she saw that his mouth was set in a firm and stubborn-looking line she hadn't seen before.

He pushed his spectacles up his nose, a gesture that Amy had seen him do so many times she knew it was a nervous habit. The thought that he was nervous gave her a little hope. Perhaps he did care.

He looked at her with those dark blue eyes. "Do you want me to take you home? I'll make any explanations if you need me to."

"There's no one to make any explanations to." She could feel his gaze and squared her shoulders, but didn't look to him. She thought she might start crying.

He shoved his hands in his pockets and stood there. "I have to meet with some people, then sail up to Bath."

When she'd been healing he had come to her room, had told her about the ships from Scotland, in particular the one that was coming and how he felt he had a duty to see that the people on board were given clothing, shelter, and food. Calum gave people a new chance in a new land.

If she hadn't been in love with him before, she would have fallen when she realized this man cared about someone other than himself. He actually cared about strangers. Calum MacLachlan was noble and honest and above all he was different from any other man she had known except her father. He was like him, because deep inside of him, he was a truly kind man.

Someone called out his name and they both looked up. A small group of tall and rugged-looking men were walking toward them.

Amy turned toward Calum.

"The MacDonalds," he said.

"Those are the men you are to meet?"

"Aye."

She squared her shoulders, then offered him her hand. "I guess this is goodbye."

He was staring at her mouth.

Amy had a hunch that Georgina was right. He wasn't thinking about her brain. "Thank you, for everything." She flushed because she was thinking of those kisses. In an embarrassed rush she added, "For saving my life."

He just nodded and took her hand in both of his. "Are you sure you don't want me to take you home?"

"I'm sure."

"I'll go with you to the end of the dock." They walked together. He jumped off the way his brother had, then placed his hands on her waist and lifted her down to the dock as if she weighed no more than a feather.

When they were at the end of the wharf they stood there in awkward silence. He looked as if he wanted to say something, but he didn't.

She looked up at him. "Goodbye, Calum."

"Goodbye, Amy-my-lass."

She closed her eyes when he called her that. Her heart was pounding in her ears so loudly that she barely heard those men impatiently call out his name.

"I have to go." His voice was gruff.

Amy nodded and just stood there watching him walk away.

> Always act the winner,
> even if you lose.
>
> *Anonymous*

Georgina marched down the streets of Portland with proud and determined strides. She hadn't a cent to her name, couldn't even hire a coach, but that wouldn't stop her. She'd walk all the way home.

She moved along the board walkways for quite a distance before she became aware of the continuing jingle of a wagon harness and the steady clopping of a team in the street alongside of her. She sped up. So did the wagon team. She slowed down and the team paced her.

She stopped. So did the wagon the MacOaf was driving,

He grinned down at her. "I thought Joe Cabinet had a house up on the hill, one of those old brick places with the white columns and velvet knee pillows on the front steps for genuflecting."

Georgina used every ounce of her concentration to keep walking. *"John Cabot* does live on the hill. *I'm* going home."

"Interesting. I thought you'd race a path right to his golden door."

She stopped. "Dressed like this?" She rolled her eyes. "I don't think so."

"You look just fine to me."

"I can't tell you how thrilled I am that you approve. Just makes me want to swoon with delight."

"Don't swoon. I don't want you to stop walking, George. I like the way you walk."

She was silent.

"Nice and fast . . . with just enough jaunt in your step to make your best parts jiggle."

She ground to an immediate halt and turned.

He reined in the wagon and sat there with his arm resting on the back of the wagon seat while he grinned at her.

"Move over." She grabbed a hold of the wagon seat and hoisted herself up. "Since you have nothing better to do, you can take me home."

He snapped the reins and took off with a jerk. Her back slammed into the seat frame, but she didn't say a word.

He began to whistle merrily.

She just sat on the wagon seat, her leg rubbing against MacOaf's. It was immensely annoying, especially when her hip would butt into his at every bump.

Of course he managed to hit every pothole and rock in the road between midtown and her home. It got so bad that she was watching the road so she could grip the railing and not end up in his lap.

She did the natural thing and pretended she didn't care. Only a few more minutes and she would be home, then she wouldn't have to see the MacOaf again. Ever.

Just outside of town she watched the familiar road unfold before her. She saw with new appreciation the trees she had passed so many times, the curves in the road where the willows grew, and the neighboring estates that grew larger and more elegant the farther out they drove.

In the distance the water was blue and the gulls screamed overhead and circled above them. She could hear the sounds of the sea. For some strange reason it sounded different here than it had on the island. There was a peacefulness to it. Perhaps because she was almost home.

They rounded the sharp bend in the road that was nearest the Bayard gates. Her hands were knotted in her lap and she waited anxiously to see the welcome sight of that large *B* scrolled into the iron grates of the walled fence and the small Bayard clock set in the gate post.

She could hardly believe it. She was almost home.

Eachann pulled the wagon to a halt and she swung down off the seat before the wagon had rolled to a stop.

The gates were threaded with a thick metal chain and a huge steel lock. There was a paper notice with ends that were beginning to curl stuck on to the gate. It read:

BANK FORECLOSURE
For information regarding
estate sale of all possessions
and date of auction contact:
Merchants Bank
Boston, Mass.
NO TRESPASSING
Trespassers will be prosecuted.

Like a cipher she walked to the gate. She grabbed the iron bars so tightly that her knuckles turned white. She rattled the gates hard and pulled and yanked on them again and again.

Her stomach rose and felt as if it were stuck in her throat. Her breaths were sharp because she couldn't seem to get any air. She kept shaking the gates and shaking them, over and over, as if by doing so she could somehow shake off the terror she was beginning to feel.

Sweat dripped down her temples and beaded on her upper lip. She couldn't let go of the gates. She couldn't will her hands to work. She leaned her head against the cool bars for a moment, then felt his big hands on her shoulders.

"George?"

"Leave me alone!" She shook off his hands and twisted away from him, running around the walls to the side and back gates, rattling them one after another, half-hoping even one of them would be open.

Every single one of them was locked with big thick chains and heavy locks. She stood there for eternal minutes, staring through grates at the leaf-strewn gardens at the back of the house. She felt as if she were in jail, looking out on the world she wanted to be a part of.

With her fists clenched tightly in frustration, she spun around and stomped back toward the wagon.

"What the hell happened? How could someone foreclose? You weren't gone that long."

"My brother lost everything before he died. I knew I didn't have much time. I had to marry someone rich and marry him quickly."

The MacOaf stood there looking as if he was feeling sorry for her. "Don't you dare," she said through her teeth."

"What?"

"Don't you dare feel sorry for me or, so help me God, I'll hit you harder than Calum did. I can take your belligerence. I can take your smart mouth and goading. I can even take your manhandling, but I

can't take your pity. And I won't, Eachann MacLachlan. Do you understand?"

His look changed immediately. He gave her a quick
and perfectly serious nod.

"Good. Now come with me." She grabbed his
hammy hand and pulled him along with her while she
hurried back along the wall. "Might as well put all
that brawn of yours to a good use."

She stopped at the back side of the estate. "Give me
a foot up."

"You're going to go inside? The sign said No
Trespassing."

She slowly turned and faced him, scowling. "You're
worried about trespassing? This from a man who
kidnapped me?"

He had the good sense to look chagrined. It was a
first.

"Yes, I'm going to go inside *my* house and change
into *my* clothes."

"Look, George—"

"Shut up, MacOaf, and give me a boost."

He shrugged, locked his fingers together, and held
them out so she could stand in his cupped hands. A
moment later she was sitting on top of the wall.

Before she could jump down he had pulled himself
up and was sitting alongside of her.

She gave him a dirty look. "What do you think
you're doing?"

"I'm going with you."

"No, you're not."

He acted like she hadn't spoken and jumped down
from the top of the wall as easily as he'd gotten up
there, which annoyed her to no end. It was a long way
down.

He held out his arms. "Jump, George."

She jumped and he caught her, using his chest to
break her fall. He held her a second or two longer than

necessary, their bodies pressed intimately together, their faces inches apart, her feet dangling in midair.

She pressed her knuckles into his shoulders and he set her down without a word. Then she was running across the gardens, down the flagstone paths and on toward the house.

He was right behind her when she stopped at one of the back doors. She tried the knob, but the door was locked. He followed her as she tried every door and window. They were all locked tighter than a safe.

"I'll break a window if you want me to."

"I don't think we'll have to yet. There's one more place I need to check." She moved to the north side of the house where the rhododendron bushes were thick as a forest and tangled with thorny bougainvillea that climbed up one side of the house.

She got down on her hands and knees and crawled into the bushes. The bougainvillea thorns were scraping her arms and snagging her hair, but she didn't care. Because she could hear the MacOaf behind her swearing and cursing and muttering. "Ouch!"

She found the small cellar window and shoved up on the sash. It opened with a loud squeak.

A minute later they were inside the dark basement. She looked around for a lamp, feeling her way across the room. A second later a flame illuminated the MacOaf's face and he lit a small oil lamp that was near the tin washtub.

"One would think this was your home instead of mine."

He shrugged and she turned and led the way across the room, then up the steep wooden steps. She prayed the door wouldn't be locked.

Again she thought perhaps luck was in her favor. But she felt her luck die the moment he followed her into the house. The place looked as if it had been ransacked.

She heard him swear viciously as he raised the lamp and light spilled across the room.

She walked from room to room, each one worse than the last. The furniture was there, but most of it was draped or overturned. In the butler's pantry by the crystal, china and silver serving pieces and flatware were all gone.

There were broken pieces of priceless porcelain scattered all across the floors and rugs. She ran into the clock room and sagged in relief against the door.

The clocks were all still on the walls. Apparently whoever did this didn't care about the Bayard clocks.

She hurried past Eachann and ran up the stairs to her room. Perhaps the upstairs would be untouched.

She opened her bedroom door and stood there too dismayed to move. The room was a disaster. She looked around and suddenly remembered the last time she'd been in there. She had been upset about the yellowed wallpaper. Now the yellowed wallpaper actually looked good compared to the rest of the room.

Drawers were overturned, their contents broken and scattered across the carpet. She could hear crunching glass from porcelains and broken mirrors as she walked toward the bed. She just sat there, trying to understand what she was seeing and why. Why did this happen?

Eachann filled the doorway. After a moment of utter silence he said, "Let's get the hell out of here."

"No!" she said more sharply then she'd meant to. "I can't. Not yet." She stood up abruptly. "I came here for a reason. I'm not leaving yet." She crossed to a wardrobe where the doors were open and her belongings were tossed about or ruined.

She spent the next hour going through the wardrobes, the drawers, the dressers, everything from which she might salvage something worthwhile. She spent another hour in the wall closet. She poked her head out once and saw that Eachann was on her bed. His arms were behind his head and his boots were crossed at the ankles. He looked like he was sound asleep.

She wasn't likely to be fooled. It didn't take long to pack up the few things she could salvage. She wondered who had done this and why. When she was finished, she changed into a silk moiré suit with a shirtwaist that wasn't exactly the right match, but it would do.

She found an old hat under the bed that was the same deep color blue as the suit. She dressed with care, knowing her only hope left was John. She had to explain and hope if she looked good enough he'd be willing to forget her disappearance and the bankruptcy. By now people would know the truth.

She packed two valises and dragged them out of the closet. She walked over to the bed, where the MacOaf was sleeping. She poked him in the arm with a finger. He didn't stir and his breathing was even and quiet.

She walked over and picked up one of the valises, walked back to the bed, and dropped it on his stomach.

"Goddammit to hell!" He jackknifed upright and shoved the valise off of him. "What did you do that for?"

She was dragging the other valise across the room. She looked up. "Stop lounging around. Let's go."

Then she dragged it a little farther. He got up and took the valise from her and lifted the other one from the bed with annoying ease.

Within a half of an hour they were back by the wagon, her valises loaded in the back and her hand holding her hat on her head. Someone had taken every last one of her hatpins.

The MacOaf looked at her and bowed. "Your pumpkin awaits, Cinderella."

"My bumpkin? Yes, you are, aren't you." She lifted her skirts and pulled herself up onto the wagon seat.

He laughed. "Good one, George."

"Stop your crowing, MacOaf, and just drive this thing back to town."

"Ah, he said knowingly. "To Jim Karat's house."

She looked at him and shook her head. She would let him have his fun.

"So what are you going to do? Lie?"

"Probably. I know one thing. I hope there are velvet knee pillows. I think after all this I might have to genuflect."

He snapped the reins and gave the team their heads. "You? On your knees before a man?" he crowed with cynical laughter. "Now that's something I'd like to see."

She slapped her hand on her hat when they hit a rut. "You think that's funny?"

"The image is enough to keep me awake at night."

She knew she was a proud woman, but certainly the idea of her begging wasn't all that funny. She stiffened her spine and chose to ignore him. Every so often she could feel his gaze on her, but she was silent.

She watched him steer the wagon right toward a rock in the road, and when he hit it, she almost flew off the seat. She turned and gave him a frosty glare.

He was wearing that wicked grin.

"You can stop aiming for those ruts and rocks. I'm starting to find you most annoying."

"Sorry, George. I can't concentrate. I keep imagining you on your knees in front of me."

"Imagine all you like, MacOaf."

He laughed harder.

"I would never beg you for anything."

"Is that a challenge?"

"No. It's the truth."

"You don't think I could make you beg me for anything?"

"I know you couldn't."

"Want to make a wager?"

"You are so arrogant. I ought to do it, just to teach you a lesson. But . . ." She waved a hand through the air. "I don't have to make any wagers with you, because after you drop me off at the Cabot house I won't ever have to see you again." She threaded her hands together and straightened her spine.

He just kept laughing.

"Oh, be quiet and turn right."

I come from the city of Boston,
Home of the bean and the cod,
Where the Cabots speak only to Lowells
And the Lowells speak only to God.

Samuel C. Bushnell

Georgina stood on the steps of the Cabot mansion and rapped the brass knocker three times. It was a huge home, but small compared to the family's other residences. The entire house was red brick with windows along the front that looked out to the bay and beyond. There were white columns on the portico, and the front steps were Italian marble, the handrails cast iron with polished brass insets in an intricate Greek motif.

She knew from John that this house had twenty-five rooms. And she would enjoy every last one of them when she was mistress. She just had to give her best performance and this house and, more importantly, her own family estate would be all hers.

She stood there, her back stiff and straight as the ships' masts out in the distant harbor. In her mind, she kept going over her speech, again and again.

Well, you see, John, it is the most ridiculous set of circumstances—

235

She heard sudden sharp and annoyingly familiar notes of Eachann whistling. She stepped back, leaned out, and looked down the street.

He was sprawled on the wagon seat watching her.

She gripped the iron handrail and leaned over it. In a loud whisper she said, "I told you to leave!"

He looked at her and cupped one hand to his ear and shook his head, acting like he couldn't hear her.

Before she could move or shout, one of the front doors opened.

She spun back around, her hand on her hat.

The Cabot butler stood there. "Miss Bayard."

"Samuel." Georgina acknowledged him with a sharp nod and straightened her skirts by giving them a little shake. She raised her chin. "I'd like to see Mr. Cabot."

"I'm sorry but Mr. Cabot isn't home."

She panicked. "He hasn't gone back to Boston, has he?"

"No, Miss. Mr. Cabot has gone to Philadelphia."

Good. Perhaps this was a good thing. Perhaps he didn't know about the foreclosure yet. "When will he return?"

"I really cannot say."

She gave him her most regal glare. "You can't or won't."

"I don't know, Miss Bayard. Neither he nor Mrs. Cabot said when they would return."

"Oh, I see. He's with his mother." She laughed and raised a hand to her chest where her heart had been beating much too fast. "Well, Samuel, why didn't you just tell me that?"

"Mr. Cabot's mother is at home in Boston. I was referring to the new Mrs. Cabot. Mrs. Phoebe Cabot. I believe her family, the Dearborns, are from Philadelphia."

Barely a moment later, right there, on that posh marble stoop with the iron rails and those tall white columns, something truly odd happened: for the first time in her life Georgina Bayard fainted.

Here's to you and here's to me,
And here's to the girl with the well-shaped knee.
Here's to the man with his hand on her garter;
He hasn't got far, but he's a damn good starter.

Anonymous

Georgina awoke to someone unbuttoning her clothes. A warm hand brushed over her neck. Then she felt a few whiffs of air brush her face. She opened her eyes and blinked a couple of times.

The MacOaf's face was above her. He was fanning her with her hat. She blinked against the sudden glare of light and the sudden horror of waking up to a face that belonged in a woman's dreams, but instead had been foolishly given to a mule.

Her sense returned and she glanced down. Her jacket was gone and her shirtwaist and her corset cover were unbuttoned and lying open, even her corset laces were untied. She was almost all bare skin to the waist.

Her mouth fell open. In a rush, she looked around her. Her panicked gaze flashed upward to all that brick. She was outside the Cabot home in full public view, lying in the back of the wagon half undressed.

She shot up, gripping her shirt closed with one hand

and swatting his hand away. "Stop waving that stupid hat in my face!"

He stopped and looked at the hat. "You think it's stupid? I guess the feather is ugly."

She snatched the hat and held it over her chest. "I'm half undressed, you fool!"

MacOaf sat back on his heels and shrugged. "It didn't bother you that night in the garden when you were meeting Jack Cabbie."

She was furiously trying to rebutton her clothes, but with the corset undone, they wouldn't close. She stuck a hand inside her clothing and dug around. She jerked out the long corset strings. "Here. Pull."

He wrapped the strings around one hand again and again like you would reel in a fish.

Oh God, no. . . .

He kept wrapping the strings around his hand until her face was only a few inches from his.

She glared up at him. "I said, 'pull.'"

"Okay, George." He grinned. "Like this?"

A second later she was flat against him, breasts against his chest, her mouth so near his she could taste him. His other hand was under her skirt and on the back of her bare thigh, holding her right where she was.

"One more move from you and I'll scream rape so loud the whole world will hear me."

"And sully your name in front of this house? I don't think so, George."

"Well, that's where you're wrong. I have no reputation left to sully." She inhaled enough air to scream for at least two minutes, opened her mouth, and hollered, "Ra—"

His mouth caught the rest of her scream; he was on her so quickly they fell back and landed hard on the wagon bed. His free hand was pinned between them with the weight of his body. She wiggled against him, trying to buck him off her, but he was too heavy. She still made as much noise as she could against his mouth.

He jerked his hand out from between them, pulled his mouth away, and covered her mouth with his hand. "Be quiet, George. Hell, you know I wouldn't force you."

She bit his hand.

"Ouch! Dammit!" He sat up, shaking his hand and scowling at her the whole time.

"Just stay away from me." She pulled her corset laces off his other hand and jerked them so tightly she almost fainted again. She knotted them off and began to button up her clothes. "Just stay away. This whole thing is your fault!"

"Now, George . . ."

"Go away." She tried to scoot out of the wagon, but he was in the way, so she jammed an elbow into his ribs. "Go back to your foggy wet island and your children and leave me alone. I don't ever want to see you again. Do you understand?"

He didn't say anything. He just stared at her from a face that showed no emotion. For just one second she thought he looked angry. He had no right to be angry. His life wasn't ruined.

She crawled past him and jumped to the ground. She grabbed her hat with a sharp jerk and jammed it on her head. Then she just turned and walked away.

An hour later she was walking down the road to her home. He never followed her. She half expected him to, but he didn't.

As she walked there was no wagon, no horse, no carriage anywhere on the road. The homes here were summer places. By now the summer crowd would have returned to their city houses.

They must know, every single one of them must know about her situation. She stumbled slightly and had to balance herself on a tree trunk. She stood there, her back pressed to the trunk for a moment, staring down the road. She had no idea what she was going to do.

From here she could see the house. The stone walls and the peaked roofline. She could see the tops of the trees and the ivy that grew over the back fence. She could see the bougainvillea that climbed up the side of the house and covered all that chipping paint and wood rot in the eaves.

Every summer for every year that she could remember back, Georgina had spent in that house. It had been the last thing to go, perhaps that was why she fought so hard to keep it. She shoved away from the tree and moved on.

It wasn't as hard to get inside this time. She used a tree limb to get over the wall and went straight for the cellar window. For a while she wandered through the house. She moved some of the furniture back into its proper place and took some of the dust cloths off certain pieces.

She sat in chairs in every room, rooms that held memories for her. Her family memories might not have been wonderful, but they were all the memories she had.

For the longest time she sat in the clock room and looked at each and every Bayard clock. She wound them herself and watched them mark time that had no meaning to her anymore.

Time only mattered if you had some place to go. She almost laughed. She didn't have anything, not even the few things she'd saved in those valises, which she'd left in the wagon. She didn't have anything, not even a place to go.

As the sky grew darker and the sun set, she made her way upstairs. She slipped off her shoes and jacket and crawled into her bed.

In less time than it took to say good night, she was sound asleep. So sound asleep that she didn't hear anything, not the opening of the front door, not the footsteps up the stairs. She didn't even hear her bedroom door open.

She heard nothing until a constable with a gun and a billy club woke her up and arrested her for trespassing and vagrancy.

No man can be happy without a friend, nor sure
of a friend until he's unhappy.

Scottish proverb

Georgina sent notes to every person she knew. No
one came to bail her out of jail. Not even those who
hadn't left for town yet. Not one person who had
danced to music played in the Bayard ballroom. Not
one person who had drunk their fill of champagne or
eaten food paid for by Bayard money.

Not one person whom she had known for years,
some of them all her life. Not one came. Even the
servants. The police told her they had been the ones
to ransack the place, taking valuables in place of their
wages.

So she sat on a dusty bunk covered with a moth-
eaten blanket and plenty of fleas. Her hands were
shaking, shaking the way they had when she was lost
in the park so many years ago. She was that same little
girl again, the one who was lost in the crowded park,
the one who sat on sand dune all alone and so very
scared inside. She propped her elbows on her knees
and pressed the heels of her hands into her burning
eyes. For the first time in her life, she didn't know if
she could survive.

A door squeaked open and she could hear her jailer walking down to the cell, his keys jangling too loudly in the emptiness.

"Yep, that's George."

Eachann?

Georgina's head shot up and relief washed over her with such a strong force that she felt too lightheaded to even stand up. But the feeling didn't last long.

She was up and clinging to the bars. "Get me out of here."

He looked at the jailer. "What do I need to do?"

"Pay her bail of ten dollars and sign an affidavit accepting full responsibility for her."

"Sign it, Eachann."

The officer looked from her to Eachann, then said, "She can't go back to that house for any reason. It and all of its contents belong to the bank."

Eachann watched her thoughtfully.

If he makes me beg, I'll kill him.

"You'll go back to the island with me?" He didn't say a word about begging.

"Yes."

"Willingly?"

"Yes. Just sign that thing and get me out of here."

Five minutes later, she left the jail in the custody of Eachann MacLachlan, the man who had kidnapped her.

The old man laughed and sang a song
As they rocked in wooden shoe;
And the wind that sped them all night long
Ruffled the waves of dew;
The little stars were herring-fish
That live in the beautiful sea.
"Now cast your nets wherever you wish—
Never feared are we!"
So cried the stars to the fishermen three,
Wynken, Blynken and Nod.

Eugene Field

His brother and the coaster had long since left for Bath, so Eachann had paid a herring boat that was going out that night to take them back to the island. Georgina kept to herself at first, sitting alone in a spot and not talking to anyone. She spent most of her time watching Eachann.

He stood in the aft and his hair was wild in the breeze, as wild as the man himself. He was so tall standing there, looking like some god who lorded over the sea and sky.

She didn't have to look at him to know he was the most beautiful man she had ever seen. His features were strong and chiseled. Superbly masculine. He wasn't bald and short.

He wasn't rich either.

But he was something to see standing there like that. She rested her chin in her hand and decided it would suit her just fine if she could spend the rest of her life looking at him.

As long as he never opened his mouth.

Georgina remembered back to that party and how she had thought Eachann would look all dressed up in white tie. Watching him here on the sea at night was more striking a scene than white tie and tails, than any clothing could ever make him look.

Eachann MacLachlan was as wild and rough as the island where he lived. They seemed to fit together. All that hard weathered granite that could withstand the strength of the sea and the hardheaded man who didn't care what she said or did or who she was. He was like that granite island. Immovable.

He spoke easily with the man he hired, an old fellow, the kind of Maine talker who had a saying for everything. He'd assumed they were husband and wife and Eachann hadn't said anything different.

As they left the harbor the old man had chattered about the storms he'd seen and how "they blowed a fit enough to make rabbit cry." He busied his two sons with taking the boat out while he looked at Georgina. "You from Boston?"

She nodded.

"Yep. Can always tell you Boston folk. Hits you right between the face and eyes."

Eachann laughed.

"Did you know them Pilgrims didn't land at Plymouth?" The old man unwrapped a tangled fishing net as he spoke. "The Pilgrims, they first landed on Monhegan island. Got themselves some good cod, they did. So the story goes, one morning a fisherman's wife looks out her window and sees the *Mayflower* hove in for some handlining. She turns to her husband and says, "Who do you suppose that is?" Her husband looks out the window. "It's got to be the Pilgrims. They've come at last!""

It was a silly story, but even Georgina had to laugh. All those women she knew, her so-called friends, prided themselves on being descended from Mayflower dames, and as such, the daughters of the first Americans.

The laughter was cut short when one of the sons caught sight of a school of herring. A moment later they were turning the boat and tossing nets in the water.

"George? Come over here."

She glanced at Eachann, then got up and joined him at the railing in the aft.

"Have you ever seen the herring run?"

She laughed. "Not hardly."

"Look there." He nodded out at the sea.

The moon was behind a big fat cloud but its light still spilled on the water, making it glisten and shine with a cool and quiet light.

Then suddenly the water was sparkling and twinkling as if lightning bugs were trapped in the sea. There were hundreds, maybe thousands, of sparkling flashes spilling and flashing all over the water.

She laughed, because she'd never seen anything like it. It was magical and eerie and new. She could feel Eachann looking at her. He was leaning with his back against the railing.

He wasn't watching the fish. He was watching her. She wondered what he was thinking. What he saw when he looked at her. Which then made her wonder what she was going to be. What her life was going to be like. Marriage to this man was her only choice.

She wondered why he was the only one in the world who seemed to know or care that she existed. She supposed Amy cared and would have come, but no one knew where Amelia Emerson was. And Amy had been adamant when she told her she would not go back. She wondered if Amy was as lost as she was, or if she was doing what she had suggested and was working a little female magic on Calum MacLachlan.

The fishermen had released their nets and they began to pull in the herring.

Georgina felt uncomfortable with the way Eachann looked at her and what those looks of his made her feel. She had that instinctive urge to lash out at him, but, to tell the truth, she was tired of fighting and she couldn't fight him anymore anyway. He was the only future she had.

She felt a horrid sense of loss standing there watching the men haul up the fish. They spilled them all over the deck where the herring flopped and flipped their beautiful silver bodies all around the deck in a desperate attempt to get back into their home in the sea.

"I want to throw them all back," she said, without looking at Eachann.

"It wouldn't do any good. Someone else will just catch them."

"Would they? You can't know for certain. Look at them fight. Perhaps they could get away and swim far out to sea."

"And get eaten by sea lions or other fish."

He was right, but she didn't feel any better for it. She excused herself and walked back to sit and watch. She felt like those herring flopping around on the deck.

At one moment when everyone was too busy and no one was paying attention, she stood and kicked a few of them overboard. It was stupid. But for some idiotic reason it made her feel better.

He knows not the pleasures of plenty
who never felt the pains of poverty.

Scottish proverb

By the time they reached the island and were in Eachann's house, Georgina had resigned herself to her future. She had no other place to live. She couldn't do anything to support herself. She had no choice but to marry Eachann.

He was building a fire in the fireplace while she sat in a chair and looked around the room. It wasn't clean and organized like Calum's part of the house.

She shook her head. "This is a hovel."

He turned back and looked at her. "It's lived in."

"I guess I have no choice anyway."

"No choice about what?"

"I have no place to go. I have nothing left. I guess this will have to be my home, especially if I'm going to be forced to take your offer."

He didn't say anything but straightened and leaned against the mantel.

"I suppose we can get along amicably, if you'll just be reasonable for part of the time. We can treat this like a . . . well, like a business alliance."

He gave her a long intense stare. Then he began to slowly nod his head. "Fine" was all he said.

"Then you agree?"

"As far as I'm concerned, it's settled."

"Good." She exhaled a breath she hadn't known she'd been holding.

"The way I figure it, with room and board and expenses, I should be able to pay you—"

"Pay me?"

"Aye. I have you to thank for this idea, George. You were the one who told me that I didn't need a wife. You said all I really need is a nursemaid. You're right." He straightened, drove his hand through his hair, and laughed a nervous and shaky laugh, the kind that sounded as if he had just escaped all the pains of hell. "To tell you the truth, it's a relief. We don't exactly see eye to eye. It would have made for one hell of a difficult marriage."

He let loose a big sigh and looked directly at her. "So now, let's come to an agreement. Let me think about this for a second . . ." He was tapping one finger against his chin while he mouthed and grunted something that sounded like a pig doing arithmetic. "I've got it. Here's my offer. I'll pay you twenty-five dollars a month."

"Are you really that stupid?"

"Okay." He grinned, then gave her a knowing wink. "Can't blame a fellow for trying."

She relaxed. "Well, I should say so." She shook out her skirt with a couple of sharp snaps, then raised her chin.

He was grinning at her.

She certainly wasn't above a little humorous jest. But really. The very idea. It was so ludicrous. Georgina Bayard as a nursemaid. She gave in and laughed with him. When her laughter finally faded she shook her head at the silliness of it all. "That was, without a doubt, the most ridiculous thing I've ever heard."

"You're right, George. You Bayards are just too sharp for me."

She was still laughing.

"I'll double my offer. Fifty dollars a month and you can have Sundays off."

Her laughter stopped as abruptly as a train wreck. Was he really that stupid? She examined his expression, searched it for a long time to see if he was doing this to goad her. His usual approach.

"Of course you'll want me to deduct your bail from the first month's pay. I know how proud you Bayards are, George. You wouldn't want to owe me anything." He looked at her as if he had just given her the best gift in the world. He stuck out his hand.

She stared at it as if it were a dead herring.

"Now, George. Don't get sly. I can't go any higher on your salary, so don't think you can wheedle more money out of me. After all, I'm being very generous."

Wheedle? She just sat there staring at his outstretched hand and wishing she had an axe.

It took her a very long time to find a calm and controlled voice. "You want to pay me fifty dollars a month to be a nursemaid to your children."

"Aye." He walked over and gave her a hard slap on the back. "That makes for the perfect business alliance."

That makes me a slave.

"Get up now so we can get to bed." He paused, then added in a pointed rush, "In *separate* rooms. I didn't want you to get confused like Amy did. You'll not have to worry about your virtue now that our relationship is master and servant. You know . . . all business."

Servant? He all but dragged her out of the chair and

up the stairs. He stopped in front of a room and opened the door. She looked inside.

It was the size of her closet. Her two valises sat on the floor and covered most of it. The floor appeared bare, from what she could see of it and the room was musty and smelled old and unused.

"I'll need to get up early and ride over to the other side of the island. I have to get Fergus to bring Kirsty and Graham back first thing in the morning. The sooner the better."

She looked up. Besides breathing, looking up was the only thing she could manage at the moment. Her feet were lead, her arms numb, and her jaw felt as if it were locked together.

"You'll need to keep a sharp eye on those little devils of mine. Especially on their schooling. I'm certain you Bayards had the best education all that money you used to have could buy. That's a real good thing too, because I can't hire a tutor for them until at least spring." Then he turned around and sauntered away whistling.

> If you want something more than anything,
> be prepared to stake everything.
>
> *Georgina Bayard's advice*

What the hell are you doing in there?"

Amy looked up from the open mackerel tank at Calum MacLachlan's angry face. "What am I doing? I do believe I'm getting seasick again." She raised a hand to her clammy forehead and swayed a little.

He swore.

She blinked up at him, then winced. "Would you please stop weaving back and forth? You're making me dizzy and I'm already quite lightheaded enough."

"I'm not weaving. I'm standing perfectly still, lass." He bent down and scooped her up out of the tank so fast it felt as if she'd left her stomach behind.

"Ohmygod! Don't move!" She gulped down deep breaths of cool sea air.

He must have been deaf because he ignored her and walked over to the side of the boat. He propped her up and kept her pinned against the rail, his strong arms on either side of her.

"Take deep breaths, lass. If you need to, go ahead and empty your stomach."

There was nothing in her stomach to empty. "I haven't eaten," she groaned.

He grumbled something that included the word *stupid* and picked her up again.

"You know, Calum, I think I'm getting sicker from you flinging me up into your arms than I am from the motion of the sea."

"You're lucky I'm not flinging you into the sea."

"You wouldn't do that."

"Don't test me." He took her below to the small cabin in the bow of the boat and set her on the edge of a bunk that was built into the wall. He opened a cabinet and pulled out a few things, evidently found what he was looking for, and came back to her. He knelt down in front of her with a cracker tin under one arm.

"Here, lass. Try to eat these."

She moaned and sagged back flat against the bed, a hand slapped to her forehead. "My stomach is somewhere around my throat right now and you want me to eat."

"You'll feel better if you eat a few crackers. Here. Come on, now. Just try one."

She raised her head and stared at the white crackers in his outstretched hand. She took one and held it up, turning it one way, then the other.

"Are you going to eat it or memorize it?"

"I haven't decided."

"Take small bites and chew it well. The salt will help your stomach."

She did as he told her. The first time she swallowed she thought it was going to come right back up. It didn't. So she took another bite, then another. Before long her stomach was not as queasy.

"Now I want to hear why you stowed on board."

"I didn't want to leave."

"But Eachann shouldn't have taken you, lass. I

thought you'd need to get home, where you had your people around you."

"I have no people I want around me." She looked up at him. "Except you."

"Lass, that's not wise."

"I don't care."

"Use your head."

"According to Georgina, I don't want to be known for my brain. She claims beauty is better because men see better than they think."

He began to chuckle, then laughed out loud. "I think in Eachann's case that might be true." He was still laughing. "I can't be with you now, Amy-my-lass. I have work to do. I can't be taking care of you."

"I can take care of myself."

His look was disbelieving. "Like you did in the cave and just now when you were sick?"

"I'll help."

"You'll help," he repeated without inflection.

"I can help you. Just tell me what to do."

"I can't, lass. Not now. I need to get topside. Will can't handle this boat alone along the stretch of coast that'll be coming soon. We'll be in Bath soon. I have to make certain those people on that ship are fed and clothed and have safe transportation to their land.

"Can I come with you? I want to know how all this started. What exactly it is you do. I want to watch. I want to help. I feel so, so worthless. If I can help someone, then perhaps I . . . well, I don't know exactly what, Calum, but I do know I need something to do."

He stood there for a long time, as if he needed to come to some decision, then he crossed the room, turned a small latch in the wall and pulled down a desktop with a drawer hidden behind it. He rummaged through and took out a leather-bound book that looked like a journal.

He handed it to her. "Here. When you're feeling better, you can read this. It will tell more about what I do than I can."

She took the journal and watched him walk to the companionway.

He stopped and looked back at her. "How are you feeling now?"

"Better. You were right about the crackers. Thank you."

He nodded at a small metal tank across the room. "There's water in there if you need it."

"Actually what I need right now isn't more water. I need to rid myself of some."

He laughed and pointed to another cabinet. "The necessary is in there."

She flushed, then muttered, "Thank you."

He turned and opened the door to leave, but turned back around. "Why didn't you just ask if you could come with me?"

"Would you have taken me?"

"No."

"That's why."

He just shook his head and left the cabin.

She opened the journal and first skimmed through the pages. On the first pages there were newspaper clippings and editorials pasted to the pages. She began to read the first one.

We have been pained beyond measure for some
time past to see in our streets so many unfortunate
Highland emigrants, apparently destitute. Their last
shilling is spent to reach this new land, where they
are reduced to begging. Their case is made worse by
their ignorance of the English tongue. Of the hundreds of Highlanders in and around the city at present, perhaps not a half dozen understand anything
but Gaelic. We may assist these poor creatures for a

time, but charity will not keep so many for very long. Winter is approaching and then what? Are they to starve and freeze in the streets?

Amy felt sick. This was a terrible thing that was happening. She read on, each article more horrific than the last. Then the pages in the book were handwritten. In Calum's own hand there were journal entries of what he had seen. What he felt. His experiences.

I saw a funeral today. A long line of Highland emigrants walked down the silent street. On their shoulders that were bony and narrow with starvation was a small coffin, not much bigger than a cradle. It was a child's coffin made of crude material, rough boards that looked like the kind of old splintered wood planks that were left to rot along the dockside. Children followed the mournful train, and when asked, they told of their friend, the small eight-year-old boy who had in healthier and more happy times played with them in their native glens.

Their looks, their faces were indescribable. The sorrow and grief were there, but there too was a look and sense of an inevitably hopeless future that creased their faces like wrinkles of age. Their faces could break the heart of a grindstone.

Their mourning weeds were little more than rags that had once been clothes. The child's mother walked along behind the small coffin, her clothing torn and her eyes empty and vacant as the promises made to these poor people by their lairds and benefactors—those desperate men whose grandfathers had protected them. Now the grandsons threw the crofters off the land they had farmed for centuries so they could graze sheep.

The procession walked on toward the grave site, where their hopes and the promises for a future

would be buried in that shallow grave along with
the coffin.

I am a clan laird, by birth chieftain, by title the
MacLachlan of MacLachlan. I have no Highland
lands, for they were taken from my great-
grandfather many years before. I have no clansmen
like my grandfathers did. Just my small family. But
I have Scots blood and I can't help but feel a strong
sense of anger at what I am seeing here. I cried as I
watched that funeral. I cried for that mother, for
that child. It could, but for the grace of God, have
been me or my brother or even Kirsty or Graham.

I vow, today, with everything I have and everything I am, that this will be no more. That no more
Highlanders will starve and die and freeze in the
streets. I will not let it happen. If I do nothing else
in my short lifetime, this will be enough.

When Amy finished reading she was crying. The
tears were pouring down her cheeks the way they must
have poured down Calum's. She read on, every newspaper article and Calum's entries. She could see what
he did, how he provided these people with more than
just food and clothing and a place to live. Calum gave
them back their pride.

She closed the book and sat there, staring up at the
wood on the ceiling. Then she closed her eyes against
all the images she saw, vivid painful images from
Calum's journal. They haunted her, those images,
until Amy finally fell asleep with tears still streaming
from the corners of her eyes.

When the bold kindred in the time long
    vanished,
Conquered the soil and fortified the keep,
No seer foretold the children would be banished,
That a degenerate lord might boast his sheep.
Fair these broad meads—these hoary woods are
    grand,
But we are exiles from our fathers' land.

Canadian boat song

When she awoke it was to the sight of Calum leaning against the wall, his black hair ruffled by the wind and probably from his habit of driving his hand through it when he was frustrated. He wore no coat, only a white shirt with the cuffs rolled up and a leather vest.

His breeches were tucked into tall leather boots and he rested one foot on the steps of the companionway. He was absently rubbing his chin with a tanned hand and staring at her like a missionary who'd been stuck with the job of converting all the tribes of Africa.

"You're awake." He straightened and his hand fell away from his chin.

She sat up, still drowsy, until she realized the boat was not moving. "We're in Bath."

"Aye."

She swung her legs over the side of the narrow bunk and spent a moment or two straightening her twisted skirt. She glanced up at him. "You're being very quiet."

"I'm trying to decide what to do with you."

"You could let me help."

"I could send you back to Portland in a wagon."

"What would you do with me when I came back? Besides, you cannot make me go if I don't want to. You have no right to tell me what to do. You are not my father or my husband."

She stood and raised her chin the way she had seen Georgina do when Eachann was trying to tell her what to do.

He just watched her for the longest time, not saying anything, but he was thinking. She could see it in those dark blue eyes of his.

"I never thought you to be such a stubborn lass."

"I never thought you to be autocratic and unfair."

"Autocratic? Me?"

"Yes." She gave a sharp nod. "It must be a family trait. You sound like your brother."

"Good God . . . that bad?" He shoved away from the wall and walked toward her. He looked at her for a long time before he finally placed his hands on her shoulders. She didn't look away.

"I don't think this is good thing, lass."

"What?"

"You being here."

"Then tell me, Calum. Where should I be?"

"Back at home where you can get on with your life the way it was before my brother made a mess of it."

She laughed facetiously. "Oh, now that's funny. My life was so wonderful before." She shook her head, then looked up at him. "My life was nothing but one big heartache. It was a mess long before Eachann ever came into it."

"You're too young for your life to be a mess."

"I don't feel young. I feel very, very old."

"But you aren't old. You are young."

"No, listen to me, please, Calum. I might be young to you, but I feel all used up. I'm a person who doesn't fit in anywhere. I just don't think like other people, Calum. Life isn't the way it's supposed to be, at least the way I thought it would be."

"It never is."

"But I'm so confused all the time. I don't even know where I belong anymore. Even my home doesn't feel like home since my parents died."

"What happened to them?"

"My father had quite a few business interests. He and my mother traveled to Baltimore. I was supposed to join them in a week, but there was a fire in the hotel, in the middle of the night. They were on an upper floor and couldn't get out." Her voice cracked.

He pulled her into his arms and just held her, while he slowly rubbed her back.

It had been so long since someone cared enough to comfort her, she began to cry into his shirt. "This is so silly."

"Grief isn't silly."

She turned her head and rested her cheek against his shoulder. "They couldn't get out, Calum."

"I'm sorry, lass." He stroked her head. After a few minutes he asked, "You have no other family?"

"No. My father was an orphan and the last of my mother's family died when I was a baby. My parents were the only family I've ever known." She looked up at him. "So you see, I have nothing to go back to. When your brother took me, my life seemed like nothing. In here." She pointed to her heart. "I was all shriveled up inside."

"Time will change all that, lass. Sometimes we have to wait. When we're young, waiting is very hard."

"I'm not that young."

He laughed. "You have a long life ahead of you."

"If I do, then I need something in my life. I read your journal. How old were you when you first began to work with the emigrants?"

"It was ten years ago. I was nineteen."

"I'm twenty, Calum."

"I'm a man."

She frowned at him, then stepped away. "What does that have to do with it? You were nineteen. I am twenty. You're a man. I'm a woman. Because I'm a woman, does that make me less capable of caring?"

He ran a hand through his hair. "That's not what I meant."

"Just what did you mean? Do you think because I'm a woman I shouldn't feel a calling, like you did? Am I supposed to sit around and drink tea and sew samplers and ignore everything else?" She planted her hands on her hips. "If that's what you meant, Calum, then that was a stupid thing to say."

He looked completely perplexed. "You're twisting my words around."

"I'm trying to make you understand how I feel. This important to me." She crossed over to him and placed her hand on his chest. "You are important to me."

He looked down at her hands as if he didn't know how to take her touch, then he covered them with his own hands and they stood like that for a while.

She tried to explain. "I want to help. Perhaps if I can help someone else, if I can make a difference in even one person's life, then my life won't seem so wasted and empty. Can't you understand that?"

"Oh, Amy-my-lass. I understand all too well."

"Then you'll let me help?"

He shook his head as if he didn't want to agree, but he said, "Aye."

She grinned up at him. "That's good, because I wouldn't have left."

He laughed and turned her around by the shoulders. "Well, you need to leave now. I have something to do here. Go up on deck. If you hurry you can watch the ship come in. It's a sight you don't want to miss."

She looked back at him over a shoulder. "Will you come?"

"I'll be up soon enough."

She went up the stairs and out onto the deck where she stood by the railing and just looked all around her.

In the distance, the hills had turned a deep heather purple. The outline of the thick pine forests that topped those hills cut a jagged line across the horizon. The river inlet looked like a thin silver ribbon coming down from those hills, where it flowed past ploughed green fields, the small farms and houses that dotted the river's rolling hillsides, on past the docks and wharves to the edge of the wide open bay.

There was a strong breeze with the incoming tide and gulls wheeled about the blue and cloudless sky, screaming and calling as if they were heralds. Amy walked to the other side of the boat, where the ship was a clear and vivid image as it came toward them with sails full, slicing through the tidal water and up the river.

An American flag flew high in the masts, its red and white stripes rippling like May ribbons in the wind. She could see the people gathered at the ship's rail, watching like she was, and she wondered how many of these ships and how many people had come up this same river before.

She could see the sailors scurry about the masts and upper decks like starlings in the tallest trees. They pulled lines and maneuvered the ship up the river toward the wharf. There was an eerie silence about the passengers. No one called out. No one pointed. They only stood and looked around them.

She heard a noise and turned.

Calum stood on the deck facing her, but he was watching the ship. No one who looked at him would have any doubt who this man was. He didn't looked like the man she'd first seen on that foggy night or like the man who had saved her in the cave.

He looked like what he was: the clan chieftain, for the MacLachlan of MacLachlan was wearing the kilt, his muscular legs showing from beneath and his feet in leather brogues. He wore a black woolen jacket with silver buttons and his red plaid swagged over one broad shoulder. A bonnet with a feather was cocked on his dark head and he stood as tall and as proud as any man could be.

The sight of him took her breath away. As if he knew it, he turned, gave her a long look, then moved to the dock where he was joined by the men he had met with in Portland, the MacDonalds, who were dressed in their own green plaids.

Within seconds the skirls of a bagpipe filled the air and the men followed the piper as he walked down the dock. Except for the lilting notes of the bagpipe, there was not a sound. Even the gulls had grown silent, as if they understood the solemn ceremony of this moment.

Her gaze followed Calum. She could not have looked away if she had tried to. The men stopped at the base of the gangplank and the piper's song rose high and higher, then stopped, the notes floating in the air for only a second.

Cheers erupted in waves from the ship and bonnets flew high in the air. The noise went on for a long time, minutes that stretched on seemingly forever. When the cheering finally stopped, Amy realized she was crying.

She felt Calum's gaze shift up to where she stood still gripping the railing. She smiled and gave him a short wave. Then another pipe began, this one coming from the deck of the ship, and the Highlanders walked down the gangplank, everything they owned tied into small bundles or slung over their backs.

She had heard people claim the sound of the bagpipes could tear your heart out, and it would have, but her heart was already gone. It belonged to the man who stood on that dock dressed in a red plaid and kilt, a tall and noble Scotsman with hair as black as sin.

Whilst in her prime and bloom of years,
Fair Celia trips the rope,
Alternately she moves our fears,
Alternately our hope.
But when she sinks or rises higher,
Or graceful does advance,
We know not what we most admire,
the dancer or the dance.

Anonymous

Calum found Amy in the meeting hall, a huge barn of a room near the wharf, where most of the work was done. He didn't call out her name or make his way through the crowd to stand at her side. But he stood there watching her as he had been for too many days and far too many nights.

He'd never seen a lass work so hard. One minute she was handing out clothing or checking the fit of a winter coat on a small boy. The next she was serving food to a line of hungry people that wrapped around the building two times.

He'd seen her peel potatoes, wash plates, fold blankets, and help a young mother feed her fussy two-year-old twins. He'd seen her try to speak Gaelic until she had everyone around her laughing. She would claim the language was just beyond her.

He knew it wasn't. He knew she was smarter than that. But he also saw what she had, that the emigrants who spoke little English had laughed with her and her antics had made them more willing to try to speak.

He'd seen her walk through the hall late at night, picking her way through all the people who had bedded down on mats on the floor. She was still handing out blankets because she was so afraid one person might go without. She had learned quickly that many were too shy to ask for something they needed and many were afraid to ask because they could only do so in Gaelic.

Everything she did, she did with sweet smiles and a burst of energy that made him tired just watching her. He had never known anyone like Amy. Granted he'd seldom taken the time to know a woman, but he was glad he'd taken the time to know her.

He respected her, and respect was something he didn't give easily. Even men had a hard time earning Calum's respect. He was a tough critic. Eachann claimed it was because he wanted the rest of the world to be as meticulous as he was and that he got angry when they weren't.

He didn't know if that were true, but he did know Amy was someone he wanted to understand and he didn't care that she wasn't exactly like he was. She wasn't slow and methodical, clinging to a routine. Watching her was like watching a dragonfly flitting from flower to flower. It was like trying to hold a waterfall in the palm of your hand or trying to capture the wind.

Now she was about twenty feet away from him, standing in a crowd of women. He could see her frown and could tell she was listening so intently to those women to try to understand their feeble attempts at English.

He'd seen her do that since the very first day. And when she didn't understand what they were saying, she found someone to translate or she took the time to figure out what they wanted.

Her hair wasn't brushed. It was in a tangled and

loose blond braid that hung down her back. Damp curls had slipped out and hung around her face. He watched her swipe them out of the way while she listened and and folded blankets at the same time. Her face was damp with sweat and her dress was wilted and wrinkled and had some child's supper dribbled all over it.

"So how long are you going to wait?" Angus Mac-Donald clapped him on the shoulder.

"Wait for what?"

Angus nodded at Amy. "The lass. How long are you going to stand around here all moonfaced before you marry the girl."

"Moon-faced?" He almost choked on the word.

Angus laughed. "Aye. You ought to have a look at yourself, Calum. Robbie and Dugald have bets going to see how long you last. Robbie claimed you've been trailing her like a bloodhound for the last two days."

Moonfaced?

Angus looked at him, then shook his head. "I know what's ailing you. And you might want to take an older man's advice. Put yourself out of your misery and just take the girl right to Reverend Munro. It's easier than fighting it, lad." Then Angus walked away.

Moonfaced . . . trailing her like a bloodhound? Marry her?

He stood there feeling as if the windows in the room were suddenly growing smaller. He looked around him, but he didn't see anything. It was as if his eyes weren't working. He shook his head and then ran a hand through his hair. He looked back to the group where Amy had been standing, but she wasn't there.

For some reason he needed to see her, right then. He just needed to look at her. So he could understand what was happening. He didn't think he could talk right now. But he needed to see her.

He scanned the room and walked through the

crowd. But nowhere in the huge room did he see her smile or her long blond braid. Nowhere did he hear her laughing.

He crossed to the door with determined strides. He passed Robbie MacDonald, who called his name, but Calum didn't stop. He shoved open the door and someone made a howling noise like a hound baying at the moon.

It was Robbie, but Calum didn't stop. He'd blacken MacDonald's damned eyes later. After he found Amy.

He walked down the wharf, asking if anyone had seen her. Then he moved past the opposite end of the hall, where an open field of freshly mown grass had become the place for the children to play and run wild and free after being cooped up for a month in a ship.

And that was where he found her . . . or at least he spotted her head.

It was bobbing up and down in a large crowd of little girls. He moved closer, trying to figure out what she was doing.

Her head and her braid flew up and then down, up, then down.

When he was about ten feet away he could see her clearly. She was skipping rope and singing some silly rhyme about fleas and knees and the number of peas in trees.

The MacDonalds were right. He was trailing her like a hound. He shoved his hands in his pockets and stood there, half relieved and half scared of what he was feeling for her.

Calum had never really needed someone in his life or felt he needed someone, especially a woman. He had thought marriage was not for him. He had been so used to living alone, being the bachelor for so long, that his loneliness had become part of his routine.

And because that was what he was used to, he was reluctant to change it. There was safety in his scheduled routine. He had thought he liked his life exactly as it was.

When things in his world became strained or didn't meet his expectations, he would fight and struggle to keep everything the same—detailed, structured, and meticulous, as if by making everything orderly that would fix what was really wrong, which was that he was alone, and deep down inside he didn't want to be.

But when he listened to that laughter, when he saw her playing with the children and jumping rope in time to some nonsensical rhyme, with her braid bouncing up and down and her skirts halfway up her calves, he just didn't care.

Because with Amy he had no routine, there was no way it was supposed to be. This whole thing was foreign to him because for the first time in his life he was in love.

And hand in hand, on the edge of the sand,
They danced by the light of the moon,
    The moon,
    The moon,
They danced by the light of the moon.

Edward Lear

On the notes of a fiddle and pipe, laughter rode out of the meeting hall and into the cool night air. Inside there was a celebration. The next day the Highlanders would leave to go to new settlements inland and new farms far from the coast, some as far as Canadian borders.

They laughed and sang and rejoiced. They toasted their benefactors with cider and beer and cried over the friends they had found at a time when their lives had seemed most bleak.

Amy watched the dancing, the reels and jigs, and listened to the lively music. She had never been happier than this last week. She supposed it should have been strange to her to feel this way. She been to a hundred or more parties and balls, had been to every kind of social event known to society. And there had been some real doozies.

She had been to birthday parties for thoroughbred horses. She'd been to opera openings and art parties and parties just because someone wanted to serve strawberries and champagne. She had been to grand balls where a duchess was guest of honor and another where an Austrian prince danced with her. His principality needed money desperately.

But she had never had as much fun or felt as if she belonged in a celebration more than she did in this room with these people.

She tipped her head back and twirled an ankle to the beat of the dance, her eyes closed as she caught the refrain and hummed it over and over. Something brushed her hand and she opened her eyes. She was looking up into Calum's grinning face.

The next thing she knew he had pulled her into the circle of dancers, his arm around her waist as he twirled her round and round until she was laughing so hard she could barely keep time to the music.

He swung her around again, then led her down the line of clapping dancers, only instead of taking their places at the end of the line, he danced her right outside onto the boardwalk and kept on twirling her down past the docks.

"Calum!" She gasped as he swung her around until she was dizzy. She had to grab handfuls of his shirt to keep her balance.

"Don't you worry now, Amy-my-lass. I've got you."

And he did. His hands were on her waist and she felt a small thrill in the pit of her stomach, the same thrill she got whenever he touched her.

She laughed and took a deep breath, her hand pressed to her chest. "You've worn me out, Calum MacLachlan."

"I doubt anything could wear you out. I get tired just watching you."

"I love this. I really do. I've never felt so much a part of something before."

He leaned against a willow tree, reached up, and broke off a twig. "It makes the world look like a different place after you've seen it through the eyes of these people."

"They are wonderful."

He was looking at her as if he wanted to say something very badly.

She cocked her head. "What is it?"

He didn't respond right away, just tossed the twig into the river and moved over to the river's edge and stood there looking out at the water with his hands shoved into his pockets.

She walked over to stand beside him, then sat down in the damp grass that edged the riverbank.

The moonlight made the water sparkle like silver glass and the music and the laughter flowed out over them the same way the slight breeze did. She looked up at him and watched that breeze ruffle his hair.

He looked back down at her after a long silence; then sat down next to her, his long legs drawn up and his forearms resting on them.

She was leaning back on her elbows and looking up at the night sky. "I don't remember ever seeing a night like this. Look at all those stars up there twinkling down at us."

"For some reason there are always more stars when you're this close to the sea."

"I wonder why that is?"

"I don't know," he replied.

"Did you ever wonder what those stars really are?"

"No."

"Didn't you ever look up when you were a boy and pretend they were something special?"

"No."

She laughed. You were probably too busy cleaning something."

He just looked at her.

"Try it now."

"Try what?"

"Guess what the stars are."

"Stars."

"Please."

"All right." He was quiet for a long time. "I suppose I've always thought they were planets like the sun or the moon only smaller and farther away."

"They could be. I think they're lightning bugs that fly really high."

He gave her an odd look and she laughed. "Go on. It's your turn. Dream up something."

He scowled up at the sky. "Running lights for ships that can fly to the moon."

"Good!" She laughed again. "Or they could be cracks in Heaven."

"I think, Amy-my-lass, that you and that furtive little mind of your can out-imagine anything I can come up with."

"My 'little' mind?"

"Sorry, your huge brain."

"You aren't suppose to notice my brain. You're supposed to notice my beauty."

"Is that because according to Georgina I see better than I think?"

"Yes. It is. Oh! Look Calum! See there. A shooting star! And there's another! Two shooting stars." She paused. "I wonder what that means. Two shooting stars in one moment." She turned toward him. "It has to mean something, don't you think?"

"Maybe it does." He wasn't looking at the stars. He was looking at her.

"What does it mean?"

He leaned forward. "Maybe it's a way to tell me I should do this." He leaned forward and kissed her, softly, quietly as if this kiss was the most important kiss he'd ever given.

She slid her arms up and around his neck, let her

fingers play in his hair. His arms pulled her against him and he rolled with her onto the grass.

His kiss was thorough and changed quickly from a tender kiss to a passionate one. He filled her mouth with his tongue and groaned when she scored her fingers through his hair and pressed her mouth closer to his.

The kiss went on forever. It made her dizzy and lightheaded and she was glad he held her so tightly. He pulled his mouth away but skimmed his lips across her cheeks and to her ear.

"You're so sweet, Amy-my-lass, so sweet."

"Oh, Calum, don't stop kissing me. Please, kiss me again and don't stop."

His mouth was on hers the moment she asked and he pressed her deeply into the grass. She linked her arms around his neck and his hands moved from her back and shoulders down her ribs, then up to gently cup her breasts.

Chills raced down her whole body and she felt as if she were flying. She gasped into his mouth and then kissed him back the way he had kissed her.

He gave an aching moan in response. Long minutes later he broke off the kiss and laid his forehead on her shoulder. His breathing was rapid and it took him a long time to control it.

Finally he took a deep breath and threw back his head, staring up at the sky as if he needed to.

She traced the strained muscles in his neck with one slow finger. "So tell me what it means when there are two shooting stars."

He looked down at her, moved his hands to cradle her face as he looked at her with such naked longing she wondered if it was really there or if it was just the starshine playing tricks on her because she wanted to see that look there in those dark blue eyes of his.

"I know what it means, lass."

"What?"

He smiled down at her. "When you see two shooting stars, over a river, on a fall night, that means, afterward, the first man you kiss will be your husband."

"Husband?"

"Aye."

"You're teasing me, Calum."

"No. I'm asking you to marry me."

She stared up at him and thought she was going to do something really stupid like cry. "I'm going to cry."

"Could you give me an answer first?"

"Yes." Her voice was choked.

"Yes, you can give me an answer or, yes, you will marry me?"

"Both." Then she buried her head in his neck.

"I love you, lass. And I'll love you longer than there will be shooting stars in the sky."

And when he kissed her again she looked way, way up in the sky and thought that Georgina was wrong. Stars are there for wishes. She knew, because she'd just had one come true.

When you get up in the morning,
Don't ye blush with shame.
Remember your mother before ye,
Did the very same.

Scottish bridal toast

Calum and Amy returned to the hall before too much
time had passed and tried to enter as inconspicuously
as possible. Calum took his glasses out of his pocket
and put them back on, then walked her through the
door, took her hand, and danced her across the room.

Slowly, one by one, the dancers moved aside and
stood in a huge circle, clapping and laughing. Before
long they were the only ones dancing. The whole
room was standing in a circle and clapping in time to
the music.

Amy looked up at Calum. "What are they doing?"

He glanced around uneasily. "I don't know. Just
keep dancing." He twirled to the steps of a reel and
the loud clapping and cheering all around them.

Amy leaned back during one step and asked, "Do
they know we're going to be married?"

"No, lass. I had to ask you first."

"Then why are people winking at us?"

"I don't know." He spun her around and finally the

music stopped with both of them completely out of breath and standing alone in the middle of the hall.

Angus MacDonald brought out a jug of whisky and filled some glasses. More jugs appeared through the crowd and all the men raised their glasses.

"Saoghal fada, sona dhuit!"

Amy looked up at Calum. "What does that mean?"

"It's a bridal toast. May you have a long, happy life."

"Then that means they do know," she said out of the corner of her mouth. "Calum, I think you told them before you asked me."

"I didn't, lass, I swear."

"Lang may yer lum reek!" Angus MacDonald shouted and the men downed another glass.

"Calum?"

"Och! What's the matter, lass?" Robbie MacDonald swaggered up. "Why are you frowning so. You should be the happy bride-to-be." He gave her a wink and slid his arm around her, which earned him a scowl from Calum.

"I'm frowning, Robbie MacDonald, because I don't know how you know that Calum asked me to marry him. Or that I said yes."

"Well, we don't know for sure, lassie, but we Scots can put two and two together better than most."

"Just because we were outside together, alone in the moonlight doesn't mean a wedding."

"No, lassie, but I'll wager those grass stains on your back mean there's bound to be either a wedding or a birthing."

Then the whole room cheered and laughed while Amy blushed bright red.

You can marry more money in a minute than you can earn in a lifetime.

Anonymous

Bright and early the next morning, a procession of women all chattering in a mixture of English and Gaelic swarmed over the dockside and onto the coaster like ants on a sugarloaf. Since they had first arrived, Calum had been bunking in the temporary quarters with the men, so Amy had slept on the coaster.

She awoke this morning to almost thirty woman standing in the cabin, grinning at her, and more women lined up on the dock, all there to make certain her wedding day had no ill winds cast over it.

To insure her luck that day, she had to get out of bed backwards—which someone had to explain to her because she wasn't certain which way was backwards. She had to turn counterclockwise three times before she put on her shoes, which someone had slipped pennies in the toes of to ward off poverty.

That one had made her laugh. If they only knew poverty was not her problem. She was made to wash her face with morning dew gathered from the huckleberry bushes by some of the young girls. She was assured that this would keep her beauty well into her golden years.

Her wedding dress was a special dress. The women had stayed up in the wee hours, sewing a wedding dress of fine linen whitened in the Highland sun and threaded with velvet ribbons fitting for the bride of the MacLachlan.

She had her feet bathed in a bowl of water filled with the wedding rings of the older women to make certain the marriage would last. Blue ribbons were laced into her hair for luck. She wore old satin wedding slippers that had belonged to Mrs. MacKinnon's great-grandmother and she was to borrow Widow Drummond's fancy lace collar.

When all was ready she had to stand at the companionway and wait. At two o'clock sharp there was a gunshot at the dock. She was to not move. A second gunshot came five minutes later and then a third shot. She walked up the companionway and down to the dock where Calum was waiting, dressed in tartan and a kilt and looking as proud as he could for a man with eyes so bloodshot it was like having two crabapples staring down at you from behind his spectacles.

He took her hand and placed it on his arm and led her down the dock to the grassy field where Reverend Munro was waiting beneath the shade of a willow tree.

She looked up at him. "Hard night?"

He looked down at her from a squint and grunted one word; "Whisky."

Considering a wedding was something a girl waited for and dreamt of all her young life, the ceremony was all over almost too quickly. But the dancing was wild and lively and she and Calum tossed coins to the children as they danced the first reel.

The food was plentiful and the cider and whisky flowed long into the dark night when the moon was high and the young girls rushed to their makeshift beds with pieces of bridal cake to put under their mats so they could dream of their future husbands. And one lucky lass, Mairi MacConnell, the one who'd caught Amy's silk stocking with the gold piece hidden inside, would go to sleep that night and dream of the future she hadn't had back in Scotland.

Calum carried Amy to the coaster along with a procession of singing Scotsmen who had drunk too much whisky and couldn't carry a tune in sporran. He did his duty and to ward off the witches he carried her over the threshold—that being the entrance to the cabin stairs in this instance—then he went back on deck to send the wedding carolers all away.

Amy sat on the edge of the bunk and waited, her hands knotted in her lap. She didn't know whether she was more excited or more worried about what would happen next.

He came down into the cabin and then leaned against the handrail for a moment. "I never knew marriage was going to make me this tired."

She raised her chin. "It isn't marriage that has tired you out. It's all that carousing last night and tonight."

He sighed and took off his spectacles and put them in a cabinet in the wall. Then he pinched the bridge of his nose. "Aye, lass, you're probably right. Too much whisky. Not enough sleep, and now I'm too tired to be a husband tonight."

With that pronouncement he yawned and stretched his big arms high, so high his hands could touch the rafters.

Too tired? Amy sat there stunned and hurt and feeling as if he had slapped her. She couldn't even look at him. She tried to reason this scenario in her mind, telling herself that he hadn't done it on purpose, that they had a whole lifetime to have a wedding night.

But it did her no good. This *was* her wedding night. And there could only be one. Ever.

She stood and began to try to unbutton her dress, pulling at the buttons and bending this way and that, trying to reach every last one. She certainly wasn't going to stop and ask him for help. She had one arm flung over her back at an odd angle and the other was reaching around her back, trying to grasp the last few buttons.

"Having trouble?"

She inhaled a deep breath. "Yes, but I don't need your help." She bent this way and that, struggling to reach the buttons and failing miserably.

She heard his laughter and glanced up, scowling. Her scowl fell away.

Calum stood across the cabin from her, in all his naked glory, with his arms crossed over his hairy chest and a teasing grin on his face.

"Oh you!" She grabbed a pillow and threw it at him, then tried to run. She only got as far as the bunk, flat on her back with Calum on top of her.

He brought his nose so close to hers they almost touched. "You're a gullible lass, you know that?"

She looked at him, and rubbed her fingertips over his lips. "I was afraid I wasn't going to get any more kisses."

"Ah, Amy-my-lass, you'll never be kiss poor."

Poor. The word rang through her conscience. She looked up at her husband and wondered if she should tell him about her fortune now.

But there was no time for second thoughts or telling truths and secrets, because he lowered his mouth to hers and kissed her long and lingered there as if he had to, as if kissing her was necessary to his being.

When he was through, money was the last thing Amy thought about.

He pulled her clothes away piece by piece. His lips and hands explored her face, neck, breast, and legs. He kissed her in ways she never knew existed: her ears, neck and breasts and body. It was a new world of experience, one she savored with each new touch and kiss, each new thrill that ran through her blood making her hot and crazy.

In an act of pure instinct, she ran her fingers through the thick black hair on his chest. He inhaled sharply when her fingertips touched his nipples. He went a little wild then, and took most of her breast into his mouth, laved the tip of it with his tongue and sucked so hard that she felt the rush of a tingling sensation in her most private place.

He pulled her to her feet and knelt before her, taking off the satin slippers she wore as if they were glass. His hands roved up her legs, stroking her, memorizing her skin, the feel of it. He told her how soft she was and he kissed the backs of her knees and drove her wild with his tongue.

In a slow and methodical way, he rolled down her one silk stocking and kissed a path up her legs, taking forever. Soon he touched her there, at that intimate spot with his mouth.

When he kissed her she almost lost her balance. She grabbed the first thing she could. His head, and clutched it to her. She needed the feeling he was creating, the thrill and the rise that made her blood speed through her body in a storm of emotion.

A moment later she cried out and fell back on the bunk, her body pulsing with something she couldn't believe could happen to her while her breaths came in broken gasps.

Calum was standing over her then, his look satisfied

and spectacularly proud, as if he had just saved the world.

He pulled off the rest of her clothes, folded them, and then knelt on the bunk, one thigh wedging its way between her legs. He started again, kissing her ankles and her calves, up her thighs and pausing to breathe on the center of her. He did this over and over until she craved another touch there.

She whispered his name and a wealth of love was in that one word: Calum. He drew one finger over her and she arched toward him. His mouth was on her waist, her belly, and her hips, everywhere, making her body nothing but sensation while his finger stroked her, then slipped inside and filled her, rubbing in and out and making her body cry.

Then he was looming over her, his mouth and tongue tracing her ear and her neck, her breast, while his hand and fingers made her wet and wild and wanting him.

He shifted his body and slid against her. His face was above her and he was watching her closely. He shifted slightly so his was stretching her open, beginning to slip inside. "Are you okay, lass?"

She nodded and he slipped inside farther. She inhaled sharply at his fullness.

He stopped, not even halfway inside her. "Amy?"

She opened her eyes.

He touched her with his fingers again until she was feeling that sensation again, the building of something wonderful deep within her. He slid in farther, his touch making her accept him more easily than before.

Then he kissed her long and hard and filled her mouth with his full tongue. He gripped her hips in his hands and pushed hard.

Her eyes flew open and she cried out into his mouth. She tried to push him off her, but he wouldn't move.

"Amy . . . hold still."

"It hurts, Calum. You're hurting me."

He groaned and rested his head on her shoulder. "Lass, please. Give me a moment."

So they lay there, her center burning with the fullness of him. She was tense and stiff and almost afraid to relax. She was afraid it would hurt again.

He began to move. "I have to move, lass. I have to. Does it still hurt? Tell me what you feel." His expression held a hint of an apology.

She looked up at him from teary eyes and she shook her head. "Not like before."

"Ah, lass, I didn't want to hurt you. If I could take the pain for you, I would."

"Just hold me. Please hold me."

"Aye, I have you now and I'll hold you forever."

He reached between them and began to touch her. Before long, she was captured by the fullness of him and his motions were starting to make her want to move with him, slowly at first, then faster and faster.

This was like nothing she'd ever experienced, nothing that ever came before it.

He pulled up one of her thighs and pulled it against his hip and moved harder, then stroked longer and more rapidly. She was breathing hard now, and so was he, like they were both running, chasing after something. If they hurried they could really fly, fly all the way up to those stars they had watched.

He moved faster and she moved with him, until they were moving against each other. His fingers gripped her bottom, pulled her tight and more open against him, and he used his body at a different angle so it rubbed against that vulnerable, aching spot.

She cried out his name, because she had to, because she needed to say it aloud.

He thrust with five hard and rapid thrusts and she

exploded, felt as if she were one of those shooting stars. She gripped his damp back with her fingers as she whispered his name again and again.

He kept moving, the same hard rhythm, for long minutes and then he thrust once, groaned, and she could feel him pulse inside of her.

In the sudden silence they lay there, sweaty and wet and their breath coming in hard shocks, neither one of them able to speak for the longest time.

Calum lifted his head and looked into her eyes. "You are so sweet. You taste like everything good in the world."

She looked into his eyes and saw her husband, a man who knew her in a way she hadn't known someone could.

She gave him a dreamy smile that he traced with his fingertip.

"I love you, Amy-my-lass. God, how I love you."

And then he kissed her again. Almost too tenderly after what they had just experienced. Holding him, having him kiss her was everything wonderful and magical.

She knew she was going to like this thing called love and marriage, because she had Calum.

He was still hard inside of her and he began to move. She met his motions this time, met him movement for movement while he built the tension inside of her all over again, watching her come in an explosion of ecstasy until finally he went with her, came hard and furiously inside of her.

As they lay there, he shifted and raised up on one elbow and looked down at her. He looked at her as if he wasn't going to stop looking for a long, long time.

She cupped his cheek with her hand and he grabbed it, and turned his mouth to it so he could kiss her palm. He lifted her hand and placed it on his shoulder. "Am I too heavy?"

She laughed. "Isn't it a little late to ask that?"

He smiled, then his smile faded. "Am I hurting you now?"

She shook her head. "No. Stay there. I like the feel of you on me."

"I like the feel of you under me."

She flushed and he laughed.

"Tell me, lass. How we can do what we just did, twice, and you can still blush?"

"A woman can't control when she blushes."

"Ah, but perhaps a man can. I'll have to test this." He traced her breast with a finger.

"Again," she asked.

"After we rest for a few minutes." He shifted off of her and then groaned. He started to get up, but she stopped him. "Don't leave me."

"I'm not leaving you. I promise I won't."

He shifted off of her but kept her pinned against him. Her head rested in the crook of his arm and her leg was flung on his warm thigh. She played with the thick curly hair on his chest, until he laughed and stilled her hand with his.

There was a noise outside and he paused for a moment, an awkward moment because his hand was just moving downward over her bottom.

A crash cut through the still night air, followed by some Gaelic curses. A man on the dock began to sing.

"Damn those MacDonalds," Calum groaned and leaned his forehead on the pillow.

"What are they doing?"

"Serenading us. Like a shivaree, lass."

They listened quietly to the off-key singing:

"There's a marriage game called 'Ten toes,'
It's played all over town.
The girls play with ten toes up,
The boys with ten toes down."

They sang the bawdy verse for a few minutes, stomping up and down the dock, singing the refrain over and over and laughing.

Finally it grew quiet outside. When the singing was surely gone, and the man had stomped off elsewhere, Amy looked at Calum and began to giggle. "Ten toes up?"

"Aye, one can never say the Scots don't have a sense of humor."

Then he grabbed her, rolled her over on top of him, and shifted so her legs fell in between his.

"What are you doing?"

He smiled up at her. "I'm going to teach you how to play the marriage game."

"I already know how. You just taught me."

"Aye, lass." He laughed and kissed her nose. "But not with ten toes down."

It is said, an Eastern monarch once charged his wise men to invent him a sentence to be ever in view, and which should be true and appropriate at all times and situations. They presented him with the words, "And this too shall pass away."

Abraham Lincoln

Georgina flopped back into a chair in the main room in Eachann's half of the house. It appeared to her as if this was once a reception or drawing room. She looked around. No artist could draw this mess. It was beyond the imagination.

She raised a limp hand to her pounding forehead. "My life is over."

Eachann's children had been home for a week. It had been the longest week of her life. She had tried to be friendly with them. She had tried very hard to be friendly. They wouldn't let her.

They fought and argued and played tricks on her. They hid when she called them and pretended she wasn't in the room when she tried to talk to them. She found sand in all her clothes and they greased the doorknobs in her room and the inside of the bathing room. No two children could wreak the havoc they had.

They weren't human. They couldn't be.

But then why was she surprised? Their father

wasn't human either. No one but David was human in this godforsaken place and he'd been gone to the other side of the island for two days, fishing and trapping lobster with Fergus.

Her shoulders sagged back into the overstuffed chair and a puff of dust clouded around her. She sneezed, then rubbed her pounding temples.

Something sharp poked her in the backside. She lifted one hip and pulled out a sharp piece of walnut shell.

She rolled her eyes and flung it over her shoulder. "What's one more shell in a room that looks like . . ." She paused in thought. "Hell?"

"Miss Georgina!" Graham hollered, his feet thudding on the hall floors. "Miss Georgina!"

"There is no God," she muttered, just as the doors burst open with such force they rattled against the walls.

She flinched. She lifted the hand that was covering her tired eyes and frowned at him. "Can you not just *walk?*"

"I was in a hurry."

"You're always in a hurry."

"I have to be in a hurry. Otherwise Kirsty would get here first."

"Heaven forfend." She took a deep breath. "What do you want, child?"

"There was frost on the eaves and the trees this morning."

"Okay." She nodded as if she knew what that meant. "Frost."

"Uh-huh." He nodded like a sage. Then said absolutely nothing else. He was too busy rummaging in his pockets, taking out rocks and string and shells and something that looked horribly like a dead bug.

"Did you tell her?" Kirsty stood in the doorway, rocking on her heels and looking exactly like a small female version of her father. Blond hair, green eyes, a look that said she had Georgina pegged.

"Yeah."

Kirsty turned to her and put her hands on her hips. "Well?"

"Well what?"

Kirsty gave a mammoth sigh. "Can we go?"

"Go where?"

She turned and scowled at Graham. "I thought you said you told her?"

"I did." He was holding up an earthworm.

Georgina shuddered.

"Then how come she doesn't know what I'm talking about."

Graham shrugged.

"Why don't you just tell me what you want, Kirsty."

"Because Graham was supposed to. It's his turn, not mine." She crossed her arms over her small bony chest just like her father.

"Fine," Georgina stood up. "Then the answer is no."

Kirsty's arm dropped to her sides. "How can you say no if you don't even know what we want?"

"Easy. One word. One syllable. No. En. Oh."

Kirsty just stared at her for a long time. The child despised her and made no point of hiding it. From the first moment she came back from staying with Fergus, she couldn't look at Georgina without a challenge in her eyes.

She was smart as a whip and had a quick mind that kept Georgina on her toes, but she also found the girl entertaining, when she wasn't exhausted like she was now. It was interesting to see what the child would say next. She eyed her for a long time. After all, she *was* the adult here. But for the briefest of moments she wondered exactly what the little girl was thinking.

From way in the back of the house, another door slammed shut. The windows rattled in this room.

"It's Father!" Kirsty jumped up and down, then raced Graham out the door and down the hall.

"Ah. The prodigal father returns," Georgina mumbled.

A few moments later Eachann strode into the room, a child on each side of him. He looked around the room. "Have you seen my riding crop?"

"No."

"It's got to be around here somewhere."

"There were five in your closet."

"They won't work. I need this one. It has a special new leather grip."

She rolled her eyes. A riding crop was a riding crop.

"Aren't you going to help me look for it?"

"I'm not being paid to look for your riding crop." He straightened and gave her a pointed look.

"I'm a nursemaid, not a slave."

Kirsty gave her a belligerent glare that mirrored her father's. "If you're a maid, why don't you clean up the house?"

"A nursemaid doesn't clean. She watches children."

Kirsty planted her hands on her hips again. "Then why do they call her a maid?"

Before Georgina could answer she heard a loud *clop clop clop* down the hallway.

What was that?

A white horse came lumbering into the room.

Georgina screamed and stepped backward. She fell over a two-foot stack of horse journals.

"What's wrong?" Eachann looked at her like she was crazy.

She waved a finger at the horse. "There's a horse in the house!"

He glanced up. "Oh. That's Jack."

"Jack is Father's favorite horse," Kirsty informed her while Graham was busy tying something to the horse's mane.

"But it's in the house!"

"Don't worry. He's housebroken."

Housebroken? "But it's a horse."

"Aye." He scoured through more of the junk on the floor.

"Horses belong in the stable."

"He doesn't like the stable." Eachann paused and glanced at her. His expression changed suddenly as if he just remembered himself. He walked toward her.

And here she thought he wasn't going to help her up. She struggled a little, then reached out her hand.

Eachann walked right past it. "There's my crop!" He bent down and pulled it out from under her and the journals, then he turned and went back over to the horse. "Thanks, George." He saluted her with the crop.

"Miss Georgina won't take us to the cove, Father," Graham whined.

"She won't." He looked back at her. "Why won't you take them to cove?"

"I never said I wouldn't."

"Yes, you did," Kirsty argued. "You said no. En. Oh."

"Take them to the cove. As you said, that's what I pay you for." He mounted the horse and rested an elbow on the saddle. "It'll do you good. You could use the exercise. A nice little walk in the sand will build strength in your legs. You need some strength in your legs, George. Then you won't have so much trouble getting up."

He rode the horse right out of the room, leaving Georgina struggling to get up so she could kill him.

Sailing blossoms, silver fishes,
Paven pools as clear as air—
How a child wishes
To live down there!

Robert Louis Stevenson

Kirsty, Graham, and Miss George walked down the hill to Piper's Cove. Kirsty and Graham ran ahead, racing to see who would reach the sand first.

"I'm first! I'm first!" Graham hollered like the silly old boy he was.

Kirsty pretended like she didn't care. "Let's play firsts! I see the first seagull!" She pointed up at the sky.

"I see the first sand crab!" Graham fell to his knees in the wet sand and scooped up handfuls of sand and scuttling crabs.

"I see the first grass." Miss George stood in a clump of grass on the dunes near a great pine tree.

Kirsty looked at her. "That's not plain old grass."

"It isn't?"

"It's called poverty grass."

Miss George looked down at the grass and gave a short laugh. "Oh, then this must be my spot."

Her voice was flip in that way adults had when they

meant just the opposite of what they said and thought.

"Somehow it seems fitting. I'll sit here." She plopped down in the grass and looked "moor-rosed."

Kirsty remembered that spelling word too. Although she could never figure out how the Moors and a rose could mean something very sad, unless the Moors trampled all the roses in Spain.

"I don't suppose there's any wealthy grass around here, is there?"

"There's no such thing as wealthy grass," Graham informed her in a tone that said he thought she was dumb.

"Rich grass?"

Graham shook his head.

"Now, why am I not surprised," she said, then hugged her knees and rested her chin on them.

It seemed to Kirsty as if Miss George was having a whole conversation all by herself.

She turned around and spotted Graham holding something shiny.

"What's that?"

"Nothing." He hid it behind his back really fast, so she knew it was something.

"Let me see."

"No." He ran down the beach.

Kirsty ran after him. "What is it?"

Graham ran past her, holding up a silver bottle. "Look what I have," he said in a singsong voice.

Kirsty tried to grab the bottle, but Graham danced away, laughing and pointing and taunting her like dumb boys always did.

She dove for his feet but missed. Graham laughed and turned to run . . . right into Miss George.

"What are you two fighting over?"

"Nothing," Graham lied.

"A silver bottle," Kirsty said at the same time.

"It's mine!"

"No, it's not!"

"Hand it over." Miss George held out her hand. Graham looked at her hand, then put the bottle in it. She held it up to the sunlight. "Doesn't look like it's worth anything. But if you two are going to fight over it, neither of you can have it." She drew her arm back and flung the bottle far out into the sea, then turned back to them. "That should teach you two to stop fighting over everything."

Kirsty and Graham looked at each other. "It was just a dumb old bottle," she whispered to her brother. "It looked really old, probably older than Miss George. And it's gone now."

Graham nodded. Like most things, he probably only cared about it because she wanted to see it.

"Let's find real live firsts!" she said.

Kirsty and Graham then ran along the water, splashing each other and seeing who could find "the first live firsts." Kirsty found the first starfish, but Graham had found the first crab. Then Kirsty chased the first sandpipers that were teetering along the shore.

Miss George hadn't found the first of anything, even though she had made one try.

Kirsty looked at her. She was standing near a great pine tree and she was staring off in the distance, out at the sea and beyond as if it was going to give her some important answer.

Kirsty turned away, then whipped her head back around. "Look! Graham. I have the first blue heron! Look! It's the first blue heron! The very first!" She pointed at a huge rock covered in windflowers, and tucked into one end of the cove, right next to that rock, stood a heron that was almost four feet high.

A second later the great bird pulled his long neck in

and took off, wings flapping as he climbed high into the sky, squawking, "Frahnk, frahnk, frahnk!" She watched him soar until he was only a small black dash in the sky.

When Kristy turned back around, she saw that Miss George had taken off her shoes and stockings and she was standing in the water, holding her skirt up around her knees while the waves slapped at them. She was laughing.

Kirsty stared at her, gaped at her if the truth be told. She hadn't imagined Miss George laughing. Really laughing anyway. She had never seen her laugh. She seemed so . . . not angry really, except when they had played tricks on her, but so . . . well, unhappy all the time. She must be lonely if she had to talk to herself.

Sometimes Kirsty had to work hard to remember that she didn't like her. Sometimes when she looked at Miss George, all she saw was the pretty lady with the long shiny hair that was the color of night and the white skin and clear blue eyes. She knew that Miss George had tried to be nice to her and Graham.

But Graham never paid attention, because he was a boy and boys didn't pay attention, and Kirsty didn't want to like her. She wanted to not like her because she didn't want a pretty woman like Miss George to take her father away from her.

Kirsty wondered what a pretty woman like her had to be unhappy about. Then she realized that she, herself, was unhappy a lot of the time and she wasn't ugly. Maybe Miss George didn't have a mother and maybe her father didn't want her around. Maybe she was lonely and scared like Kirsty.

Another wave came in and slapped her legs and Miss George laughed louder, so Kirsty turned around because it confused her when she saw her being a real person like her and Graham. She wanted to think of her as an enemy like Miss Harrington and Chester Farriday. They were easy to not like.

She heard a horse whicker and turned. Her father was riding Jack and they stood high on the rise above the cove. She waved, but he didn't wave back. Her hand fell to her side and she just stood there, feeling silly and ashamed for waving at him.

He wasn't looking at her. She followed his gaze. He was watching Miss George.

Kirsty stood there for a long time watching Miss George. She was walking through the water, not paying any attention to her or to Graham.

"Look! I got the first lobster!" Graham was standing on a rock ledge. He was tugging a lobster trap that they'd found in an old boat on the other side of the island. Fergus fished for lobster all the time and he had told them how to use it.

Kirsty ran over to look at the lobster. "For something that tastes so good it sure is ugly."

Graham was squatting down beside the cage and he was poking a stick inside the trap and watching the lobster grab it. "Look at those pinchers! I bet he can pinch even harder than you can."

Kirsty looked at the lobster, then back to the spot where her father had been. He was gone now. She glanced out at Miss George, who was walking up the sand, her skirt flapping in the wind and her hand shading her eyes.

Kirsty was very, very quiet, then she looked at Graham and said, "If you want to test those pinchers, I have a great idea."

"Sure." Graham nodded.

Boys were always so easy.

Whenever the moon and stars are set,
Whenever the wind is high,
All night long in the dark and wet
A man goes riding by.
Late at night when the fires are out,
Why does he gallop and gallop about?

Robert Louis Stevenson

Georgina had come here every night, to this spot just
below the hemlock tree that looked as if it sprouted
right out of the granite cliff. It was cold tonight, colder
than it had been the night before. Graham had told
her there was frost in the mornings now, icing the
trees and ground.

Had this year been like all the other years, had she
been at home in the family town house in Boston, she
would have never noticed the moon or when the first
frost came or if the night was colder than the night
before.

She would have been too busy, flitting from soiree
to soiree, toasting friends who weren't really friends
with glass after glass of champagne. Laughing and
dancing, probably with John Cabot, whose nose came
to her shoulder and whose bald head had been known
to catch the glare of the glittering gaslights in a
ballroom.

She leaned back against the trunk of the tree and
watched the orange moon rise, a bright ball of fire

against the deepest purple sky you had ever seen. That moon was so bright it almost hurt to look at it.

The leaves had begun to fall the past few days, floating down the ground every afternoon when the sea breeze blew in. Now the harvest moon turned those leaves bright gold.

It was beautiful here on this isolated island, especially at night. She left the tree and walked along the trail, listening to the leaves crackle under her feet.

She went up the hillside, back into a meadow where a winding path led to a small bridge near a pond. A pair of swans were sleeping in a cluster near the bridge, their heads tucked safely under their wings.

Georgina walked along the edge of the pond, where the pussywillows were thick and the elderberries grew wild. In the last hour the wind had slowed to just a light breeze and the air seemed quieter, the sea in the distance sounded calmer.

She stood near the bridge, watching the lazy swans floating on the still water while they hid from the night. She looked way up at the stars and thought about Amy. She wondered where she was and what she was doing.

She wondered what her own life would be like now, where she would go from here. What would happen to her?

She tried to believe she had a future, yet she didn't feel she did, not deep down inside. She felt as if she had absolutely no control over anything that was happening to her.

With an eerie suddenness the air grew still. She glanced up and could almost see the stars freeze and the golden moon turn silver.

As if the someone had just called out his name, Eachann MacLachlan rode over the hillside. At first he was nothing but a dark silhouette riding the air like

some legendary midnight image galloping out from
Sleepy Hollow.

His mount jumped a stone fence and thundered
down the hillside. Closer and with amazing speed and
grace. It was a sight that took her breath away.

She barely found that breath, caught it quickly
when he and his horse turned sharply and rode
toward the bridge. Right at her. She didn't run,
because for some reason she thought he might be
trying to scare her. She didn't know how she knew it,
but she just did.

He reined in the horse and just sat there, high in the
saddle, looking at her as if he wasn't surprised to find
her there.

She met his gaze unflinchingly. She started to say
something, but for the life of her she couldn't think of
anything to say.

He swung a leg over the front of his saddle and slid
to the ground with a horseman's ease. He closed the
distance between them and stood there looking down
at her.

She thought for one crazy minute that he might just
grab her and kiss her. And for that same crazy minute
she wanted him to.

"You'll freeze to death out here dressed like that."

She shook her head. "I like the bite in the air. It's a
relief."

He smiled then, one of those smiles that should
have warned her. "Are things getting too hot for you
around here, George?"

"Hardly," she lied.

He just laughed, then braced a boot on a rock and
rested his arms on his knee as he stared out at the
bridge and the pond. After a moment he looked
around, then said, "It'll freeze over soon. The winter's
coming early this year."

She didn't respond, there was nothing to respond

to. She didn't really care about the weather, never had to unless it kept her from doing something she wanted to do. She stood there next to him and wondered what he was thinking. What he thought when he looked at her. What he thought when he looked at his children. "Tell me something."

"What?"

"What do you do all day while you pay me to take care of your children?"

"What do I do?"

"Yes."

"I work."

She nodded and waited for him to explain. When he didn't she asked, "What do you do, MacOaf?"

"I breed and raise horses. Like Jack, there." He straightened and clucked his tongue twice and the horse walked over to stand next to him. He stroked Jack's muzzle, then turned to her. "He's sired four colts this year."

"Four?"

"Aye."

She nodded. "I see. And who takes care of the colts?"

"I do. And when they're here, Will and Fergus help me in the stable. Why?"

She took a deep breath. Someone was going to have to hit him over the head to make him see what he was doing to his children. "I think if I told you, you still wouldn't understand."

He gave her an odd look, then just shrugged it off. He straightened and grasped the reins. In one incredibly graceful movement he swung up into the saddle. "It's getting late and cold." He held out his hand. "Here. I'll give you a ride back to the house."

She just stared at his hand.

He turned his foot. "Step on my boot and I'll pull you up."

She hobbled around for a second, then managed to get her foot on his. A second later she was behind him on the horse.

"Put your arms around my waist."

She slid them around him and locked her fingers together. Her wrists pressed against his stomach, which was solid and hard.

He cast a quick glance over his shoulder. "Hang on, George!" And they took off like the wind.

A whisper in the silence:
Yet I know by their merry eyes
They plotting and planning together
To take me by surprise.

        Henry Wadsworth Longfellow

Georgina tied a bow in the blue silk ribbon on her only nightdress, then turned around, stiffly. Her backside and the insides of her thighs felt like someone had beaten them. She had only been off that white beast of a horse for a little while and she was already sore. Tomorrow would be unbearable.

"I'll give you a ride back to the house," she mimicked in a snotty voice as she limped across the room. "I'd like to give him something," she muttered and punched a fist into the palm of her hand.

But deep inside she knew what she wanted to give Eachann. And it wasn't a good sock.

Her shoulders dropped and she just stood there, feeling sorry for herself. Try as she might to ignore him, to tell herself he was an oaf, she couldn't ignore one thing—he fascinated her. He did so in a way that no man had.

From that first night in the garden he had made her feel all those girlish dreamlike things she had told herself she would never feel. She didn't want to feel them, but she did.

He was a good opponent; he didn't give an inch. She liked that about him, because she knew she was one of those people who would push an inch into a yard if given the opportunity.

She almost wished she were less moral, then perhaps she could just march into his room, seduce him passionately until she became tired of him, then she could get on with her life. Whatever that life was going to be.

She glanced around her. If this room was any indication of what her future would be, she might as well give up now. The room was so small and still smelled musty even though she'd kept the window open.

She shuffled over to close the window, but stopped and looked outside. She took a deep breath and then blew it out. Fresh air was supposed to be good for what ails you.

She leaned against the window frame and looked out. The moon was still high and no clouds had blown in to hide the stars. They were everywhere tonight.

She started to close the window and changed her mind. She looked up at the sky again. Chewed on her lowered lip for a second, then quickly picked a star and made a wish.

She slammed the window shut and felt her cheeks flush because she was embarrassed, which was as silly as her making that wish, because no one could possibly know. She was all alone.

She shuffled back over to the bed and pulled back the covers. She leaned over and turned down the lamp. She got under the covers and wiggled this way and that, trying to get comfortable in the small bed.

She punched her pillow a couple of times. She

missed those down pillows she used to have, then flopped her head back down and pulled the sheet and blankets all tightly around her chin.

Then, as she closed her eyes, a handsome, grinning, and too-arrogant face swam before her. She sighed and slowly turned her lips toward her pillow, pressing her mouth to it slowly and tenderly.

A second later she screamed so loudly she woke up the swans.

My arms around her taper waist
Her lovely form I pressed,
Her beauteous face reclining
Upon my manly chest.
I kissed her twice upon the lips,
I wish I'd done it thrice.
I whispered, Oh it's so naughty,
She said, it's oh so nice.

Anonymous

By the time Eachann ran into her room, Georgina was hopping around the room on one foot, hollering and yelling because she had a lobster hanging from the other foot.

"Get it off me! Get it off!" She hopped all over the place. "Get it off!"

"Hold still! I can't get it if I can't catch you!"

"Don't you yell at me! This is all your fault!" She plopped down on the bed and rocked back and forth. "Ouch-ouch-ouch-ouch! Get it off. Please."

Eachann knelt in front of her and tried to pry the lobster's claw loose. "Strong little bastard," he muttered.

She screamed again.

"Oops. Sorry about that, George. It slipped."

She kicked her foot a few times, but the lobster just hung on, flopping back and forth as she flung her foot all over the place.

Eachann grabbed her by the waist, picked her up kicking and hollering, and dropped her on the bed, then straddled her, sitting on her fanny and facing her kicking feet.

"Get off me!"

"Hold still, dammit!" He grabbed her foot and pried the lobster loose. "There! Got it."

He raised to his knees and then slid off her. They faced each other on the bed and he held up the lobster. "See?"

She held her toes in one hand and rocked on the bed. "That was so mean."

"How the hell else was I suppose to get it off?"

"Not you! Your children!"

"Oh. They are a handful."

"How would you know? You're never around!" She rocked, then grabbed her ankle and lifted her foot up so she could examine it. There were little zigzags deep in her toes from the serration in the lobster claws. She frowned at them, then mumbled, "They hate me."

"No, they don't."

"Yes, they do. Your children hate me!"

"Now, George. Don't cry." He patted her gently on the back.

"I'm not crying." She turned and wailed into his chest.

"Okay . . . okay. You're not crying." He slid his arms around her and held her. He just held her like that for a long time.

She lay her head against him. Her toe hurt like the very dickens, but her pride and her feelings hurt more.

After a minute or so more of his rubbing her back he took a knuckle and tilted her chin up so she had to look at him.

His voice was little more than a rasp. "I like you, George."

She blinked, trying to believe that he'd really said what she thought he'd said.

"You do?" she whispered.

"Aye. And I wanted to do this by the bridge tonight." His mouth came down on hers. It wasn't a hard kiss, but it was a passionate one. His hands slid to her head and held her there while his tongue wedged between her lips. He filled her mouth, then slid one hand down her back and pulled her flush against him.

She kissed him back, kissed him with all the passion she had been hiding for so long. Her hands went up into his hair.

His hands slid to her breasts.

She stilled, suddenly frightened of what was happening and happening too fast. She broke off the kiss, shaking her head. "No."

He watched her closely for a moment and she had the feeling he was trying to gauge if she really and truly wanted him to stop.

"Please, not now."

He nodded, his expression a little frustrated. The moment grew awkward.

"I need to get to bed," she said in the way of an explanation. It was all she could think of at the moment. "I need every moment of rest to keep up with your children."

He walked to the door, then, just before he left, he turned and said, "You're a good sport, George."

And she was a good sport. Until two mornings later when she woke up and discovered that his children had painted her face blue.

> If you unthinkingly set up a tack in another boy's
> seat, you ought never to laugh when he sits down
> on it—unless you can't "hold in."
>
> *Mark Twain*

Georgina marched over the meadow and down the trail that led to Eachann's stables, where she could see horses turned out in the neighboring field. The wind had come up from the northeast and was strong and cold, the kind that blew in sharp gusts that flattened her dress to her legs and yanked long strands of her hair free.

She shoved the hair from her blue face and stormed on, not even missing a step. She threw open one of the stable doors and stood there in the entrance while the wind whipped past her and spun the straw around.

Fergus and Will were busy mucking out the stalls.

She slammed the door and threw the bolt, then turned and stood there, her hands hanging at her sides in white-knuckled fists.

The men both turned around at the same time.

Will's eyes grew huge and he swallowed hard.

But Fergus just stood there as if he had grown roots. He squinted at her, then muttered, "Those wee devils."

Will's mouth quivered and began to tilt up into what looked like a smile.

Georgina raised her finger and pointed at them. "One laugh, one smile out of either of you, and you're both dead." She looked around. "Where is Eachann?"

"In the field with the horses."

She spun around and threw open the latch, then stormed out the door, heading for the grassy field beyond.

Some colts cantered playfully in a wide circle around the fencing and a small herd stood huddled together the way horses did whenever the weather took a sudden change. She could see Eachann's blond head on the other side of the herd.

She called his name, but the sound was swallowed by a gust of wind. She looked for a gate, saw none, so she crawled through the fence and stormed toward him.

A nearby horse looked at her, threw its head up, and rolled its eyes. A second later it bolted as if it had just seen the devil himself.

She cursed under her breath and stomped across the field, her feet sinking in soft damp spots that were hidden by the thick grass. She stumbled twice and had to throw out her arms to help catch her balance.

One of the colts must have thought she was a playmate, because it pranced over with its tail and head high; it circled her a few times, nudging her straight back with its muzzle and playing with her hand.

At the best of times, she had little patience. Now she had none. She chased the colt away. She'd been plaything enough for one day.

When she was midfield, just near the herd, a gray stallion flattened its ears and bit another, even larger, and stockier horse. The gray kept bullying the other, nipping at its flanks.

She might be a sound sleeper. She might have a blue face because of it, but she wasn't stupid. She could see the fight between those horses coming.

Before she knew what happened, Eachann threw her over a shoulder like a sack of oats and all but tossed her through the fence.

"Stay there!" he ordered, crossing the field toward the horses. He approached the gray and it backed away, then lowered its head.

Eachann didn't appear the least intimidated. He just kept walking right straight toward it. The wind carried back his soft words, murmurs and whispers, easy talk that seemed to calm even the gusting air.

With an eerie suddenness, the horse quieted. By the time Eachann stood next to it, the animal was poking its muzzle in his chest and acting like a faithful old hound. The other stallion stood nearby, completely contented to just eat the grass and swish its long tail.

Eachann stroked the horse, then he was coming toward her. He stopped at the fence and watched her with a look of someone who knows exactly what he's going to hear.

"I've had it!"

"Now, George."

"Don't you 'Now, George' me! Look at this!" She pointed at her face.

"Why would they paint your face blue?"

"To make me look like a Pict! What in God's name is a Pict?"

"The old tribes of Scotland. They painted their faces blue when they went to battle." He squinted and searched her face. "What did they use?"

"I don't know. But it doesn't wash off!"

He looked away, and just stood there, rubbing the back of his neck with one hand. He glanced up at her. His eyes were beginning to crinkle at the ends and he looked like he was chewing on a belly laugh.

"Don't do it!" She poked her finger in his chest. "I'll tell you what I told Fergus and Will. Not one smile out of you."

He lifted his hands in mock surrender.

"This is not funny, Eachann."

He managed to compose himself and looked at her with a serious expression. "Come inside. Let's see if we can find something to take it off."

She was inside the stable before him, but followed him into a boxy room with bridles and halters, saddles and ropes, and other tack scattered everywhere.

"Watch where you step." He pulled a bowl off of a shelf, then pointed to a bench with two saddles on it. "Sit here." He left for a few minutes while she sat on a saddle with her blue chin resting in one hand.

He came back inside and hunkered down in front of her. "Close your eyes, George."

He began to clean her face. After a while he said, "It's not as bad as you think."

"That's because it's not your face that's blue."

He stood and set the bowl down.

"Well?" she asked hopefully. "Is it any better?"

He was silently studying her.

"Eachann . . . How does it look?"

He didn't answer right away. Finally he said, "It matches your eyes."

She stood up, snatched a halter off the bench, and threw it at him, then slammed out of the stable to the sound of his laughter.

If seven maids with seven mops,
Swept for a half a year,
"Do you suppose," the Walrus said,
"That they could get it clear?"
"I doubt it," said the Carpenter,
And shed a bitter tear.

Lewis Carroll

Eachann's children were smart. For the next few days they stayed in their rooms doing their lessons and behaving like perfect angels.

However, Georgina declared war like the blue-faced warriors of old on Eachann's side of the house. She'd had enough. She couldn't take the clutter any longer.

The blue on her face was slowly disappearing. If she kept busy, she wasn't prone to look in the mirror, which was safest for everyone concerned, particularly Eachann MacLachlan and his children.

She attacked the rooms with a vengeance. In the main room she swept up enough walnut shells to fill Eachann's bed—and that's where she put them. She spent one whole afternoon just stacking horsemanship journals and papers. The man didn't throw anything out. She found three-years-old newspapers and two more riding crops, one boot—she never did find the match—shirts, socks, saddle soap, and currying combs.

In one corner of the drawing room there was a

wooden crate filled with nuts, bolts, nails and wooden pegs, wire, and some metal things that looked like huge belt buckles. There were strips of leather and metal, five stirrups, something that looked like a wood plane, two spoons—one slotted—a rasp, a hammer, five horseshoes, a piece of silver metal that looked like the grate door on a woodstove, and three doorknobs and some pipe.

When Eachann caught her dragging the crate down the front steps, he stopped her. "What are you doing with that?"

She placed a hand on her back and straightened. "I'm getting rid of it."

"What? You can't. That's mine!"

"But there's nothing worth keeping. I don't even know what half of this is. What are you going to do with it?"

"That is my parts box."

"Pardon me?"

"I'm saving those things to use for 'parts.' Parts," he repeated firmly. "If something breaks or gets lost, I'll have a replacement part in this box."

She looked at the box, then shook her head. "Then take it somewhere. It doesn't belong inside the house."

He grumbled something, then picked up the box as if it were filled with gold bricks, and he left.

By Thursday, she had cleaned all the rooms but his bedroom. She'd spent one whole night just rearranging the furniture. She moved the overstuffed chair nearer the door and the small sofa near the fireplace.

The tables had all been in foolishly inconvenient places and none of the chairs faced each other. There was no conversation area at all. Everything had just been shoved against whatever wall was available.

The room had been such a mess that she actually found a piano she hadn't known was there.

When Eachann came in the room, Georgina was sitting by the fire admiring the room. She watched him leave a trail of clutter—his coat, gloves, and a riding crop were on the floor behind him. He emptied his pockets and dumped all the contents into a delicate crystal vase she'd found stuffed with dirty socks.

He turned around, took two steps, and ran into the chair. "What the hell is that doing there?" He scowled at the room. "What did you do?"

"I just fixed up the room a little."

He was still looking around. "Where did the piano come from?"

"I don't know," she said. "I found it in that corner."

And from then on, the week got worse. He came in one afternoon, went into the kitchen, looked around, then came back. "I forgot to tell you. I sent David to the mainland."

She had just sat down because she had a pounding headache. "Fine," she said, rubbing her temples.

"There's no dinner."

She waited for the rest of the sentence. When it didn't come she opened her eyes and looked at him.

"You need to make something."

"Me? I can't cook."

"What are we going to eat?"

She stood up and crossed the room; she paused. "Perhaps you should have thought of that before you sent David to the mainland." She reached over to a bowl on a small table. "Here, have an apple. It doesn't have to be cooked."

The next night she tried to cook something for the children. She found a cookbook with basic instructions and she worked hard. The whole time she was remembering all those times she reprimanded one of the servants, the maids, or the cook. She hadn't known what hard work was until now.

Eachann sent word that a mare was ready to foal, so he wasn't there, but she was sitting at the kitchen table with his children.

They'd spent five minutes arguing over which one of them got the first serving. She'd spent over an hour shelling peas and now Graham was blowing them out his nose.

"Graham, stop that right now! Hasn't your father taught you any manners at all?"

The boy just shrugged.

Kirsty gave a slight gasp, then she looked at Georgina. "Graham farted."

Georgina dropped her fork and looked at the child. "I'm so glad you shared that with me."

Kirsty looked a little uneasy. "I just thought you'd want to know."

She threw down her napkin. "Why? Why would I want to know that? The truth is you said that for the same reason you say and do everything. You want to offend me." She stood up. "Go to your room. And Graham, if you blow one more pea out your nose you'll go with her."

Kirsty just sat there.

"I said, 'Go to your room.'"

"I don't want to."

"You have one minute to move or . . ."

She could see Kirsty was waiting to hear the severity of her threat. It took Georgina about a minute to come up with a good one. "If you don't go up to your room right now I'll let Graham be first in everything for a week."

A second later Kirsty was trudging up the stairs.

> Children want limits. Limits make
> them feel safe.
>
> *Unknown*

Georgina was waiting for Eachann when he came in. She was sitting in a chair in the shadowed corner of the room. She watched him for a moment.

He paced the room like a caged animal, then stopped and stared at the fire. After a minute he sat down in a chair and leaned his head back. He had his hand on his forehead. He was rubbing his temples.

He didn't look happy. He looked agitated. And what she was going to say to him was going to make things worse. It had been this way almost every day. They couldn't be around each other without one of them getting angry.

"Eachann." She stood up.

He looked up from his chair, startled.

"I need to talk to you."

"What about?"

"Your children are completely undisciplined and rowdy. Their behavior is beginning to turn mean. You have to do something."

"What?"

318

"I don't know. You're their father."

He ran a hand through his hair. "I don't know anything about children."

"You can't control them by running away or shoving them off on someone else."

"They scare the hell out of me, George."

She knew how hard that was for him to admit. He was a proud man.

"What was your father like?"

He shrugged. "I don't remember. I don't know how to be a father. I can't be something I don't know how to be."

"Why not? Did you always know how to be a brother to Calum? Were you born knowing how to raise horses? You can raise horses but you can't raise your own children?"

"I know I let them run wild. But I don't know how else to show I care for them."

"Did you know how to be husband?"

"No," he said almost too quietly. "Maybe I was afraid to be a father to them. I just didn't have anything to give anyone after their mother died." He took a deep breath and stared up at the ceiling. "I know that's selfish, but it's true."

"You need to get to know your children. If you paid any attention to them at all they wouldn't be doing all this."

He sat there with his head back, staring at the ceiling as if he were searching for something he'd lost. "Sibeal was so good with them. I never had to do anything. She did everything. She had wanted to do it all. Even when they weren't babies anymore." He looked at her then. "They were more hers than mine."

"But she's not here for them anymore. All they have is you. I know you care about them. I can see it in your face when you look at them. I saw the haunted look in your eyes when you pulled us from the water

319

that first night. You care. But if you love them, you have to become part of their lives. You have to learn to discipline them. You need to find some way to show these children that you love them."

He sat there for the longest time, thinking and not speaking. He shook his head, then looked at her. "Sometimes, George, when Kirsty looks up at me like I'm some god, I want to run as fast as I can. I'm no god. I'm a man and not even a good father."

"You can't be anything to them if you don't get to know them. She's just a scared little girl. She lost her mother. You don't pay any attention to her unless she does something wrong and lately not even then. You need to spend time with your son and your daughter. You need to learn who they are."

He was quiet for a moment, then he gave a cynical laugh. "I think I know who they are. Little heathens who would paint my face blue and put lobsters in my bed."

The strangest things are there for me,
Both things to eat and things to see,
And many frightening sights aboard
Till Morning in the Land of Nod.

Robert Louis Stevenson

Calum and Amy came back to the island that day
with the news of their marriage. Georgina went to bed
that night thinking things in her life would be better
with Amy around.

But the reality was that Calum and Amy were
newlyweds. She saw little of Amy after that first day,
and when she did, she was always with Calum.

Georgina was happy for Amy and Calum, but
watching them almost tore her heart out. They were
so in love. They touched. They kissed. They were a
couple. In fact they were never alone.

Watching them just made Georgina more aware of
the fact that she was all alone. Very much alone.
Loneliness was an ache deep inside her.

As the days went on it became harder. She would
catch Eachann looking at her with the same uncomfortable tenseness that she had whenever Amy and
Calum were with them.

Eachann had spent more time with his children.
He'd even talked to them about the tricks they had

played on her and made them apologize and promise to behave. They had too.

He included Graham in most of his daily activities. He took him to the stable, taught him to ride, and had him helping with the chores.

But Kirsty was left with Georgina. They were getting along somewhat better, but only because every time she started to misbehave, Georgina called her on it. So far, it worked.

So as the days passed their life took on more of a routine. As the weather grew colder and the nights longer, they all spent more time together.

Just that night they were all sitting around a toasty fire. The frost was high and cold and the first snow had come and gone the week before.

Eachann was teaching Graham to play chess. But Graham was hiding Eachann's chess pieces in his pockets when his father wasn't looking.

When Eachann finally caught on, he gave his son a stern look. "Hand them over."

Graham had begun to empty his pockets into his father's big hand. There were chess pieces, string, rocks, a moonsnail and an earth star, two-dried up worms, seashells and a sticky peppermint, small pieces of paper and some keys and old buttons.

He was still emptying his pockets when Georgina looked at Eachann and smiled. "You can tell he's your son."

Calum burst out laughing.

"What's so funny?" Graham asked, as he added a twig shaped like a fork to the pile in his father's hand.

"You have a lot of things in your pockets, son."

"I know," Graham said perfectly seriously. "I'm saving them for parts."

Eachann laughed along with everyone else and ruffled the boy's red hair.

Amy and Calum exchanged a kiss, and when Georgina looked away it was straight into Eachann's serious gaze. The look he gave her warmed her all over, held hers intently as if he were trying to gauge her thoughts.

She turned away, afraid he might actually be able to see what she was thinking, that she didn't want him to stop looking at her, that she didn't want him to treat her like his children's nursemaid.

She felt awkward and out of place, scared because she so desperately wanted to walk over to him, to touch him, to trace his jaw with her hand, and to have him hold her.

But she just sat there, looking calm on the outside and feeling anything but calm on the inside.

The weather grew wild that night too. The wind blew and rattled the windows. There was thunder and hail and enough racket to scare the fur off a rabbit.

It was late when Georgina finally went to bed. She'd been in the kitchen, eating some of David's sweet potato pie. She was carrying it and a fork to bed with her.

She heard the sound of crying before she even realized what it was. She stopped in the upstairs hallway and listened, then followed the muffled sound.

It was coming from Kirsty's room.

She stood outside the door, then slowly turned the knob and opened it. The room was dark and it took a moment or two for her eyes to adjust. She tiptoed inside and moved silently to the bed.

It was empty. Then she heard the sobbing again and turned. It was coming from the closet.

The rain and wind rattled and tapped against the window and howled over the house. The heart-wrenching sobs grew stronger with the storm.

She opened the closet door and looked down.

Kirsty was huddled in a dark corner, her knees

drawn tightly against her chest and her head buried in her small hands. Her shoulders quivered and you could hear her breath catching in short abrupt gasps.

Thunder crashed over the house so loud it almost made Georgina jump. The little girl moaned pitifully.

Georgina stepped inside and sat down on the floor next to her.

Kirsty looked at her in horror. "Go away," she wailed. "Go away."

Georgina didn't say anything. She just reached up and shut the closet door. She drew up her knees and sat there in the dark, eating pie and waiting.

Kirsty was still sobbing.

Georgina waited for a long time. Then more thunder rattled the room. She set down the pie and slid her arm around Kirsty, who was shaking. "Here," she said, and pulled the child into her lap. "Sometimes I'm afraid of storms."

"I'm not afraid," she muttered into her hands.

Now what? Georgina waited, then said, "I'm afraid of many things."

"I'm not."

"I have nightmares that frighten me."

The child didn't say a word.

"I'm afraid that I'm not smart." *I'm afraid that your father is smarter.*

Silence.

"I'm afraid because I'm all alone. I'm afraid because I don't have a family. I'm afraid because I don't have any friends." *I'm afraid because I am poor.*

Kirsty looked up at her.

"I'm afraid my face will always be blue. I'm afraid I might find a lobster in my bed. I'm afraid I might sneeze and my brain will fall out. I'm afraid I'll eat this whole pie."

Kirsty began to giggle.

Georgina held up the fork. "Want some?"

Kirsty ate some pie with her. After a few minutes she finally said, "I wasn't telling the truth. I am afraid of storms."

"That's why you're hiding in here, isn't it?"

Kirsty nodded.

"I used to hide under my covers. I'd pull them over my head whenever there was a storm."

"How come you're not afraid anymore?"

"I learned to think about something else, something I really liked, and then I forgot about the storm. So I always think about my favorite things when I'm scared."

"There are things that still scare you?"

"Yes."

She felt Kirsty relax against her; she wasn't crying anymore. She was munching on the pie and not paying any attention to the storm outside.

A few minutes later she turned her small face up with its pie-crust crumbs on her chin. She looked up at Georgina. "I didn't think grownups were afraid of anything."

"Everyone is afraid of something, Kirsty." She hugged the girl a little tighter. *I'm afraid I'm falling in love with your father.*

There was a young maid who said, "Why,
Can't I look in my ear with my eye?
If I put my mind to it,
I'm sure I can do it
You can never tell till you try."

Anonymous

Georgina found the old clock the next morning. It was in a room on the other side of the house. She was standing there staring at it when Calum came in.

"It's one of your family's clocks."

"Yes, I know."

"Do you have any of the clocks?"

She shook her head. "They were all auctioned with the house."

Calum crossed the room, took down the mantel clock and handed it to her. "It's yours."

"No."

"We don't need it," he said. "And I think you might."

She looked at the clock as he placed it in her hands and felt as if she might do something really idiotic like cry.

"Go on," Calum said. "Take it."

"Thank you." She started to leave the room then hesitated at the door.

He was watching her as if he expected this. Before

she could ask her question, he answered, "I'm sure."

She smiled then and left, carrying the clock upstairs to the small bedroom that was hers. She went inside and crossed directly over to a small pine dresser.

In it was everything she owned in world. She set the clock on the dresser top, wound it, leaned down a bit, and opened the small walnut door. With a flick of one finger she started the pendulum in motion. She started to close the door but saw the Bayard signature on the inside.

She ran her finger over the carving, then took a deep breath and closed the small door. She stood back and looked at the clock. It was a walnut clock, the kind with a moon face on it. It ticked and tocked and kept perfect time.

She stood there for a long time, thinking back over the years, over time that had been spun away by the hands of so many Bayard clocks. She remembered her life, her childhood and how her family had lived.

Part of her wondered what kind of life her ancestor who crafted this piece had had. Did he and his wife have a house filled with love? Did they care about their children? Did they love their daughters as much as they loved their sons?

For a long time past, years and years, deep down inside of her she had thought it was her fault that her parents hadn't cared about her. She thought there was something missing in her.

But last night, as she sat in that closet with Kirsty and held her while they both spoke of only happy things, she had learned something important about herself.

It wasn't that she was unlovable. But that her parents were incapable of giving love to her.

Last night she had sat inside a dark closet giving her heart to a child that wasn't even part of her. Kirsty wasn't her own flesh and blood. But blood ties didn't keep Georgina from feeling something for Kirsty. She did. She felt as if Kirsty needed her right then, as much as the little girl needed her father.

There was a freedom in knowing that. It was as if she were finally turned loose to be what she wanted to be. She realized that no matter what she had done, her parents would have never loved her. Who she was didn't matter and if she had become a Cabot or a Lowell or nothing at all it wouldn't change the fact that her parents were the ones who had the problem.

Whatever Georgina chose to be—maybe only a nursemaid to two lonely children on an isolated island—that choice wouldn't change her value as a person. It wouldn't make her more accepted.

She didn't have to be a Bayard. She didn't have to be a wealthy woman with the right name. She didn't have to live in a mansion to be someone.

Maybe being someone was nothing more than sitting in a dark closet with a little girl every time there was a wild storm.

Georgina felt a sudden sense of freedom, as if she had just learned the secret to happiness, something that had been hidden from her for the longest time.

She smiled and turned around, then stopped.

Hanging on the back of her bedroom door was a shimmery green silk dress, the one that had belonged to Kirsty's mother.

Georgina went over to the dress and touched it. It wasn't a Worth. It wasn't from Paris and it wasn't particularly spectacular. But that dress meant more to her than all the clothes and all the possessions she had lost. She closed her eyes and stood there for a moment. She bit her lip and took deep breaths. But it didn't do any good. The tears came anyway.

The world is so full of a number of things,
I'm sure we should all be as happy as kings.

Robert Louis Stevenson

Kirsty hopped the last few feet to the stable. Making wishes every time she landed sure—with her ankles still pressed together. It was a game she played all the time, because it helped her forget that deep inside she was scared, so scared that sometimes she wanted to go and hide in a closet.

Her first thought when she opened the door and snuck inside was that it smelled like she thought a stable should smell, like hay and horses and dirt.

It was darker inside than she imagined, but she didn't let it worry her. This darkness was different. It wasn't the scary kind. She was inside her father's special workplace, a place where he spent too much time, too much time with his horses instead of time with her.

Her shoes crackled on the straw and she walked past the stalls where the horses were kept when they weren't in the field near the goose pond. There was an open door just ahead and she moved toward it, holding her breath because she thought her father might be inside.

She didn't know how he would react to her being there. He had never once asked her to come with him. So she thought he didn't want her in the stable.

Maybe he thought she would get in the way. She wouldn't get in the way. She'd even promised herself she wouldn't ask too many questions either. Sometimes adults got tired of her questions. But she knew why. She knew they only got tired of them when they didn't know the answers.

She slowed her steps the closer she came to the open door. She took a deep breath and peered around the door. There was no one on the inside. Nothing but a jumble of saddles and harnesses, bridles and other tack stuff.

The room was a mess. She just bet Uncle Calum would love to fix this room all up. She was glad Uncle Calum was home and she liked Aunt Amy. She liked her because she never treated them like children. She listened to them. Really listened, as if what they had to say was important.

She heard a horse whicker in one of the rear stalls and she went back there. She could see the horse tossing its head as if it were calling her to come over there.

So she did.

She went into the stall next to it and climbed up on the sideboards, stood on her toes, and rested her arms on the stall wall.

"Hello, Horse."

The horse turned its head and looked at her from the softest eyes. She was a pretty horse. She had a lovely gray mane and tail, but the rest of her was white. She knew from listening to her father that you didn't call this a white horse. Only horses with all-white manes and tails and pink skin were called white horses.

Two stalls down was a white horse just like Jack. Kirsty ran down to it.

White horses were supposed to mean good luck. She remembered a poem and recited it aloud: *"White horse, White horse, lucky lucky me. White horse white horse, bring my wish to me."* She closed her eyes real tight and made a wish.

"Kirsty!"

Her eyes shot open and she whistled. *That was fast.* She gave the white horse a thank-you pat and jumped down from the stall, landing with her ankles together and her arms out for luck. "Hello, Father!"

"What are you doing in here?"

"Nothing, I just wanted to see what the stable was like."

"Why?"

She shrugged. "Just because."

"Does George know where you are?"

She nodded. But she wouldn't tell him their secret. That George had told her to come here on purpose because her father had been spending time with Graham and not her.

Her father crossed over to the open room and she followed him, then stood in the doorway and watched as he tossed the coil of rope in a corner.

"This is the tax room," she said, wanting to impress him.

He glanced up at her. *"Tack* room."

"Oh" She stared at her toes and felt foolish.

"That was close." He was grinning at her as if he were actually proud of her, even though she had messed the word up.

"What were you doing?"

"Separating two of the stallions that were fighting."

"Oh. Why do horses fight?"

"The same reason people fight. Because they want to be the master." He took something out of a box.

"What's that?"

"A new bridle. I'm going to put it on Jack and go for a ride."

"Oh." She'd asked too many questions because now he was going riding to get away from a silly little girl who talked too much.

He stopped and held out his hand. "Do you want to come with me?"

"Riding Jack?"

He nodded.

"Just you and me?"

"Aye."

"Oh boy, do I!" She took a hold of his hand and skipped along to keep up with his long strides.

Soon they were riding over the meadow and down the path to the cove below. She leaned back against her father's chest. "Do you think if you put your ear to a tree trunk you could hear it grow?"

"I think that trees grow too slowly and quietly for you to hear it."

It was getting darker and colder. The sounds of night came quickly this time of year.

"Why do crickets sing?"

He looked at her. "What?"

"I asked why crickets sing."

"To attract a mate."

"Oh." She was very quiet, thinking very hard. "Miss George is very lonely."

"She is?"

Kirsty nodded. "She told me in the closet. Maybe we should tell her to sing so she can attract a mate."

He looked down at her; his face was a little sad.

"Are you lonely too?"

"Aye. Sometimes I get lonely."

"Do you miss Mama?"

"Aye. I do."

"So do I."

"Look. There." He pointed up at the moon.

"There's a ring around it," she said. "That means rain will come soon."

"I'm surprised you can remember that. I thought you were too little. I used to take you riding when you were but a wee thing."

"I always remembered."

They rode along the sand in the cove, then he led Jack up to the path near the big old hemlock tree by the house.

She tugged on his shirtsleeve. "Since you're lonely and Miss George is lonely, maybe you should marry her."

"Would you like me to marry her?"

"She's very pretty."

"Aye. She is."

"And she likes to hide in the closet during storms."

"That's important."

"Yes. And she saved me from drowning. We shouldn't forget that."

"No. We shouldn't."

"And Graham and I need discipline."

He began to laugh then. He laughed really, really hard. And it made Kirsty feel all warm inside because she liked to make him laugh.

He dismounted and lifted her off Jack. "You know what I think?"

She shook her head.

"I don't think you need discipline."

"You don't?"

"No. I think you need this." Then he picked her up in his huge arms and right there, under the bright pearly moon with the rain ring around it, he gave her one of those great big hugs, the kind the kids at school got from their fathers, the kind Kirsty had wanted all her life.

All good things arrive to them that wait—and don't die in the meantime.

Mark Twain

Georgina was sitting in her room, staring out the window at the frosty night. There was a sharp blue wind and the stars snapped in the deep purple sky like sapphires. She looked at one of the stars for the longest time, then turned away just as the door to her room opened.

He stood in the doorway, filling it the way a painting fills a frame. "Can I come in?"

"Yes." She was standing there stiffly, but she couldn't help it. The tension between them had gone on for so long now that she didn't think it would ever change. She was destined to go through life wanting something she couldn't have.

He sat down on the bed. His knees were slightly spread and he rested his elbows on his thighs. He just stared down at the floor. "I'm sorry, George."

"Why?"

He looked up at her. "For everything that's happened. The kidnapping, jail, the stupid deal we made."

"Stupid deal?"

"Aye. I was angry because you wanted to marry someone else."

"Tom Cabbage," she said.

They both laughed and for just a moment the tension relaxed.

"Aye." He stood up and held out his hands in supplication. "I'm asking you to forgive me."

She took a step, then another, and put her hands in his and felt his close around hers. "You fool. There's nothing to forgive. I wouldn't want to go back to what I was before."

His mouth was barely a breath away. "I want to kiss you."

She smiled. "You know." She shook her head. "You really have to stop asking, MacOaf. If you see something you want, take it."

He kissed her then. Kissed her as if she were the most important thing in his world. It was almost more than she could bear.

When he finally pulled back, his gaze was locked on her mouth. It seemed to fascinate him and he traced the outline of her lips with one finger. "I think I was caught from the night of your party, there in the garden."

She slid her arms around his shoulders and looked up at him and smiled. "Me too."

His mouth closed over hers and he was kissing her deeply and with all the passion and power that seemed to always be between them, from the moment they were in the same room, from that first instant in the garden.

That passion was there and they had both known it, both had been fighting it. For once it felt so good to just give in to it, to let him love her and she him, anyway they wanted. No doubts. No regrets. Nothing but honest emotion.

His mouth moved to her neck and ear and he whispered, "God . . . you taste so good to me."

She smiled against his cheek. "Better than doughnuts?"

"Aye," he said with a deep laugh that was scratchy with passion. "Better than doughnuts. And maybe, even better than blueberry pie." His hands moved from her face to her bosom, and one large hand slid around to her back and down to her bottom, and he pressed her against him so her feet were between his and their bodies were touching from mouth to hip.

His tongue was in her mouth, filling it, and his other hand was inside the neckline of her dress, playing with her naked breast and making her aware of how his touch could excite her and make her knees weak.

She buried her hand in his hair and held his mouth even tighter against her, kissing him back until he was the one who was moving. He growled something earthy into her mouth and then he swung her into his arms, never breaking their kiss.

By the time he placed her on the bed her dress was already down to her waist and they were fumbling with each other's clothing.

He muttered something about the damn buttons.

"Tear it," she told him.

In a heartbeat he'd ripped the dress in two and it was off of her. Her underwear was gone a moment later. Her corset hung from the ceiling lantern and her linen drawers were frayed and lying across the room where they landed on a chair.

His hands moved over her skin, down her back, and they cupped her bottom.

She pulled at his shirt.

He broke the kiss and stared down at her, his gaze hot and suddenly lazy. "Tear it."

She looked up at him.

"Go on. Tear if off."

She grabbed the shirt in two fists and jerked it apart. Buttons flew around them and pinged onto the stone floor. She ripped at the long sleeves, at the cuffs while he only stood there, not helping, just watching her.

She looked at his belt, suddenly unsure.

"What the matter, George. No guts?"

That was all it took. She had his belt off in two seconds, then she grabbed the waistband of his pants in each hand and pulled apart as hard as she could. His breeches split in half to the inseams.

She shoved him back on the bed, knelt down, and pulled off his boots. One crashed against the wall and the other knocked over a washbasin.

He laughed, lying back on the bed completely naked as he pulled her up his long body so that her breasts and hips and thighs touched his all the way upward.

"My turn." His hand cupped the back of her head and pulled her mouth to his. Then she was beneath him, and he was kissing her so thoroughly and so completely that she thought of absolutely nothing. She only felt: the crisp hair on his chest against the tips of her breast, his body pressing onto her, and his hips rotating, rubbing against her.

He wedged his knee between her thighs, then reached down and pulled one leg up so he pressed himself against the heart of her. His hand stroked her inner thigh and she raised her knees and lifted her hips.

He seemed to know what it was she wanted because he used his body to stroke her for long minutes while his fingers teased in soft tickling strokes from high on her inner thigh down to her ankle and then back again. Over and over, he rubbed adjacent to the center of her and whispered into her mouth and ears about how she felt and what he needed and how good this was. That he'd waited so long he thought he was going to die.

His mouth closed over a breast and his tongue teased her, then he sucked hard and pulled on her nipple, then did the same to the other. His tongue was licking her ribs, her waist, sucking in her belly, her hips, and then stroking down her thighs to her ankles like his fingers had.

He drove her mad with his mouth, just kissing her inner thighs and raising her legs so he could kiss the backs of her knees.

He sat back on his heels, knees between her legs and he just looked down at her. His gaze went from her mouth to her breast, down her body until he was staring between her legs. He raised his gaze to hers, then touched her with one finger, sliding it inside so slowly she lost her breath and closed her eyes.

He pulled out. "Open your eyes."

She did.

He slid his finger back inside. "Watch me." Then he moved in and out of her, never once breaking their locked gazes. She could feel the pleasure start, in the center of her, then it moved down her legs and thighs and to her feet until she couldn't breathe because it was rising each time his finger moved.

Her hips rose up, needing him, and he slid another finger inside and she came. Hard and fast and with a cry of release that she knew was her voice, but that sounded too far away to be real.

He let her come down, giving her all the time she needed to take in each second of the pleasure. He wasn't rushed. But he watched her as if she were the only thing that mattered.

She started to sit up, but he shook his head and pressed her back on the bed with one hand.

When she looked at him, he just smiled. Then he lifted her one thigh and kissed the inside before he placed it over his shoulder and lifted the other the same way.

She realized what he intended and panicked. "No, Eachann!"

"Yes," he said. His hands slid to her bottom and lifted her to his mouth.

She moaned so loudly she bit her lips to keep from doing it again and again.

"Yes, my love," he said against her. "Let go and let me love you this way."

He kissed her with all the passion he always used in her mouth. And she pulsed against him over and over, and each time he let her feel every second of it.

He waited, then did it again, until she lay there trusting and helpless.

When he came into her with his hips pressing her deeply down into the bed, she knew why sex had the power to drive people to do what wasn't rational.

She understood love that caused wars and a love so powerful that a small human mind had no way to stop from needing to experience it.

Never did she think that a man and a woman could create this kind of magic. And she couldn't imagine the freedom of being able to love like this whenever she wanted for the rest of her life.

"I love you," he whispered, then said it again and again with each motion of his body.

He made love to her in long strokes and with such power but tenderness, watching for her needs and talking to her so she knew that he was feeling the same things, that she was making him wonder at how anything could be so good.

His face was flushed with desire and excitement from all they were feeling.

When he finally gave in to his pleasure and pushed deeply into her, he moaned her name as he filled her with warmth and power and warm life.

She had no idea how long they lay there, damp and not moving and if they had taken everything from each other and there was nothing left to give or to take.

It seemed like hours later, but it had only been minutes and she started to get a cramp in her calf, then she moved too quickly.

"Oh . . . God!" she squirmed under him, "My leg!"

"What?" He arched up and looked down at her. "What the hell's wrong?"

"Cramp! Cramp!" was all she could say as she tried to bend down with him on top of her.

He rolled off her. "Where?"

"Leg!" was all she could say.

Then he was kneading her calf muscle, which knotted so painfully she wanted to holler.

After a minute he made her flex her foot a few times even though she groused that it hurt and soon she was okay. She turned back to look at him.

A second later they both were laughing and rolling around her bed.

"It's all your fault," she said laughing. "You had my legs everywhere."

"You weren't complaining, George. You kept moaning for more."

"I did not!"

"Aye. You did, 'More . . . more . . . Eachann,'" he said in a falsetto voice, his eyes closed while he shook his thick head and mimicked her.

She just lay there, not saying anything. She let him have his fun and acted as if it didn't bother her. He stopped laughing and looked at her as if he had realized he wasn't going to get a rise out of her. She just smiled and rubbed her hand over his chest affectionately for a few seconds.

When she had milked the moment for all it was

worth, she slowly reached out and touched him, drew her finger along him and watched his reaction.

His laughter stopped, and suddenly he was the one who was holding his breath.

It only took her a few more minutes to discover something new, a power she had over him that was intriguing and made her understand that she had a hold over him, the same kind of hold that he had over her.

And here she had been fighting against him so valiantly because she was afraid of how she felt, afraid that she was losing her sense and her control, that if she gave into Eachann she would lose herself to his man and the passions he created in her that she couldn't stop no matter how hard she tried.

There was a freedom in her discovery. And for the first time she realized that love wasn't something that controlled you and took over who you were and what you were. She sat up and pushed him back.

She spent the next hour doing to him every single thing he had done to her until she got her revenge and he was the one who was begging, "More . . . more . . ."

And hours later when she lay curled in his arm and the moon had gone down, she listened to his breathing and felt the depth of his sleep.

She never had been a gracious loser and she discovered she was even a more gloating winner, because she laughed and murmured, "And they call women the weaker sex."

> You can marry more money in a minute than you
> can make in a lifetime.

Anonymous

Less than a week later, Eachann and Georgina were
married in a simple white clapboard church that sat
on a barren stretch of coastline just outside the small
town of Rockland.

Had any of her old crowd seen her, they'd have
never thought this was the same Georgina Bayard.
She wore a pale green silk dress. No Worth gown.
There weren't five hundred guests. Only the groom's
small family.

No one would have believed it was the same Georgina Bayard that stood in that simple church with the
crisp winter afternoon sunlight falling through the
clear glass church windows.

Kirsty and Graham stood on either side of their
father and walked him down the short aisle to where
his bride was waiting for them. At this wedding it was
the children who had someone to give away.

When the ceremony was over, they walked down a
stark pine floor instead of a white satin carpet. There
were no diamond rings set in precious platinum. No

champagne or caviar. There was no pageantry. No grandeur. Just love and laughter and happiness.

An hour later Georgina stood in the crisp winter air as the coaster cut through the sea, heading for the island and home. She held up her hand with the plain gold band Eachann had given her. Eachann came up behind her, linked his arms around her waist, and whispered in her ear. "Did you want diamonds, George?"

She shook her head and looked up at him. "All I want is you."

He kissed her and the children came over and danced around them as if they were a maypole while Calum and Amy laughed and did some kissing of their own.

Georgina looked at her husband and said, "Since I couldn't marry for money, I married for love."

Kirsty looked up at Georgina. "But Father has a whole lot of money."

"Yes, dear," Georgina said. "I'm certain to you he does. Lots and lots of pennies." Then she laughed.

"Not pennies," Graham said. "Dollars."

She looked up at Eachann.

He grinned down at her and handed her an envelope. "It's your wedding present."

She opened it and just stood there. Inside was the deed to her estate. She looked up at him. "You bought my home back for me?"

"Aye."

"Oh, Eachann. This must have cost you everything. It's too much. It's very thoughtful, but we'll sell it. You can't spend all your money on this. It's not practical."

Everyone was watching her with such funny looks that she looked back at Eachann in confusion.

"Slide the wedding ring off, George."

"Why?"

"Just do it."

She took off the ring.

"Now look inside."

She turned the ring. To G from E and there were some numbers engraved on the inside. She frowned up at him. "Two, three, seven, one, four? That's not the date. What is it?"

"A bank account number."

"A bank account. Oh, that's sweet." She put the ring back on. "Just how much money is in it?"

"I don't know." He scratched his head and turned to Calum. "How much is in the bank?"

"Together? Both accounts? Or just yours?"

"Just mine."

Calum stood there thinking a second, then looked from Eachann to Georgina. "Over two million dollars."

She stared at Eachann in utter silence. Then, for the second time in her life, Georgina Bayard MacLachlan fainted.